CHRIS H. STEVENSON

ISBN: 978-1-68046-704-8

Published by Satin Romance
An Imprint of Melange Books, LLC
White Bear Lake, MN 55110
www.satinromance.com

Published in the United States of America.

Cover Design by Ashley Redbird Designs

This work is dedicated to Deborah Carroll, who meticulously edited and researched this work. She is responsible for many of the character's personalities and motives, as well as the makeup of the main female lead. Martha's vineyard was her location idea, having lived and interacted there.

CHAPTER ONE

C andace Sabella sat at the wardrobe mirror pretending to primp again. She actually had her eyes on the two bridesmaids standing behind her, who looked approvingly upon her reflection as if to say, *Good luck, sweetie. You look like a million bucks.*

Most brides would have welcomed any glowing comments and best wishes. Yet nobody knew just how forced this wedding was and how much she hated the prospect of seeing it through. People might have heard rumors and suspected something, but those people belonged on the side of the groom and sworn to secrecy. An open mouth could cause lots of problems for snitches and rumor mongers, even death. The wedding guests had been handpicked by the groom. The priest, if he suspected anything at all, was paid to keep his mouth shut. Since Candace's parents couldn't be located, the groom had provided his own man to give her away. The groom had picked out the wedding dress without her say or approval, but it was pricey, even extravagant. All of it was staged, wrapped up tighter than the meat inside a nut shell.

This man Candace was to marry had complete control over everything and everybody, including beautiful women. The stakes had been too high for her to refuse his demands.

The organ music crackled to life and then drifted up the stairwell to the second story dressing room. Candace didn't know the tune, although she suspected the wedding march would kick in as soon as she made her expected appearance.

She bit her lower lip, a nervous tick. A reckless impulse came over her —one that made her heart race. Could she pull it off?

Candace slid her stool back and made a half turn in her seat. She addressed her bridesmaids. "You'd better get down there. You don't want to be late for my wedding." She half chuckled.

"But what about your train?" said the taller one. "You shouldn't let it drag on the floor."

"That's okay. I'll gather it up. I have to make a quick trip to the ladies' room, and then I'll be straight down and join the procession." She watched her bridesmaids leave, then stood up to listen to their footfalls hurry down the steps. She plucked a pair of scissors off the makeup counter and slid the train fabric through the blades. She began to make a small cut and then thought better of it. She fingered the beret-type veil over her head, realizing that she couldn't do away with either piece on the church property. *Evidence.* They'd be found soon if a search was ordered.

Candace pulled up her train and wrapped it around her neck several times, then slipped out of the door and hurried down the hallway. When she entered the restroom, it was empty. She locked the door behind her. In the next minute, she was standing at the second story window. When she pulled it open, it gave out a creaking groan. She parted the drapes and kicked a leg over the window frame. She hung for a moment, a breeze rustling through her satin dress, her bangs fluttering against her forehead. She stood fully upright and leaned out as far as she could to grab a hold onto the rain gutter. After a short leap, her hands caught both sides of the aluminum pipe, and she swung around until her legs straddled it. The sides of her heels gouged in the metal, so she kicked them off. She performed a hand-over-hand slide to the bottom, picked up her heels and ran for the tree line at the edge of the church property.

Under the cover of a small windbreak of trees, she stopped and contemplated her escape route. She hadn't broken a sweat, but there was a lot of distance to get clear of the church grounds—actually a long haul— much further than she thought.

She took off, weaving inside and around the trees, running as fast as she could, stepping on sharp bark and twigs. When she got halfway to the main road, a change of plans made her stop. It might have taken her five minutes or more to get to where she was now. She couldn't be seen on the street in her wedding clothes—too many potential witnesses. She would have to hide out somehow, wait for dark and then make her exit under the cover of darkness.

Candace bolted for the largest tree she saw on the edge of the driveway. A glance over her shoulder revealed no one leaving the church, which was a stroke of luck meaning no one yet suspected her absence.

When she stopped in front of the giant tree, winded but feeling strong, she wrapped her arms around the base and kicked her heels into the thick bark. Losing purchase was a problem, forcing a backward slide until she began a bowlegged shimmy upward.

When she reached a high branch, her strong hands and arms took her out on it, where she kicked her legs back and forth. She gained speed and height from her full body swing. When her swinging momentum was at the highest, she bent at the waist and kicked her body up on top of the branch with a smooth ease. She crouched to catch her breath. Then she smiled. A gymnast couldn't have done it better!

She figured it wouldn't be long before a gang of people would come bursting out of the doors and scatter throughout the parking lot, checking all the cars, roaming the lawn and nearby trees. She was right. A few minutes later the main doors swung open, and a flood of wedding guests started searching the property.

She had been right about everything except for a few people who scanned the ledges and roof of the tall building. She could hear excited voices in the distance. Some people screamed out orders to others, while some cupped their mouths and called out her name. There was nothing funny about the people swarming over the property. Their movements were quick and desperate. Three cars left the parking lot and screamed down the church road, heading out onto the main street. Through a slit in the branches, she could see others running for the straight tree line break where she had been only minutes before.

She trembled with the fear of what the groom might do to her if she was found hiding in a tree. His thugs might rough her up some with his approval. Mostly, she feared a ride back to his mansion where he might exact a heavier toll on her. The thought of it made her shake uncontrollably.

CHAPTER TWO

Antonio Madera looked around from the church's stage. The wedding song droned on from the organist. He was past the point of tapping his foot. Now he was breathing heavily and perspiring around his upper lip. About a dozen guests rose from their seats and looked around. He glanced back at the priest and sighed. The ring bearer stood glued to the carpet, as did the flower girl. The bridesmaids looked nervous, and they'd broken formation. What was it now? Seven minutes? Ten minutes? It was plain ass *too* many minutes!

A lone bride's maid walked from a side hallway, approached the stage and stopped. She held her palms face up and waggled her head. Her hands shook. Her open mouth and raised eyebrows spoke volumes.

Antonio quickly bent down, while his thin salt and pepper comb-over crashed over his forehead like a wave. He shoved it back up and said, "Where is she?"

"I don't know, Mr. Madera. She was here one minute and gone the next. I searched the back rooms and found nothing. I'm *so* sorry."

Antonio stiffened. He glared at the organist and swished his hand to cut the music. The organist pulled her fingers from the keys and flicked a toggle switch. He looked out into the crowd, spotted two of his bouncers and gave them the up-and-at-'em gesture. Some wedding guests rose from their seats. People snapped their heads around. Murmurs rose. A voice cracked the relative quiet. "What the hell, man?"

"What is the nature of the problem, young man?" asked the priest.

Antonio glared at Father Dennis. "You know about as much as I do."

The priest cocked his head puppy fashion. "I must insist that we continue with this ceremony or postpone it. This is highly irregular."

"You're getting paid, aren't you?" asked Antonio. "You can wait like the rest of us."

"I detect some venom in your tone, young man. I have a schedule to keep."

Antonio raised a stiff middle finger. "Here's your next appointment. Sit on this!"

The priest's mouth gaped. "I should take that as a personal insult."

"Take it anyway you want, you old crone."

"Oh!" The priest put a hand over his chest.

A collective groan rose from the crowd. A woman jabbed a finger at Antonio. "How dare you talk that way to a man of the cloth. May you be damned by Almighty God!"

Antonio stepped down from the altar, joined his men and marched off to a side hallway that led to the back of the church. He could hear shoe and heel clicks following some distance behind. As soon as he thought he was out of earshot, he said, "You guys split up, and check both sides, first the bathrooms, then the anti-rooms and utility closets."

Three more of Antonio's employees caught up with him. He ordered two younger men to the second floor and the tallest man out to the parking lot.

"Find her!" Antonio said.

His men rushed to do his bidding. Someone behind him yelled, "How can we help, sir?"

"Hell, I dunno. We're missing a bride. *I'm* missing a bride. Search the church property. Holler out if you find her."

Somebody else called out, "You heard that. We've got a lost bride. Spread out. She might be in danger!"

Bodies rushed past Antonio, clipping his shoulders. It was a stampede. Some of his personal friends surrounded him and asked stupid questions for which he had no answers. He shooed them off. He stormed off, made a left down a hallway, and came to an open door on his right. He entered a vacant classroom, needing to sit down and gather his thoughts.

Trying to squeeze into one of the student chairs proved impossible, so he took a seat behind the teacher's desk and massaged his temples. It was inconceivable that his young bride would disappear just when the ceremony was ready to start. She just wouldn't, she couldn't, do this to him! Something had happened. Maybe it was a straight-up kidnapping or maybe a fall resulting in unconsciousness. Maybe she was sick and holed up in a bathroom stall somewhere.

Someone peeked around the door frame. "Naw, nobody in here." The head disappeared.

Thirty minutes later, his full contingent of bouncers and body guards found him, and they all talked at once. The message was the same. His bride was not anywhere on the property. She'd vanished. He knew she had arrived in a bridesmaid's car, and he'd just been told the car was still in the parking lot. He debated whether to call the police. They weren't exactly fond of Antonio and his business dealings, but they'd frequented his shops, club shows and sex theaters just as much as any strangers or regular customers. *Fuckin' hypocrites.*

They saw Antonio as seedy, an undesirable shit stain on the city. No. The cops would not expend the energy to help him unless they thought he might blackmail them, which wasn't a bad idea. Maybe it was time to threaten them with the black book which had all the names and phone numbers of his most influential high-profile customers. How would it look for dignitaries—phone numbers plastered all over the pages of that book for all the world to see? It wouldn't be the type of notoriety they were looking for.

And to think, his fiancé had a priceless engagement ring on her finger. He would pull out all stops to find her. She would pay for the insult.

Antonio Madera took a deep, filling breath. His scream came out like a steam whistle.

CHAPTER THREE

Ryan Barlow pulled the same turn to St. Elizabeth's church lot for a smoke break on his way home. He drove down the winding blacktop road and stopped halfway between the frontage street and the church parking lot. The location marked his haven for a smoke break, and now he had a two-month old Toyota with all the bells and whistles. He didn't care about the last beater he owned, a deathly old Suzuki Samurai that came with a windup key and three tires in the grave. No, this vehicle was a source of pride, a technological marvel. It *talked* to him. It wished him a good morning. Not like some other bitch he knew. *Dear Lord, I didn't mean that!*

He strolled toward his favorite oak tree, the one that had the largest trunk and thickest boughs. He could stand in the cooling shade, the canopy overhead wiping out all but a few slivers of sunlight. He arrived at his usual spot next to the trunk, pulled out his pack and lit up one. He looked down and noticed a pile of dirty butts he had dropped in the past, too close to the tree to be chopped up by the church's huge riding mower.

Ryan brought his eyes around to the church between the trees. The parking lot was filled with expensive late-model cars and SUVs. There was no service on Saturday. But there was definitely an activity going on.

Something hit his shoulder. Dust specks fell in front of his eyes. Now there was a tap on his head. A piece of bark hit the grass. He looked up expecting to see a squirrel, but then furrowed his brows and stepped backward.

A female crouched on a thick branch ten feet up from the ground. She was wearing a fluffy bridal dress. A long bridal train was tied in a knot around her neck. Her face looked elfish, framed by short, black, pixie-cut hair that sported purple ribbons.

Ryan flicked his cigarette away. "What in the fuc...damnation are you doing up there?"

"You've got to help me," the bride said, nearly losing her balance, and sending down a shower of bark bits and wood dust.

"Climb down out of there. Are you trying to kill yourself?" He looked around, expecting to see someone catching him talking to a bride in a tree.

"I can't get down," she said, "It's too hard with all this on. Help me."

"How'd you get up there?"

"I climbed—shimmied."

"Then climb-shimmy back down." He couldn't believe he was having this conversation. He wondered if he was the target of some hidden camera.

"Do you have car?" she asked as she looked through the tree limbs.

"Yeah, what about it?"

"Okay, good. You've got to get me off the property."

The bride turned, dropped her train, and hugged the trunk. She bowed her legs; her heels pressed into the bark. She began a slow duck walk down.

Ryan had the good grace to avert his eyes—his vision offered a straight shot up her wedding dress. He glanced up, giving in to the curious spectacle. Of all things, she wore a racy purple thong.

Ryan heard an "Ohhh!" and saw her falling backward. He threw his arms up, fashioning a cradle. He braced his legs for the impact. When he caught her, it was like a small child had alighted in his arms. He caught a glimpse of her and saw a beautiful face that was screwed up and flushed pink. She looked very young, which made him feel like a pervert for checking her out. She kicked and wiggled out of his arms, pulled her train up and ran for his car.

"Wait just a damn..." He ran after her. She threw open the rear passenger door of his car, slid in, then slammed the door shut before he caught her. He looked in and saw her crouched low, knees on the floorboard, the dress billowing up like the petals of a huge white flower. His first instinct was to drag her out by her heels.

"Get out!" he said.

"I can't. They'll see me."

Something clicked in his mind—the realization that this escapee bride could be in trouble or even danger. Still, he couldn't understand why it was any of his business.

Ryan cornered his car, hopped in, and started the engine. He pulled a U-turn and drove up the church driveway to the frontage road, made a left and sped up. *You've got me so God-damned rattled I forgot my seatbelt. Where did my pack of smokes go?* He wanted to ask the obvious, like what are you doing in my car? But he wasn't completely daft.

"You're a runaway bride," he said over his shoulder and made a hard left.

"I'm not admitting anything," she said.

"You'll tell me the truth, or I'll take you to the police station."

"No. Don't do that. Just take me to your place. I need to make plans, and I'll explain there. Then I'll leave. I promise."

Lord and Master of the universe, why me? I only went to check in on my wife and shop for food. I just had a routine cigarette break. Then a little bird falls into my arms from out of a tree next to a church. She forces her way into my car and wants me to take her to my place.

Ryan made an abrupt course change from his normal route home. He pulled onto the town's Main Street and pulled up along the curve of the Sunrise Beach Police Department. He got out and marched around to the passenger door, flipped it open and grabbed the bride's legs. He pulled. She latched onto the opposite door rest.

"You're leaving right now," said Ryan under his breath. "Leggo that door!"

She mule kicked him in the face. "Help. Help me! He's trying to rape me!"

"Jesus Christ, shut up!" Ryan refastened his grip, pulled and tore off one of her white nylons. He gave a frantic backward glance, expecting to see a cop converge on him at any moment. Seeing no one alerted to the struggle, he tried to drag her out again.

"I've been kidnapped!" shouted the woman.

"Okay, okay. You win!"

Ryan slammed the door and got behind the driver's seat. He took off slowly, glancing in the rearview mirror. All he could see was the fluffy dress obscuring most of the rear view. "Get that dress down," he told her. "And that was a dirty trick."

"Your trick was dirtier."

"Settle down, and I'll take you home. What the hell's your name anyway?"

"What's yours?"

"I'm the one asking the questions here. I'm the idiot chauffer."

"Candice Sabbella. Now what's yours?"

"Ryan Barlow. At least that's a start. It looks like you bugged out from your wedding. What the hell happened?"

"I'll tell you later. It's complicated."

It's always complicated. There are always strings, conditions, if, ands and buts. The stories might have different twists, but they all come out the same—trouble. She's a feisty little thing. The roles should have been reversed; the groom should have slipped out the back door. Which means that the groom is made of some stern stuff if he can tolerate the likes of Candace Sabbella.

Ryan spoke over his shoulder. "What kind of name is Sabbella?" *How do you make conversation with a bride in your backseat?* "Are you Mexican or something?"

"Sabbella is Italian—tribal. My other half is Native American —Abenaki."

"Tribal...okay, whatever that means."

Candice sneezed, then sucked a breath. "Your car has that new car smell. Is it naugahyde or vinyl?"

"What difference does it make? It was a custom option—Corinthian leather."

"Oh, whoop dee doo. It's *Corinthian* leather."

"Where's your house, smart ass?"

Ryan felt the pulse buck in his neck. He made two right turns, ending up on a beach road. He slowed down for cross foot-traffic—people carrying inner tubes and surfboards. He would be home any minute now, and maybe the nightmare would ease up. Or could it get worse?

He heard his back window go down and then felt a body movement. "What are you doing back there?"

"I just heaved the veil and train."

"Now that was real smart. How old are you anyway?" He had his house in sight. It stuck out like a pencil in a stack of toothpicks.

"I'm twenty-seven."

"Give me a break. You look like a teenager."

"I'll bet you weren't thinking that when you looked up my dress."

Dear God in heaven, hallowed be thy name. She had him there. He couldn't deny it, but how could he have caught her so quickly if his eyes had been somewhere else? So she was a woman. He relived the vision of the purple thong but felt a bit guilty about it. Not too much. But *enough!*

Ryan slowed and made the gentle arc up and into his driveway. He pulled the remote out of the dash saddle and poised a finger over the garage door opener.

"If we're home, don't let anybody see me like this," she said. "Take me into the garage and pull the door down."

He didn't answer. The garage door opened, and he slid the Toyota inside. He got out and opened up the left rear passenger door, since her head faced that way. She looked up at him with an 'are we safe?' expression. He nodded. She grabbed her high heels and crawled out. It was then he noticed just how petite she was. Candice couldn't have been much taller than five-three or five-four and about a hundred and ten pounds. He stared at her chest, which was cinched up tight in some type of corset arrangement that looked like a medieval torture device. The gown looked very expensive, more costly than what his wife had bought on their wedding day. Tiny crystal beads adorned it. Some other material looked like satin.

She blew her bangs upward. "I know. Itty bitty tittee committee. But it's the corset smashing everything in."

He wasn't even about to field that one. After he pulled his grocery bag out of the trunk, he let her pass him, which was a mistake, because he had to reach around her to unlock the kitchen door. Her hair smelled like flowers or fruit juice, he couldn't decide which. He'd had trouble identifying his wife's scent the day of their wedding. She'd told him it was Taboo. How fitting that such a label was applied to their broken marriage.

Once inside the kitchen, Ryan set the grocery bag on the counter. Candice dropped her shoes and stared across the dining room and into the sunken living room. She looked out the rear glass slider, which revealed an enclosed backyard. He watched her walk over the tiled floor, drinking in the sights. She looked up at the thick rafters in the high ceiling.

"It looks new, but it smells funky old. What kind of a beach house is this? I'm sorry. Where are my manners? It's nice to meet you, Ryan Barlow. I appreciate what you've done for me. I'm sorry I got you into this." She rose up on her tiptoes. "Your eyes remind me of the sky—very blue with some grayish clouds, and you've got to be standing six-two or more."

The words caught in his throat for a moment, and then he managed, "Yeah, great." He didn't know what to do with her. "Look, you might be in the mood for some coffee or something to eat, but I think a couple of straight shots are in order, so you can spill your guts or have a good cry. Maybe both. Then we can get you out of here." He didn't mean to sound so blunt and unaccommodating, but the situation dictated it.

She looked around. "Do you live here alone? I don't want to get you in trouble. I know I should have thought of that."

"I'm alone now. We can talk about that later. Your poison? Or do you even drink?"

"Make it a double tanqueray gin with a lime twist. I'm no prude."

He almost laughed out loud while heading to the liquor cabinet. He poured himself a glass of straight tequila and made her a double in a rock glass. He offered her a seat on his button-tuck leather sofa. Before she sat down, she crossed the floor and pulled the living room drapes closed. When she returned, she sat down, took a healthy pull of her drink and made a face.

Ryan looked at the drapes. "So you don't want to be found."

"I've got to stay low and off the streets. My life depends on it."

A life always depends on it. "Okay, I get that part of it. How did you think you were going to hide from a search party while you were up in that tree?" He figured he'd start with the basics. He had to test her sanity.

"I didn't want to run all the way out to the highway looking like this. I thought if I stayed in the tree until dark, I could get away easier. Nobody would think about searching the trees. I was going to wait it out. Besides, I went out the ladies' second story bathroom window and down a drain pipe. I thought I would only have time enough to make it a little way before I had to duck for cover."

That part of her story made sense, in a twisted sort of way. The next question had everything to do with her skipping out on her wedding.

Ryan took a sip of his drink and cleared his throat. "There had to be a reason for you running away. I'm thinking that you paired up with the wrong guy and changed your mind at the last minute. Nothing else makes sense."

Candice pulled her full-length gloves off and slapped them over the armrest. "That's about the size of it."

"Aren't you sure? Why didn't you just tell this guy to piss up a rope and end the engagement before it came down to walking the aisle?"

She gave him a stern look. "You don't tell this guy what to do. He runs a syndicate. He's a major boss. He makes his own laws. He has people murdered, and he's a thief and a braggart."

Ryan didn't flinch or make any outward expression of fear. "Okay, so he's carrying a lot of nasty baggage."

"He's got more nasty baggage..." She rolled her eyes. "...than a Carnival Cruise ship."

"Okay, it's over then. You're safe for now until I figure out what to do with you."

"It won't be over until he finds me, and he won't stop until he does."

Ryan sloshed his drink down his shirt. *Oh no, you don't. You're headin' on out of here.*

She stood up abruptly and set her drink down. When she turned her back on him, she said, "I can't breathe. Get me out of this."

Ryan looked at her back. "Now how am I supposed to do that?"

"See those things that look like bodice stitches? Unlace them all."

"Uh, no. Not here. We'll do it in the bedroom. Besides, you don't have anything to wear. My wife left some clothes that might fit you."

"Then you're happily married?"

"Well, kind of. More married than not, I guess. It's okay for now. She left me. Temporarily."

Candace turned around. "Looks like we're in the same boat. Lead the way before I suffocate."

"Follow me." He started up the stairs. She followed. He couldn't hear her footfalls behind him. But he heard her voice.

"You have great butt for a tall guy."

CHAPTER FOUR

He rifled through the chest of drawers, pulling garments out and tossing them on the guest bed. He found almost everything required: panties, several tops, jogging pants and shorts, some socks and a pair of old Nike tennis shoes. He changed his mind about the shoes, went to the closet and pulled out a pair of one-size-fits-all sandals. He saw her eyes scanning the clothes. She blinked.

"This stuff is a little large," he said. "You can pin it up or something. My wife isn't really fat. She's just tall and voluptuous. You'll have to make do." *This little gal was no bigger than a June bug and a most unexpected guest to have to dress.* He glanced at her forearms and saw some defined muscles, which surprised him. Then he remembered handling her body and how rock hard it was.

She turned around and said, "I'll manage. Just *puleeze* get me out of this."

He started at the bottom, undoing a small bow and then worked the cross-hatched lace, pulling it free. After the first five rows her torso began to expand, and he was relieved to see her body filling out a little. Candace looked thinner around the waist than he expected. She moaned when he got to the tenth row. When he finally undid the top snap, he splayed the two halves open like butterfly wings, exposing a tanned and muscular back. Her brassier strap was thin and purple.

"You a bodybuilder?" he asked.

"No." She turned around, grazing his stomach with her breasts which had frothed forth.

She started to yank the dress up and off her shoulders. "I'll stash all of this under the bed."

He turned quickly, jaunted out of the bedroom and down the stairs into the living room.

"Thank you, Ryan!" she called out to him.

"Yeah, yeah," he murmured.

He retrieved his drink, gulped it down, made another one in a chimney glass and plopped down on the sofa. He couldn't bring his mind to heel. He had a mysterious woman stripping down in his guest room and donning his wife's clothes. He wasn't merely asking for trouble. He was begging for it. What if Gloria walked in right now? How would he explain it? They were so damn close to patching up their marriage that to lose their progress was unthinkable. He'd never be forgiven for another woman a second time.

All the counseling in the world couldn't save him from this mess. His wife would get out the nails and rope and hang him from a cross. She had good taste, too...in lawyers. She might get half of everything in a divorce, including one of his balls, and she'd be happy as a tornado in a trailer park doing so.

Ryan heard small footsteps leaping down the stairs. Candace appeared wearing some nylon Yoga pants, a blue T-shirt and the sandals. The T-shirt was skin tight. Thank the Maker she wore a brassiere.

"I found some safety pins and pinned the shirt back," said Candace and sat on the sofa beside him. She picked up her drink and gave him an opened mouth smile.

He glanced at her thighs. "You are a damn bodybuilder," he said. "Don't lie to me."

"Nope. I do other things to stay in shape. Do you wanna know what?"

"Let's forget about it. Now who is this groom who was left standing at the altar?" He watched her knock back the rest of her drink. She coughed and beat her chest. He took her glass and refilled it. He sat down after giving it to her.

"Antonio Madera. He's—"

"Jesus, I know who he is." Ryan gritted his teeth. "He's that porn king who makes the news every so often. A lot of agencies have been trying to shut him down and drive him away from the east coast."

The guy was a murdering hustler, the grand mal seizure of law breakers. Antonio Madera was a fat, greasy little penguin with an overshot jaw and a rat-like face that could stop a clock. He had guards, hired assassins and more whores than Las Vegas. But that would mean...

"Don't look at me like that," she said. "I didn't have anything to do with his racket. I got engaged to him. It was a dumb thing to do. Well, I'm not too dumb." She held up her finger, to show off her engagement ring. "I could buy a cheap condo if I live long enough. I can chase after my dream if I want to."

He found her arrangement with Madera disgusting. "But I mean *you*... and *him*? Were you out of your mind?" Talk about low standards! She'd scraped the dregs from the bottom of the barrel to end up with Antonio Madera.

"I had to do it," she said.

"You're a damn fool for hangin' around with that dude. I don't want anything to do with this." He paced the floor.

She reared up from the sofa, clasping her hands. "Please keep me. I need to be safe."

"You're out of your mind. You need to leave."

She dropped to her knees and hugged his thighs. "I'm begging you. I need you...I need your help," she wailed. "God, please help me!"

He pushed her away. He thought about the God comment. She had called on God.

He glared at her. "All right. You stay. But only until we can find you another place."

She moped, sat on the sofa, and wiped her eyes. "Thank you for being kind to me."

He was not a heartless man. "But why him? That man could ruin your rep for good."

"I was low on money. He found me in a small club and offered me three times the pay. It was easy for me to switch to his flagship. I got A-one service, protection, and my choice of shifts. I was his sugar shack queen. As far as the other thing, I didn't have to do much to get him off and keep him happy." She made a pumping jack-off movement with her hand.

"I think I'm going to be sick. What the hell did you do on his flagship?"

"Pole dancer. It's a flagship club, not a boat."

"A stripper? Why did—"

"Not a stripper. An exotic entertainer. Haven't you ever been to a club?"

"Why the hell would I go to one when I'm married?"

"Where's your wife now?"

"She's at her parents." Now she might ask him if he had any kids. He would have to explain that his wife had had two ectopic pregnancies as a young woman, damaging both of her tubes.

"That's my point. I cater to single and unsatisfied men. It's a distraction—a fun thing. There's nothing dirty about it."

"Those girls just swing their asses and flail their arms around. That's not dancing."

"*Oh, you!*"

"Let's talk about something else."

"You brought it up. What do you do for a living?"

"I paint book and magazine covers for elite publications. New York City buys most of my work. It's good pay with a lot of freelance opportunities."

"When do you go to work?"

"Any time I want. I work on the third floor here, a private studio."

"I didn't know this house was that big. You must be doing okay."

He figured he'd said enough about his income and property. He wouldn't tell her the house was bequeathed to him by his great uncle who had been regarded as one of the greatest oil painters on Martha's Vineyard. He had taught Ryan everything about style and methods of creating fine art. Even back in his day, his great uncle knew that this house would have historical value. His family had been whalers and settled the area in the 1600s.

Ryan thought his runaway bride-stripper-dance girl could have layers. One of those layers could have *thief* written all over it. He didn't know her well enough to trust her. She seemed okay. She sounded honest. There was no doubt about the trouble she was in. She was somebody to talk to. There was Billy and Ross who visited him, but they were the wrong gender. That's what he got for going to a high school reunion with the best of intentions and then suffering from a prank that went viral on the Internet. If it weren't for no-good, stinking Julie Monroe, he wouldn't have been cut off from his wife.

Candace must have read his thoughts because she stared at him without moving.

She lowered her voice. "You want to tell me about it? You're taking it really hard. I can tell."

"Not right now. Or maybe not ever."

"You must love her."

"I do with all my heart. Let's just say it was a misunderstanding and leave it at that."

"Can we go out in the backyard?"

"Why?"

"I want some fresh air. It's fenced in, so I'm sure it's safe."

They put their drinks down and stood up. Ryan led the way through the rear slider and out into the back property. Candace looked from the fire pit to a hammock off to the side and then to the flower beds. The sand was clean and raked, and there were patches of bright green ice plant here and there. He led her to the back fence of the property, turned and pointed upward.

Candace gazed up and whistled. "Oh, my God. It's a Victorian decked out in gingerbread. It's got Martha's Vineyard written all over it."

He always got that reaction. He owned one of the few three-story Vics in his city. "We're on the edge of Aquinnah, east of the Gay Head Lighthouse."

She turned on her heel. "Oh, what an awesome place. You are so lucky to...I mean you must have worked really hard for all of this."

"My beach is private on the other side. It comes with an old boardwalk. The Shenandoah is moored at the Vineyard Haven Marina." He had just given out too much.

"What's a Shenandoah?"

"A forty-one foot sailboat with an auto pilot."

She whistled again. "You would give Antonio a run for his money. He's a landlubber, though."

"Ever been sailing?" It was not an invitation.

"No, but I'd jump at the chance. I just don't know anything about it." She looked up at the sky, turning three hundred and sixty degrees around. "I don't suppose he'd have a helicopter after me unless he called the cops. I'm not sure if he would do that. He usually takes care of business himself. But then he could give the cops a slick deal to help him. He's hard to figure."

After they stepped through the back gate, Candace pointed down the beach. "What's that boat down there?"

"That's not a boat. That is the ultimate in luxury. That is a sixty-seven and one half foot Class D Galaxy sport yacht. See all those rocks in the water out there?"

She nodded.

"Well, that's a breakwater. And he uses that private pier there to moor his yacht."

"Then he's rich."

"Theo Albright is swimming in it. Let's get back in now."

Ryan showed Candace the complete house, visiting every room from the bottom up. Her eyes got wider with each new scene. When they stopped at the octagonal tower doorway on the third floor, he pointed to the inside. She eyed some canvas rolls and single stock. Ornate picture frames hung on wall rods. Finished paintings were stacked near the doorway. A drafting table took up the area near the front windows, and next to it sat two easels. Track lighting ran in strips under the oak beam rafters. The floor was mottled with confetti specks of dried paint. A side table next to the easels held quart bottles of brushes, knives, and spatulas. Tubes of oil paint were stacked in neat rows inside a small open-ended box. Three antique spindle chairs were stacked upon each other. A small cot, wool blanket and a pillow sat against a wall. A tiny fridge served as a platform for an even tinier microwave. The place smelled of oil paints and thinner.

She nodded. "Even though it's bad for you, I love the odors in this place."

How ironic, he thought. Those smells were what drove him to sleep on the couch for the last three months, stricken from the second floor master bedroom and the embrace of his wife. He'd always tried to keep the fan going and the windows open. He did realize that toxic fumes could make a body sick. The efforts of his safety venting had done little good especially when the chemicals had been absorbed into his skin. Sometimes he'd collapsed on the master bed without taking a shower. Gloria had bitched and cast him from their bed and out of the room. She'd claimed he'd ruined her satin sheets and other expensive bedding. Sometimes she had him take two showers in a row, but some of the smell still lingered. It *was* his fault.

"I think it's *beautiful*," said Candace. "A little artist's nest."

"A studio."

"Yeah, that. I used to dabble with paints in junior college. I did real well."

He wanted to say he was impressed but decided against it. He would not encourage her. He had to get rid of her and fast. She could stay a couple of nights, but she was not about to camp out and get him in trouble. He hoped she wasn't the kind who mistook his kindness for weakness. That would cause him to rip her a new one. Although she'd have to push his buttons for him to snap at her.

They sauntered back down the stairs, sat on the living room sofa and finished their drinks in silence. Ryan stabbed the buttons on the remote, lighting up the wide screen TV. He scanned the channels until he found a National Geographic special. It was about the blue whale, the last of the titans that still struggled to live in a polluted habitat. He kicked back and checked his watch. It was six in the evening, and he dreaded going upstairs to work on a series of covers that were on special order. Science fiction motifs were not his specialty, but he'd managed it before and hadn't been rejected. He'd done the samples in watercolors, so they were already approved. It was only a matter of going through the final brush strokes with oil.

He watched the program for a half hour, then glanced to his side. His guest's head leaned against the armrest, lolling forward. She'd fallen asleep. Just great. He clapped his hands sharply. She started and opened her eyes. She tried to hold her head up, but she was still groggy. She conked out again, emitting little wheezing snores. Damn his luck. She'd passed out straight away on his sofa which meant he couldn't invite anyone into the house with her in plain sight. He could cover her up with a blanket, but she might kick it off. What to do?

He stood up and walked to her. He studied the position of her body, adjusted his hands, and jabbed them under her legs and around her middle. He rose with her in his arms. She was a little heavier than he'd first thought. He cornered the couch and walked her up the stairs, getting a whiff of her fragrance. It reminded him of strawberries this time. But what the hell did he know about women's perfumes? Jack squat, that's what he knew! Did he care? Well, maybe.

He took her into the guest room and laid her on the bed. He couldn't help but notice that the little girl with a woman's face reminded him of some classic beauty out of *Vogue Magazine*. He pulled a comforter from the closet and flung it over her. He left, closing the door behind him, and headed for the first floor.

He paced back and forth over the kitchen tiles,his head down. He felt in the mood for another drink, but he had work to do. He didn't need to make any drunken skid marks with a paint brush. Not on a custom order. He had a cigarette instead, smoking it down to the butt. Then he went into the kitchen.

Ryan put the coffee on to brew, walked to the fridge, opened it up and checked the inventory. Hot dogs, mustard and relish took up the top shelf next to three pounds of bacon and four dozen eggs. The celery in the side door was reserved for the slathering of crunchy peanut butter. Two pounds of hamburger meat sat on the second shelf next to four packages of hamburger buns, which also served as hot dog buns. On closer inspection, the hamburger meat was gray. He smelled it and crinkled his nose. He double wrapped it in plastic grocery bags and tossed it in the kitchen trash. Half a can of bean sprouts sat in their original can covered with a foil top. He estimated the sprouts to be a week old, maybe more. They also hit the kitchen trash. The bottom shelf was crowded with designer water. He took a certain amount of pride in knowing he was environmentally conscious and protective of his teeth and bladder. None of that sewer water straight out of the tap for him.

He swung the freezer door open and smiled. He had a dozen turkey potpies stacked next to cords of chicken burritos. "Now that's what I'm talkin' about." He shut both doors, then stepped in front of his cabinets and pulled open two doors. He counted ten packages of Kraft macaroni and cheese and two dozen packs of beef Top Ramen. "Oh, yeah. We are loaded down with the staples for the week." He frowned and slammed the doors.

Who was he kidding? He didn't have the ingredients to make a halfway decent meal. It wasn't like he didn't have any money to buy food. He was just a creature of habit and had been since Gloria had left him. His best buds, Billy and Ross, paid no mind. They didn't have discriminating palates and hardly chewed their food. Fresh fish from deep sea fishing was a special treat. White bass and halibut were choice eats, and Ryan usually had tartar sauce on hand. He thought he had some in the fridge, but he must have been mistaken

A half loaf of bread sat on the counter, but he could see mold on it. He tossed that out, too. Now there wasn't any toast for breakfast. He slapped the counter out of frustration. It would be EGGS AND BACON, and that would be it!

He didn't think she would wake up for a late dinner, and if she did, she could munch on a hotdog or something.

He plodded up the stairs and entered his studio, flicking on the bright track lighting. Next he turned on a small fan and opened a window. He set a work timer, sat down in front of his loaded easel and looked at what he had. The landscape was that of an arid planet dotted with some pretzel-like trees. The grass and shrubbery had grays and blues in it. Red hillocks raised out of the background. Two white moons sat in the low horizon, while a third one reposed higher up and was dark gray and cracked in half. A red dwarf sun lay stationary off to the right almost out of frame. He needed to render the shadowing to finish off this piece. The cover painting was number five in a seven-book series called Custodian of the Stars. He felt pleased with his progress, ahead of schedule at this point.

Ryan turned on the radio to his favorite blues station and turned it up. He took some deep breaths, then laid out his brushes and paints. He began dabbing the bulk of the shadowing, and when that was finished, he used a fine-tipped brush to bring out the detail. He stood up at times to get the best angle on the panorama. At other times, he sat and steadied his painting hand. He only looked at his timer once, knowing that he hadn't reached his time quota. But he'd made swift progress.

It took two hours to finish panel number five. He'd forgotten to lay a cloth over his thighs again. He had smears of paint on his new Levi pants. There was nothing like the lack of the presence of mind to change into his old stained duds before starting. That was one of the major complaints from his wife. She never enjoyed trying to wash his clothes and rid them of deep paint stains and odors. If they were beyond salvaging, she'd burn them in the fire pit out back. What kind of self-discipline could he expect of himself anyway after sucking down almost a quart of tequila, coupled with the stress of inviting a high-risk stranger into his house? Who wouldn't be lax and forgetful?

He set his brushes to soak, tidied up and went to his studio fridge. He pulled out a half-filled bottle of Crystal Champagne and poured himself a hefty slug. He sipped it, finding it a little flat but palatable. He sat back down and turned up the radio. *Number five painting done.*

CHAPTER FIVE

C andace saw the nightmare vision of her working on Antonio Madera again while he sipped his favorite Scotch whisky and thumbed the buttons on a TV remote. She felt numb, eyes closed, mouth shut. He was a pig, and she felt nothing for him other than financial gratitude. He had a different exotic dancer almost every night to frolic with. So what did he care if a woman felt anything at all? There was no love between them, no real joyful pleasure. It was a repetitive duty that disgusted her on one hand and angered her on the other. The connection with the man was so meaningless that she could have been trying to arouse the feeling from a piece of fruit and wanting to smash the pulp out of it.

When it was over, she sat as far away from him as she could on the long sofa and dropped her eyes, knowing that he was tucking himself back in. Antonio surfed the channels for his favorite porn sites that could only mean that he was expecting a repeat.

She woke up shivering and staring into the dark. After taking in some slow measured breaths, she began to calm. And then she thought of her life.

She'd had enough boyfriends and one-nighters in her day. Those who wanted straight-up sex without any commitment. Those who were possessive and wanted total commitment, including the Mamas boys of the bunch. Others lavished her with clothes, cars and appliances. There were guys who had offered her a home and security. Men, who begged and pleaded, were another ilk. Dozens showered her with rings and proposed marriage. Many of them wanted domination and control because they viewed her as an everyday lowlife whore.

Sexual perverts and black hearted deviates flocked to her as well as those who were just plain crazy and living in an alcohol- and drug-induced world. The guys who were addicted to and overloaded on anti-depressants were some of the worst cases. Those drugs were the anti-Christ of the lot, up there with meth, cocaine, heroin and crack. Those substances sent the mind sailing out of the universe, leaving an empty, soulless shell behind.

Just once. Why hadn't she ever met that guy who was ordinary and in touch with his feelings? Where was the tenderness and honesty she craved? Where was that sensitive and loving person who could cry just as hard as she could and not be ashamed? Where was he, that man who could hold hands, snuggle, and kiss without expecting anything? Where were the small, unexpected gifts? She wouldn't care if he was as dumb as a box of rocks—if his heart was in tune and his karma aligned, it didn't matter. Intelligence could not stand in for the core of one's existence. Where was the lover, the passionate and caring gentleman she had dreamed of and ached for?

She was so tired of running through the game maze, the false fronts of deception, excursions into nothingness. She felt like the spark of life had been ripped right out of her heart. She had kissed so many frogs to find the prince that her lips were chaffed. The white knight in shining armor that she'd expected to save her was nothing more than a stuffed shirt filled with the fat from gluttony that had arrived on a mangy, lame pony. She wasn't asking for much. She was praying for normalcy—just a common balance of all the emotions that made up a human being.

Then there was Ryan Barlow—a surprise acquaintance. And she wondered about him. He had a tough exterior, but she did, too. He seemed introverted, bothered by people or company. His art studio looked like a second home, and no guesswork was needed to know that he spent his days and nights in that cramped little space, sitting there, slump-shouldered and filled up with lots of stress, pressure, and frustration.

Candace had his number.

He was forever honest and loyal to a wife who had left their home. He'd thought enough of his wife to honor a commitment and try to patch things up. Candace could see that, feel it, almost taste it on him. That was the wonderful part of him—a man who loved beyond the surface and down into the depths.

But he had a major conflict going on; he was frightened of her and maybe rightfully so. She was a wrench stuck in his gears. She was a hazard—a danger. He had virtue. But he held so much in that there was no accounting for his real personality. He cared and didn't know it or didn't want anyone else to know it. He moved with the grace of a gentleman, someone who was afraid to step on somebody's toes. A kind heart beat inside his chest, and he seemed threatened by it.

And oh, was he beautiful! He had mesmerizing eyes that could drag a woman clear across a dance floor. He had full lips, hair like spun gold and a goatee that gave him a regal distinction. Although he was gangly, the man could wear a pair of Levi's that could make nuns wet. Ryan was tall, but he almost seemed to downplay it with a forward stoop. It made her laugh watching him walk around with such a determined look on his face as though he was programmed. It was like his body had to go down and forward to gain speed. And what a body! He had nice proportions with a slender physique, but firm in all the right places. The words *dreamboat* and *pretty* came to her mind.

How could she approach him and ask him to be her friend? Did she dare do such a thing? Could she find out if a man like that would show just a hint of attraction for her? It would tell her if she'd found the type of man she'd been looking for all her life. But there was a snag in her plans. He had a wife. However, what if his wife decided to divorce him? Could she make a move then? Hell and damnation with what he owned and what he had. This guy could probably charm the daylights out of a woman if he lived in a pup tent next to a garbage dump. He was that *fine*. Yet she hardly knew him.

Who and what are you, Ryan Barlow? Am I crazy thinking about all this? Is it wrong to be protected, sheltered by a man like you? Why do I get the bellybutton tingle around you? Why did I feel light-headed when you carried me up the stairs to bed? Oh, yeah, I was awake the second you clapped your hands. It felt good, safe to be in a pair of strapping arms. I wanted to look up into your eyes so desperately.

Candace sighed and threw her legs over the bed. There was just enough light in the room to see the outlines of things, that and the crack of light spilling underneath the door. She pushed off the bed and took cautious steps across the room. Then she heard something that sounded like a radio voice.

CHAPTER SIX

Ryan continued with the min-celebration after knocking out number five. His next painting was a ship interior with a crewmember sitting at a navigation station. The last one was frontal profiles of all the characters against a cave backdrop from which two pairs of glowing eyes shone. Easy peasy. He stroked his goatee, pleased with himself in spite of the distractions. He knew how to work under pressure and had never lost an assignment.

He pulled his paint-smeared contract in front of him and turned some pages. When he looked at the payment clause he smiled—seventeen thousand five hundred, less delivery and supplies. He had a nine-day wrap-up date and felt certain he would make it. Complications might extend it to eleven days. He changed the radio channel, coming to rest on his favorite talk show, Coast to Coast. He heard Art Bell's voice on his Somewhere in Time program and turned it up over the fan noise. Tonight's program dealt with the old Grass Man out of Ohio. The last program he'd caught covered the Chupacabra.

He listened to the program for fifteen minutes, grabbed his glass and turned around. He damn near pitched the empty glass over his head. His heart valves felt like they'd locked up.

Candace sat on the edge of his cot, looking at him with sleepy eyes.

She had her elbows stuffed in the cot pillow which sat on her lap. With her palms propped under her chin, she blinked, trying to get him in focus.

Ryan sucked a breath, threw his chest out. "What the hell are you doing up here?"

"I couldn't find you."

"This is my private studio. No one is allowed up here while I'm working. No visitors. Just so you know this is off limits to you."

"I woke up and didn't know where I was. I'm afraid of the dark."

"I put you in the guest room. You should have stayed there and slept."

"I didn't know where you were. Then I heard the radio and followed the noise. I just didn't want to be alone. I think I had a nightmare."

"You think?"

"Well, I did. I needed to be around somebody."

"Okay, you're safe. Go back to bed."

"What are you listening to?"

"You're impossible. You know that? It wouldn't interest you."

"I listen to Coast to Coast all the time. I like George Noory."

He walked to the fridge and refilled his glass. He sat down at his station and glared at her. She looked like a sad little mouse with ruffled hair. She must have felt comfortable because she leaned forward with her legs spread wide open. He couldn't decide if she had bad manners or was uninhibited. She could have used some pointers on ladylike behavior. Gloria would have drummed her into shape fast. And he could swear she was an older teen who didn't know any better. *I'm in big trouble if you're jailbait.*

He stared her down until she looked away. "Now what?" he asked, perturbed. "Do I have to babysit you?"

"I'm not a baby. I'm a woman." She furrowed her brows, bringing her eyes around to meet his. "Why can't I just sit here?"

He rolled his head around in slow circles, feeling another tension headache barreling down on him. "I'm about to go to bed. I've had a full shift."

Candace moved the pillow to her side and brought her knees together. "I want to sleep near...I mean, I'll sleep on your bedroom floor and not bother you."

"I'm not going to win this one, am I?"

A grin cracked across her face. "I hope not."

"Keep your clothes on. Stay on the floor, and don't bug me for anything. Shut the bathroom door before you flush the toilet. No night raids on the fridge. You got all that?" She had more moxie than a junkyard mongrel. She'd have to follow some rules.

"You don't have anything to raid. I snuck a look in your fridge" She stood up. "It smells a bit rancid in here."

"And no bitching about smells. I've had enough of that shit. I'll shower, change out and run the air conditioner."

"Hoy!" She skipped out the door.

Ryan scanned the local radio channels and landed on the current news station. He heard the reporter's voice loud and clear.

"And she has been missing for twelve hours. The local police department has now become involved in the hunt, considering the circumstances of the disappearance. Normally a forty-eight hour time stipulation applies. Not so in the case of the bride Candace Dee Sabella whose disappearance has launched a major search by volunteers, friends, and law enforcement. Next up, we have one of the witnesses, a bridesmaid who might know more about the incident. Any sightings of Candace Dee Sabella should be reported immediately to the nearest law enforcement agency. Once again, here is the physical description and statistics of the vanishing bride: She is twenty-seven years old, pixie-cut black hair, one hundred and eighteen pounds and..."

Ryan snapped off the radio. He bit down on his bottom lip and closed his eyes.

It wasn't difficult to make scrambled eggs and bacon. It had been a routine of Ryan's for months now, and he loved the meal as much as he loved anything else on a menu, although nothing could be faster and more filling than a takeout triple hamburger with pickles, lettuce, bacon, and onion rings. He was sorry he didn't have any hash browns, toast, and ham.

His young visitor had eagerly joined him for breakfast and sat watching him scurry about.

When he set the breakfast table and placed the utensils, Candace put her palms on the table's surface and stared at the platter heaped with bacon and eggs. Ryan had no problem dishing up his serving and taking the first mouthful. He poured a glass of milk and washed the food down. He eyed her over the rim of the glass and said, "You sleep well last night?"

She nodded. "I managed to pass out. I can't stand thinking he's around somewhere trying to find me. Did you hear?"

"You were quiet enough. I hardly knew you were there."

She walked to the fridge and plucked three eggs out of a carton. She tapped her nails on the shells of each egg in turn, broke them and then ate the yolks raw.

He watched, fascinated and was relieved that she tossed the shells in the kitchen trash.

She resumed her seat and pushed her plate to the side. "That's how you get real nutritional value from food." She dabbed her mouth. "You weren't very quiet last night. Are you a Gulf War Vet? Because you really go through some changes in your sleep."

"How so?" He already regretted his question.

"You thrash and babble. Sometimes you whine."

He stopped his fork in mid bite "Oh. Yeah. Not a vet. It's stress over deadlines mostly. Sometimes I get the shivers, sometimes some over-drinking that causes mild delirium tremens—your typical nightmare stuff." He hated to admit such things, but he'd learned as much from his wife about those incidents. It was another one of her reasons for exiling him to the couch. He didn't need to reveal any more skeletons in his closet. This girl would sleep elsewhere from now on.

"You didn't approve of the cooked breakfast?" he asked, gulping his sixth mouthful.

She frowned. "It's just that I'm used to different things, and I'll need to adjust."

"What different things?"

"Oh, seared Ahi tuna, strawberries, apple, pear and peach slices, tossed salad, yogurt..." She looked at the milk carton with some disdain. "...and fresh squeezed orange juice."

"Sounds like everything an iguana would eat. What about some good dinner stuff? What do you splurge on?"

"Umm..." She looked lost in thought. "Okay, rare steak filet mignon with blue cheese and mushrooms. Crab and lobster, fresh lean fish, ending with gelato garnished with strawberries. That's a guilty pleasure."

"Now you're talkin'! I didn't use any grease to cook this. It was Teflon."

"Teflon isn't going to provide vitamins and minerals."

"Who gives a flying fu…I take One-a-Days for health."

"Did you ever think of what you were missing in your diet?"

He thought about that for a moment. "I guess I'm feeling beat and could use some energy."

"If I can use that old laptop in your master bedroom, I'll search out some herbs and foods that will do just that."

"Then go ahead, and make a list, and I'll pick the stuff up. Miss Health Guru."

CHAPTER SEVEN

C andace put a palm under her chin and studied her breakfast host. *You're not fooling anyone, Mr. Ryan Barlow.* This man was caring and concerned, but he was a mess in the worst possible way. He seemed to mask most of his issues or have flimsy excuses. His cholesterol had to be off the charts, and he was just asking for a blood clot to bust loose and slam into his heart, what with sitting at a desk all day and into the night. She wondered if he followed any type of exercise regime and pondered how often he smoked since he carried a pack around with him, but seldom lit up. *A crutch for nervousness?* She didn't see any ashtrays around the house. It was possible his wife made him smoke outside. A drinking problem might have been high on his roster, too. The kitchen cupboards held some straight liquor. She'd seen him drinking champagne from a small fridge in the artist studio. Maybe his wife had been responsible for all his bad health habits. How much could his wife have loved him if she'd never been concerned about his nutrition and exercise? What kind of a woman would allow her husband to sink into a pit of ill health without lifting a finger to help him? Staying fit was easy—fun. It was the most natural thing in the world.

She felt safe with him though. Ryan didn't act like the kind of person who would take any shit off of anyone. Leos had such fire and stubbornness—a fixed sun sign would explain a lot in his makeup, if he believed in such a thing. He hid himself by choice. No flag waving or big socializing with lots of people—except for a few choice guy friends, along with his wife. He might have had war experience and, possibly, carried a gun or was wired up to one of the island security agencies that furnished patrol services. Law enforcement officers could be some of his best friends. It was nothing more than a gut feeling she had, but she believed she had found a safe haven with this very mysterious man.

Then her thoughts congealed into an ugly, filthy mass—a mass that went by the name of Antonio Madera.

They sat in relative silence looking at each other. Ryan broke the silence, offering her coffee, but she begged off and asked for fruit juice. She had to settle on bottled water. He had to warm up to her somehow and tell her what he'd heard on the news last night. She was paranoid enough without him setting her off. She might have known that a full-scale manhunt for her was under way. If she knew of the hunt in advance, she had good reason to feel terrified. He still wondered why she had to stay with him and not somebody else. What was wrong with her parents or an ex-boyfriend?

When Ryan picked up the silverware and plates and dumped the leftovers, he headed for the dishwasher.

"I can do that if you want," Candace said and stood up.

He rinsed the plates and loaded them in the dishwasher, added soap and turned on the machine. He wasn't about to let her perform any domestic chores. He did not want her to get familiar. She would not be allowed to contribute so she could expect favors in return. He wouldn't throw her away like a dirty tissue, but they had to make plans for her relocation.

And it would have to be soon.

Ryan clanged the silverware as he cleaned them in the sink. Between his clanging and the dishwasher noise, he almost didn't hear the front door open and the heavy footsteps cross the floor. When he turned around, Billy Powell and Ross McDaniel, having let themselves in as usual, clomped across the kitchen floor and stopped.

"Fishing paaartaaay!" the two chorused. Ross twirled a bass lure around his finger. Billy's black Rottweiler, Ginger, pranced into the kitchen, gave Candace a sniff and then greeted Ryan with a paw handshake. She then turned around and assumed a seated position next to her master's side, tongue lolling.

Ryan stood frozen to the spot, knowing that it was Sunday and his time for blue water fishing with the boys. It had slipped his mind. Candace looked at him with eyes turned into slits.

Billy Powell stared at the backside of the small brunette and stepped around to peer at her. He stiffened and jerked back.

Ross came in from the other side and said, "Whoa, yeah. Lord, Ryan. You didn't tell us about this one." He cocked his head puppy fashion. "Pleased to meet you, honey. And stop the presses. Who are you...and *what* are you?"

Candace gave the gruff-looking men an attentive glance in turn. "I'm Linda, and you are...?"

"I'm Billy Powell," said the six-footer who had the darker tan. He extended a gnarly hand attached to a thick, veined forearm. Candace shook it. Her hand vanished inside his palm. She removed it and looked at Billy's hand closely. She reached out and ran her fingers over the many gouge scars.

"I worked as a scallop shucker when I was a little guy—cut me up a teeny bit. I once won a competition for being the fastest shell food shucker on the island."

Ginger extended a leg up to make it a double greeting. Candace gave the massive dog a paw shake.

"Ginger always needs to introduce herself," said Billy. "But she's shy about it."

"She is quite a lady," said Candace and gave the dog a soothing head pat.

"I'm Ross McDaniel," said the two hundred and fifty-pound plus burly man who stood six-two. "I'm the one with the most legitimate occupation. Harh!" He kissed the back of her hand. "My pleasure. Are you a bodybuilder? Sorry, couldn't help but notice." He stared at her legs.

Candace looked confused—hesitant. "I wonder why everybody asks me that. I'm a figure skater."

Ryan let out the breath he had been holding.

Billy stood mute and then gave Ryan a raised eyebrow.

Candace excused herself and went to the bathroom. She gazed at her reflection in the mirror while she ran the sink water. This was not a good situation. Now there were two strange men who had seen her. There was a good chance they might have pegged her. Her picture might have been on every screen and monitor on the East Coast. There might be flyers tacked on every telephone pole and taped on all the storefront windows. She felt like a damn fool for not having any type of plan to deal with people who blundered unannounced into the house. She hadn't even thought of a disguise or figured on some type of a warning device. There could be a huge reward posted on her. How far would someone go to snatch her and claim that reward?

Billy and Ross did not look stupid. They had eyed her keenly, and it had sent shivers down her spine. Both wore suspicion across their faces. Their movements seemed too cautious in her presence. Their eyes roamed all over her. Since they were Ryan's friends, it was a good bet they weren't tied in with Antonio's squad. *Relief.* So there was a measure of safety there that might keep things on a secret level. That depended upon how loyal they were to Ryan. Best friends would cover for him and keep their mouths shut. If things got too dicey, she could befriend the two and ask for their support—maybe even give her another place to stay. She'd have to work them though, play them like rubes. That was not her favorite way to draw people in, but she had to use her wiles and wit if things got too hot. All three men would have to honor some kind of pact together. It would have to be a unanimous pact.

She had to watch Ryan and follow his lead. He could lead his two friends down a dirt road to nowhere. He could pitch them a story and get them to buy it. He would need all his talents to fool the two and get away with it. There was a good chance that Billy and Ross had no idea who she was. But then again, they knew Ryan had a wife, and suddenly, he had a female guest in his house whom they'd never seen before.

You'll have to be the puppet master, Ryan Barlow. That's the only answer. We're both on stage now, and you're the director. I have to follow your lead. Get us out of this. If you can't, I'll make a run for it. Neither one of them could catch me. That's it. Take one, scene one, Ryan. Do us proud. If we screw the pooch, then it's been nice knowing you.

Candace returned from the bathroom and took her seat at the table. She studied both men carefully, trying to read the expressions on their faces. They studied her right back, both of them rooted to the floor. The only sound coming from the room was the panting dog. Something was off. Yet she couldn't put her finger on it. Suddenly, she wondered what the three of them had talked about in her absence.

Ross broke from his stupor and sidled up to Ryan. The giant cabinet maker leaned his head in close and said, "Are you out of your mind?" under his breath. "Damn, Ryan, whatcha got going on here? Gloria will pitch a major hissy fit."

She could tell that Ross was digging for information. His voice had an edge of panic in it, which might have meant that he was loyal to Ryan's wife. It was hard to know if Ross approved of Candace or not. Would they tell Ryan to kick her out, or would it be one of the 'Bros before Hoes' moment? That was the ultimate secret society of men, where women were cast aside, neglected, or forgotten for the sake of male machismo.

Ryan stepped back a half foot. "Show a little respect for my cousin. She's here for a few days, and I'm going to give her some art lessons."

This is where it started. This is where she had to keep up with Ryan and act it out. She felt sure she could think fast enough and slide right into his thoughts—new identity—art student cousin. Okay!

Ross smirked. "You can do better than that," he whispered uselessly. "She's a looker like that little gal on the Laverne and Shirley Show."

Billy hadn't missed a beat. "Cindy Williams. Only this gal really takes the hot out of the..." He trailed off, looking embarrassed.

They had pegged her look perfectly; she'd heard the comparison before, which meant these men were observant—tuned in. The news of discovery inched closer now, making her shift nervously on her chair. *Oh, Ryan. Change the subject or use some misdirection. Get them off their stride somehow. I'm counting on you!*

Ryan brightened, looking at his two hulking friends. "How about some coffee, guys? I can whip up some eggs and bacon in a heartbeat!" It was an asinine thing to say. They'd always blitzed out of the house and got to the marina where they bought live bait and prepped Billy's old shrimp trawler for the trip. Ryan wasn't even dressed for the occasion. He only had his bathrobe on, but that had happened before.

Billy said, "There ain't no reason we can't make this a foursome."

Ryan blinked. "I was hoping to spend the day with Linda. We have a lot of catching up to do."

"You guys can catch up on stuff while you're on the boat," said Ross.

"I get seasick easily," said Candace, latching on to the conversation.

Ryan could see that she was playing the part to the hilt by trying to discourage contact with his friends. The little gal had to be a mind reader.

"I've got Dramamine," said Billy and turned to face Ryan, letting out a chuckle. "How long do you want to keep this up? What else do you have up your sleeve, dude?"

"What do you mean by that?" Ryan didn't exactly know what Billy was talking about, but the accusations were unsettling. He didn't know what else to say.

"He means," said Ross, "that we know who this woman is. This is the missing bride, Candace..."

"Candace Dee Sabella," Billy finished it. "Her picture is plastered all over the news channels and has probably gone viral on the Internet. It's a huge news story. It's got viewers jonesing for the latest updates. People are taking bets whether this girl is a runaway, a kidnap victim or a corpse."

Ryan had seen as much as they had on the news. He suspected Billy and Ross had been playing billiards at the White Horse Saloon last night and had seen the eleven o'clock news. Billy had been a recovering alcoholic for the past six years. Ross never drank around Billy. It meant the two had been stone sober when watching the newscast.

Ryan's friendship with the two would be sorely tested now. He felt like an idiot for betraying their trust and lying about his guest. How could he ever think he wouldn't be found out? Then there was Gloria. Their counseling sessions over the recent months, compliments of Billy's sister, Joyce, had gone so well that he and his wife were a hair's breath away from reconciliation. He wondered if Billy would rat him out to his sister and spoil the couple's chance for saving their marriage.

"You guys aren't going to tell on me, are you?" asked Ryan. "I have a lot to lose with this. My situation with this girl is temporary." He looked at the pensive expression on Candace's face.

Ross guffawed. "We're not traitors. You should know that. If you get caught, you don't even know Billy and me."

"That's a deal," said Ryan.

Billy rubbed his palms. "Good. That's settled. Ryan, we're going angling for the big ones. Get your ass ready."

Ryan glanced at Candace. "I can't leave her here alone."

"Afraid she's going to run away?" said Ross. "Harh, harh, harh!"

"Shaddap!" said Ryan

"Problem solved," said Billy. "You know that wheeled trashcan I made into a dock trolley? I brought it with me. It's real easy to pull my truck into your garage, lower the door, stash her inside of the can, make the trip and load her aboard the Shamrock. She won't see the light of day, and no one will see her. We do it in reverse order for the ride home."

"What kind of fish?" asked Candace.

Ross stared at her. "I don't expect you to know too much, but halibut, albacore and white sea bass for starters."

Candace nodded. "Good, fresh, lean game fish. I'm all for that."

"You don't really get seasick, do you?"asked Billy.

"No. I don't. And if I did, I would prescribe a mix of horehound, marjoram, rosemary and basil."

Billy blinked. "I have no idea what you just said. But that must mean you have a good inner ear."

"Yes, I do. It comes with my occupation."

"Oh? And what might that occupation—"

"Shaddap! There's no need to interrogate her." Ryan wasn't going to win this one either. He told Candace to change into pants, a loose top and wear the sandals. She skipped up to the second story. Ryan could hear drawers opening and closing, small feet thudding across the carpeted floor.

Ryan pointed his finger in the air, set his remote on the dining table and said, "One minute." He stomped up the stairs and entered his bedroom. He picked out some old torn Levi's pants, a button down collar shirt along with his best basketball shoes. It took him five minutes to dress and slap a baseball cap on his head. He met the others in the kitchen, but Billy was missing. Candace was there and waiting. It irritated him that she had cut the pair of gray Yoga pants off at mid thigh and tucked a T-shirt inside them. He wondered where she'd found the scissors; she'd likely found them in the second story bathroom medicine cabinet. And, oh shit. She had forgotten her bra. He felt woozy just thinking about what the sea spray and wind would do to her top and the distraction it would cause. She wasn't exactly small there. He could still swear she acted like a teenager who didn't know any better. At least he hoped she knew better.

They filed out of the kitchen door and into the three-car garage. Billy handed the garage door opener to Ryan, then lowered the truck's tail gate. He extended a hand to Candace, but she leapt into the back of the truck and stood next to the large blue trashcan. He followed her in. Pulling a pocket knife from his pants, Billy stabbed the top of the can lid several times for ventilation holes. He flipped the top open and lifted Candace into the container. He shut the lid and checked the tautness on the wraparound bungee cords.

When the three were in the cab and Ginger was in the back, Ryan raised the garage door and shut it after they pulled out. Billy pulled onto South Road headed north. After twenty minutes, they drove through West Tisbury, picking up State Road and taking it straight to Vineyard Haven. When they pulled into the city proper, candy-colored gingerbread houses and mansions flanked the road, giving way to an occasional townhome, condo and cottage. Many of the houses were very old, sandwiched between newer, contemporary models. The lots were large and festooned with imported hardwood trees. Kentucky blue grass graced the front yards around statuary, ponds and small fountains.

After awhile, Billy entered the Vineyard Sound Harbor and Marina and parked his truck close to the docks. Everyone assisted in lowering the can to the pavement. Ross took the steel handle and pulled the large container along. They wouldn't attract any attention. There were lots of sailors who pulled carts, wagons, and trolleys from the parking lots to the docks. The carryalls were filled with coolers of food, clothes, tackle, line, and tools—everything needed for a day sail or an extended blue water excursion.

They reached Billy's '73 forty-one footDeFeverPassagemaker trawler without incident or curious eyes. Billy laid a flat of plywood down, allowing Ryan and Ross to maneuver the trashcan aboard. They rolled it just inside the main salon. Ross left with the empty live bait cooler.

Billy entered the cabin, turned some valves, pushed some buttons, and checked the gauges. He then opened the lid and pulled Candace out of the can. She was wet with perspiration from her neck down. She fanned her face and took a deep breath. Ryan expected her to throw a bitch fit, but it never came. She sat on a plush chair and looked around the main salon, picking out every nuance and detail. Her eyes seemed especially drawn to the furnishings.

The big diesel engines rumbled to life, sending a shudder through the hull. Ross arrived and secured the live bait cooler in its niche. He was proud to say he'd bought finger mullet, sardines, and cigar minnows.

Ryan cast off the bow line while Ross took care of the stern. The last time Ross crept down the catwalk to the bow he'd lost his balance and gone overboard. Since then, he was chosen to manage the easier chore of casting off at the rear of the boat.

"I hate it when you guys have to fork over the bait money," said Billy after Ryan checked the fish in the live bait tank, closed the lid and slapped his hands. "It's just been a tight week for me."

Ryan's eyes widened. "You know damn well that me or big Hoss would foot the bill. Diesel gas isn't free. Neither is the wear and tear on your vessel. You don't owe us anything."

Billy gave Ryan a shoulder pat. "You guys have taken up the bait and tackle bills for the last two months. But I did manage to get us a surprise."

Most of the time Billy found work ridding boat hulls of mussels and barnacles. It was a tough job, sometimes requiring scuba gear for boats that were not dry-docked. He also solicited work from the tourist boats and every so often commercial charters. He patched an occasional wood and fiberglass hull for reasonable prices. To save expenses, he lived aboard the Shamrock, a wide, blue-hulled six-sleeper with all the amenities of a real home.

They motored out of the bay and headed into the open ocean chop.

After they'd sailed thirty miles out, Billy anchored next to a formation of rock and rips that the locals called 'Lose your Shit Shoals'. It was a good spot. They'd had luck there before.

Billy opened a large wooden lure box and pulled out three multi-colored lures. Ryan had never seen them before. "Here is your surprise, blokes." Billy beamed. "These are Buttcrackers. It's a new lure that is supposed to catch anything."

Ryan rolled his eyes. *Buttcrackers. That's our big surprise?*

Ross peeled a tarp open and pulled out three Tuna King poles equipped with open reels. He handed Candace a smaller rig that was sturdy and loaded with heavyweight line.

They used the live bait for the first round. Candace, Billy, and Ross struck right away. A halibut and two albacores were hefted onto the deck. Candace caught the twenty-pound halibut. Ginger ran up and down the deck, licking the fish. Billy threw her some live bait, and she chomped it down.

Ryan got the impression that the little gal had fished before. She could bait, overhead cast, hook, reel them in and land them. She fawned over her catch and said, "Beautiful white fish." She stroked it.

After six hours, the fishing party collapsed, exhausted, to the deck, except for Candace, who still had a pole in the water and Ginger watching the action. It seemed to Ryan that she was just gaining her stride. To his shock, in the next five minutes she snagged a five-foot long blue shark and hauled it on board. Ryan seldom caught any sharks. And he loved shark meat.

After they gutted and filleted the fish, Billy called it quits, up-anchored and started the engines. Ross stowed the fishing rigs. Ryan put the fish on ice. Candace asked the men if there was anything she could do. The front of her shirt had become soaked from the sea spray, and her breasts stood out like accusations. She elicited more than a few double-takes.

While Billy sat at the helm, the others took seats in the salon. They looked at each other and broke out into grins. They'd caught thirty-two sizable game fish and had thrown ten of them back into the sea. Ryan and Candace were offered ten of the catch. Ryan thought that he had enough room for them inside his deep freeze in the garage. Still, it was no contest that Candace had caught more than any of them.

Ross wiped his forehead with a greasy towel and said, "Little lady, you're just plain good luck. You're going with us next Sunday!"

Billy advanced the throttles, sending the huge bow into the swells. "You can say that again. Ryan, I swear to God if you kick this girl to the curb, Ross and I will disown you."

Candace gave Ryan a lingering smirk. "I would like that, guys. I had fun, and it was great exercise!"

Ryan couldn't think of a snappy comeback. On the one hand, she was a liability. Everyone was looking for her. He could be arrested for harboring a fugitive or charged with kidnapping. That had no appeal. On the other hand, she was a complete mystery and more self-sufficient than any other woman he knew. But why did Ross and Billy assume that she would stay with him for another week? Would they blackmail him? Or were either one of them attracted to the little package and willing to shelter her? What would they expect from her? He shuddered to think. But he had to admit that both men were gentlemen and would do nothing to disgrace her.

When they pulled up at Billy's slip and tied off, Ross set the gangplank board, and Billy packaged up the catch in plastic bags. They would have to make several trips to get everything loaded. Just before Candace was placed inside the can, Ryan packed some ice cubes in a towel and had handed it to her. She looked at him in disbelief.

"You won't overheat so bad on the way back," Ryan told her.

She said nothing and only shook her head. She felt immense relief in getting out of the house, even if it was undercover. She had her two new guy friends to thank for it. Ryan had gone along with it though, thank goodness. Billy and Ross had enjoyed her company as the new girl on the boat. They had responded to her with praise, even showed sympathy for her situation. They were both likeable, warm souls. She felt safe in their protective cocoon. It wasn't impossible to imagine that they might go the extra mile and take care of her. Both were insufferably sweet, offering her complete relaxation. And when was the last time she had been admired for her fishing skills? A long time ago.

Fishing on the high seas was not new to her. Several playboys had taken her out and showed her the ropes at catching the big ones, the great sword and marlin. Her first water skiing lesson had been behind a speed boat at the Colorado River in California. Water sports were no stranger to her. She had fibbed about never sailing before. Giving away everything exposed too much, too soon. Holding things back was a protective measure. No one had to know any more than they suspected. It was 'cover your ass or pay the price'.

Yet the best thing about the trip was at the very end. Although Ryan had cared enough to carry her to bed, it seemed like a duty rather than a pleasure. Before she had entered the trash can for the transport back to the house, he had given her an ice bag, knowing that the ride back would be sweltering. It was the first act of kindness he had shown her since they'd met. His heart had opened up a little. There was hope for this man. She wondered if there was any hope for her.

CHAPTER EIGHT

Antonio Madera kept the Hummer's speed just above a crawl. His seat occupant, Tony the 'Twister' Razzuto, watched the right side of the neighborhood while Antonio took the left. They were on the outskirts of Aquinnah now. Antonio had other men searching the north and eastern parts of Martha's Vineyard, trying to spot anything out of place—a hint that Candace Sabella was, by chance, somewhere out in the open. He knew the chances of spotting the girl were slim to none. Law enforcement and others had joined the search, upping the odds. The ferries and airport were under surveillance. The charter boats were being watched.

Antonio did not see Candace Dee Sabella as his fiancée any longer. She was a witness and a threat that would have to be silenced. It would be easy enough to make it look like an accident. He could have her strangled and tossed into the bay. He could cut her up and bury her in a landfill. He could even have her found dead out in the open and stage a murder scene. As long as she lived, she had Antonio by his Puerto Rican privates.

Tony Razzuto, who got his 'Twister' moniker from his penchant for twisting arms and breaking down doors, hailed from the Bronx and was Antonio's right-hand man and go-to guy. He had more muscles than a horse and had a spotless record of seeing a job through. He'd capped a couple of Antonio's enemies and left no traces.

"What exactly are we looking for, boss?" Tony asked for the third time.

"I dunno. It's something I can't explain. My grandmother said I was psychic. I think those feelings are working overtime on me because I've got something stuck in my gut. Don't make me explain it again. Keep your eyes peeled on your side."

Antonio drove for another fifty minutes, weaving a maze through the neighborhood until he pulled over to the right curb and glared at something that looked out of place. Two girls were sitting in the front yard grass of a small condo, having a tea party. They had a spread of cups and saucers on the ground, where they poured imaginary liquid into the cups from a teapot. The scene was not that unusual. Except for one item that stuck out, screaming for attention. The blond girl nearest to the walkway wore a bridal veil. There was no mistaking it for anything else.

Without being obvious, Antonio pointed his head at the scene with a nod. "Tony, see the veil on that girl's head?

"I've got it. The net thing."

"I want you to snatch it."

"Geez, boss. If I get anywhere near 'em, they'll run like hell."

"You idiot. Take your tam off, smooth your hair back and get my briefcase from the back seat. You're a salesman. Got it? Trek down the walkway, lunge left and yank the veil off that girl's head. Then get your ass back here."

"Gotcha."

Antonio watched Tony prep himself and then slide out the door. Like it had been choreographed, the big man walked down the walkway, waved hello to the girls, and then lunged. He came back at a fast walk and jumped in the Hummer. Antonio hit the gas and drove for three blocks. He parked in front of a small open lot with the engine running. He snatched the veil away from Tony and stared at it, running his fingers through the delicate net. But it was the barrette hoop encrusted with multi-colored crystal beads that got his attention. He had personally picked out the piece for the wedding, in addition to everything else Candace wore.

"You see something, boss?"

"It's hers, Tony. I know it. I bought the fuckin' thing. She's somewhere around here. I want you to come back and get in that house tonight and see if our little girl is stashed up in there. Bring her back to me if you find her."

"What if I don't find her there?"

Antonio spread out a map and brought it up to his face. "That street was leading north and south. I'd wager Candace was heading south. That'll be our grid search area. I need all the guys out here to sweep it."

"That means combing every inch of this hood and down into Aquinnah."

"Now you're using your brain."

"Thanks, Mr. Madera."

CHAPTER NINE

It had been two days since the Sunday fishing trip, and Candace had made dinners for Ryan after having him pick up grocery selections that went with the fish plates. He couldn't believe how precise and adamant she was about the food types and ingredients. Her diet regime seemed very *veggie* and holistic to him. He'd digressed, admitting that he would give it a try. She'd explained that changing his food and beverage selections would increase his energy and stamina, ward off sickness and clear his mind, just like she'd promised him. She taught him about acids, toxins, negative accelerants, and residues. He had listened, tempted to take notes, but refrained from such an outward show of interest.

He assigned her sleeping arrangements. She would stay in the second story guest room, use the restroom there and enjoy whatever privacy she needed. She had managed to do some chores around the house that he suggested and felt were proper payment for her lodging. He didn't want to impose a regimen upon her, but he needed rules, so she could stay busy and safe within the confines of his house. He still had no idea what he would do with her, whether he would take her to her parents' house or some other safe haven. She was difficult to live with. She might have had a falling out with her parents. She couldn't return to work since the club where she danced belonged to Antonio, and he would be checking all his other establishments.

The police might not afford Candace protective custody. Antonio Madera had influence with law enforcement and city politicians, so the rumors said. Candace had said her fiancé and ex-boss carried a black book that incriminated persons of power, those same persons who had partaken of his club entertainment and clandestine meetings with his girls. If anything, cops and dignitaries would expend more time and resources to help Antonio locate and secure his missing bride.

Ryan made Candace sit and watch the morning newscast. Sure enough, a segment came on detailing her disappearance and her physical description.

"An all-out manhunt is underway," said the reporter. "Here is the jilted groom with a few words to the general public." Antonio Madera's face appeared on screen in smudged pixels. His voice was dubbed over with a mechanical disguise.

"I beg of you," pleaded Antonio. "Please keep a watchful eye out for any reports or sightings." His voice cracked, and he wiped away an imaginary tear. "She means so much to me."

Upon viewing Antonio's declaration of love, Candace scrunched her face up and swore under her breath.

"She is also described as an A-list pole dancer in gentlemen's clubs," the reporter added hastily. "And she might be found in one in the Boston area."

Ryan changed the channel and turned the volume down. "You had to see that," he said. "This is what's going on right now. I think it even hit the AP wires. You're famous. But not in the best of ways."

"He's a rotten phony," she hissed. "I think he has the authorities in his back pocket. He said there was a time when people in high places sneered at him. I'll lay you odds he used some weight to blackmail some of those people."

Ryan softened his voice a tad. "Candace, what is a pole dancer exactly? Do you climb up something and swing around like a trapeze act or something?" He wondered if he'd blundered into a hornet's nest.

She stood up, did a few deep knee bends. "I don't have a pole, but I can give you an idea of a stage dance. Find Michael Jackson's *Thriller*." She glanced at him. "Man, are you *sheltered*."

Ryan clicked on a music selection archive, scrolled to the title, and turned the volume up. The song began with her doing a prance while lip-syncing the song. He watched her, fairly mesmerized at her calisthenics and gestures.

She took up the entire living room, matching the video performance without looking at it. Ryan traded views between her and the Jackson performance. The video took an incredibly long time to finish, but she wasn't done yet. She called out the names of what he supposed were gymnastic moves. She fell over the sofa backward into a kneeling position on the cushions. Then she grabbed the head rest and flung her body up into a full handstand. She scissored her legs open and closed several times, then tucked and rolled off the couch onto the floor.

"This is a lay-over into the splits." She arched her back, kicked over, and came down in a split leg position. Her groin hit the floor with a thump. She bounced up. "That's a stage dance."

Ryan shifted uneasily in his seat. "So I guess that's choreography. You seem to know what you're doing. Thanks for that, I guess. Sorry I don't have a tip." Shit. He couldn't believe he just said that.

She sat back down on the couch. "That's a freebie. It's the least I can do, you know, something for payment. Just let me know anytime you want one."

Ryan cocked his head. He heard the hum of an engine and then a door shut. He looked at his watch. It was 10:00 AM, Tuesday morning—a half hour before the counseling session with Gloria!

He pushed off his seat. "Quick, follow me!" He led Candace through the kitchen and into the laundry room. He opened the water heater closet and motioned her inside. He ran around to the front room just as Gloria keyed through the front door.

"Hey ya, baby," he puffed. "I've been waiting for you."

"Hi ya, your own self." Gloria grinned.

His wife, Gloria Jean Barlow, wore her brassy red hair up most of the time. Today, it rested on her shoulders—a new look for her. He adored her hazel eyes and five-eleven stature. She was a little soft with about twenty-five extra pounds, but half that weight had migrated to her bosom, which gifted her with thirty-eight double Ds. She was Sicilian by birth, having a large extended family. She owned the Mermaid's Salon, an upper-class hair dressing establishment that was gifted to her by her parents. Ryan had painted a Mermaid motif on the front of the salon facade. He was very proud of the rendering.

Ryan approached her and gave her a hug. She endured the contact until his hand strayed and cupped one of her breasts. She stepped back and waved a finger at him, saying, "No frisky stuff until Joyce gives us the all clear. Hugs are fine. Nothing else."

"I just wanted to hold one."

"Hold your lust for now." Gloria tilted her head back and sniffed the air. "Do I smell a weak hint of my old Taboo perfume...or am I crazy?"

He had to think fast about that, knowing that Candace had probably sampled it. "I just shot some around the house, so I would have nice memories of you."

"No way."

"Way."

She looked at him. He had put on his best black slacks and a green pullover. "Okay, buddy boy. Let's get there and see what's up with our progress."

They stepped out the door and entered Gloria's pearl white Cadillac. She backed out of the driveway and drove down the road. He looked at her from the corner of his eye, watching the rise and fall of her chest, the sway of her hair. At forty-two, they'd always joked about her being his cougar. He loved the moniker. And the sex was ballistic. Her Italian blood stirred her into frenzies. He'd been without her touch for so long, just looking at her made him stiff.

They made it to Joyce Powell's office in Vineyard Haven in record time. Joyce's small establishment was called Loving Hearts. It had only two offices and a large room reserved for group meetings. She had graduated from Yale University. She often did work in Seekonk and sometimes even in Newport, Rhode Island, taking the ferry from Woods Hole back to the island. She had small satellite offices in those cities, which she shared with other marriage counseling and healthcare professionals.

They walked down the short hallway and entered the group room. Joyce sat behind a small desk and smiled as they entered.

Joyce, Billy Powell's sister, was thirty years old with strawberry blonde hair. She topped out at five-foot-eight and had a slim figure. She had her hair pulled back in a long ponytail and wore thick-rimmed Buddy Holly glasses. She had that prim, studious aura that made her attractive to a certain group of men who liked the school teacher look. She had earned her money for school by cleaning and decorating high-end homes on the island and mainland during the spring and summer months. It gave her enough to open up her marriage counseling business two years ago. Billy helped with some of the expenses. Joyce had just enrolled in a private pilot's course, to avoid the long drives and ferrying time she had to spend between classes and lecture circuits.

This would be a closed session as it had been for nearly three months. Ryan and Gloria would be alone with Joyce for an hour. There would be no charge for the visit as usual. Gloria offered her free salon visits and total makeovers for the counseling.

Joyce said, "Pull up a couple of chairs in front of my desk. We don't have to go to circle."

Ryan and Gloria pushed two plush chairs up close to Joyce's desk and sat down.

"Well, now," began Joyce. "Have you been in communication with each other, and how did it go?"

Gloria took that one. "We always talk on the phone. The exchanges are respectful and pleasant. He stops by my salon every so often to see how I'm doing."

Joyce raised her eyebrows. "Wonderful. Now, Ryan, you know the story. I want you to repeat your incident and purge it further. You will tell the truth and explain it to your wife."

Ryan had explained the events before. Joyce always had him repeat the happenings while she read his face and studied his body language. He couldn't deceive either woman and had to come clean.

He began, "Ross and Billy found out about my reunion coming up at Martha's Vineyard Regional High School. I still have no idea why they bugged me to go. When the date came, I got all spiffed up in formal clothes. There was a lot of drinking and a dance contest. Then a pool party went into full swing. I met a girl there, Julie Monroe, and she was an old flame of mine during my school days. She looked pretty good. The years hadn't aged her that much."

"You said that she approached you."

"She did. We talked about old times and—"

"Refresh my memory, Ryan. What were the old times?"

He'd had to admit this segment many times. "Well, we talked about love—doing it under the bleachers and in the broom closet. Just spontaneous stuff. It was fun chatting with her by the pool, but I swear I kept my distance from her."

"He told me he was going to his high school reunion," said Gloria. "I thought it would be a good break from his work."

Ryan continued, "Well, as I said before, I was laying out on a lounge chair by the pool. I'd taken my shirt off. I drank too much and passed out. Somebody said I had a smile on my face. I think it was Julie who spread my legs. She leaned her head over my crotch. A girlfriend took that photo in front of the lounge chair. It looked like it was a candid photo of a girl performing on me. It was staged perfectly."

"What do you mean by *performing*?" Joyce queried.

Ryan glanced at his wife. "I mean going down on me. The photo hit Facebook and some other social media sites. It kind of went semi-viral on the Internet. A friend of Gloria's, who remains nameless to this day, recognized me, and emailed the picture to Gloria. I tried to explain, but... wife here...wouldn't have it. She packed up and left. I think you know the rest. But it was a joke and in really bad taste, and I ended up suffering for it."

"Again, tell me how you felt about it, Gloria," said Joyce.

"I thought it was disgusting. Especially the grin on his face like he knew exactly what was happening. It looked authentic. Every one of my friends said that, too. Julie Monroe got scads of emails, but she pulled her Twitter, Facebook page and her website. She didn't want to admit to anything that had caused such a ruckus."

Joyce scribbled some notes and looked at Gloria again. "How do you feel about this now, another week after the last visit?"

Gloria twisted a ringlet of her hair. "I'm willing to give him the benefit of the doubt. Deep down, I know what he's like. He wouldn't do such a thing in public. He's kind of shy. On the other hand, I'd put him on the couch for so long that I thought it could have been the reason he slipped up. I didn't give him any sex. That might have driven him to it. That's why I initially believed he could have done such a thing with an old girlfriend."

Joyce cocked her head. "So what are you saying, Gloria? Are you still conflicted about this? Or could this be water under the bridge?"

Gloria looked at Ryan with sad eyes. "I think I want to patch it up," she said. "As long as he doesn't come to bed smelling like a paint factory and going through bouts of the night sweats and babbling." She gave a chortle.

Joyce looked at Ryan with a steady gaze. "Do you want to work on that, Ryan?"

"I'll do anything I can to her get back. I'm sorry about the hygiene stuff and the other nighttime things. I promise to work on it."

Gloria reached out a hand and patted his forearm. "Ryan, as long as you make an effort, I'll be satisfied. I'm willing to give it a go. But no more high school reunions!"

Ryan relaxed. "I've been waiting to hear that, honey. When do you think you'll be—?"

"Don't rush it. It could be at least four days, a week or more. I have some things to take care of. I won't cancel the no fault divorce just yet. I'll need a little time. I'll call you every day and see how you're doing. I'll be there when I get there."

Joyce discussed the benefits of a reconciliation, outlining some terms and conditions. She seemed pleased and relieved with the decision for them to return to being a happily married couple again. She asked them what initially brought them together. Ryan admitted that he was a breast man. Gloria, her face pink, confessed that she thought Ryan was a sex pistol and drove her crazy in the boudoir.

When Joyce stood up and dropped her note pad on her desk, a light knocking came from the entrance door. Ryan expected it was another appointment, but when he looked, he recognized his fishing buddy Ross, peering around the corner of the door.

Joyce brushed her hair back and smoothed her skirt. "You're early, Big Hoss. But I'm ready."

Ryan couldn't understand why Ross had showed up at Joyce's place of business. He didn't have a wife or even a girlfriend for a counseling session.

Ross crossed the room and gave Joyce a peck on the cheek. "I've got reservations at Noel's Seafood. So you can eat to your gut's delight."

Joyce dithered. "That sounds wonderful. Just give me a minute..." She dug through her small purse and brought out some cosmetics and a little hand mirror.

You hulking, clumsy reprobate. You have a thing for Billy's sister! Now who in the hell would have known that? Does Billy know? Or did he arrange your semi-courtship or whatever it is?

When Ryan looked at Gloria, she had her eyebrows raised. She fairly glared at the two. So much for deep buried secrets and surprise love affairs.

Joyce looked at the couple. "You two are ready. My work here is done. Blessed be, and good luck to you lovers. Call me if you run into any snags." She waggled a finger at Gloria. "Don't you forget our trip to theLofty Pines Horse Stables. We're going to ride and bond with nature again!"

Ryan and Gloria stood up and left the building. They were headed down the road a moment later. Ryan couldn't help but smile after what he'd just seen. He expressed his thoughts to Gloria about Joyce and Ross. Ross hadn't even noticed the couple sitting in front of Gloria's desk.

"She sure didn't tell me about Ross," said Gloria. "We're damn close, too. Nope. Not in a million years. Can you imagine though? It's kind of a Mutt and Jeff thing. If they get any further with their relationship, I just hope he doesn't hurt her. Although Ross is very sweet and has a tender way."

Ryan broke out in a peal of laughter. "Jesus, Gloria, you *would* think of something like that. He's smitten with her. The next thing I know he'll invite her fishing!" Ryan thought of the consequences of his statement. What if Candace was still with him? He would have to get rid of her soon. Like in a day or so. His wife and the little gal could never meet. Period. Edit, cut, and fade to black.

Gloria dropped Ryan off and gave him a kiss through the window. He watched her pull out and drive away. He'd just been with his wife and wondered why he missed the company of that stupid little pole dancer. Why did he even care? She was convenient. That's why. She was a non-threatening sounding board. Nothing more.

He unlocked the front door and entered the house. He called out for Candace. She appeared, peeking around the kitchen wall. She sighed, then walked into the living room and sat down on the edge of the sofa. He sat in his recliner.

"How did it go?" she asked.

"It was a typical marriage counseling session. It went better than expected. She wants four or more days before she moves back in." He didn't want to tell her just yet about getting her out of his house. He had some time to think of a safe haven for her or ask her about any discreet friends that might take her in. He didn't mean to be heartless, but he had no choice in the matter. He liked her okay and felt sorry for her. Yet he was not attracted to her, he reminded himself again.

Candace looked at her lap. "Then I haven't got much time."

"We'll figure it out," Ryan said. "Besides, if things go south, what's the worst that can happen?"

She continued the downward stare. "He's not going to go through with the wedding even if he gets me back."

"Why not?"

"Because I have some nasty dirt on him. I was a witness to something. He blackmailed me into marrying him. A wife can't testify against her husband. I didn't have a choice in the matter. He said if I didn't marry him he would break my legs or hurt my family."

"Which all means?"

"He's going to kill me and make it look like an accident."

CHAPTER TEN

It had been a day since Ryan's counseling session. It was late evening just after dinner. He'd finished panel number six by working on it for seven hours. He was tempted to break open a bottle of Crystal champagne, but Candace had convinced him to taper off the alcohol a bit. She had prepared the meals, all of them seafood based, but the other ingredients were different. She had loaded him up on fruits and vegetables, including a mix of avocados, oranges and then something she called yokum. He'd eaten dozens of raw oysters for the first time in his life. He didn't know whether the fact that his wife was returning had anything to do with his better frame of mind and increased energy or whether the change in his health was the result of Candace's bizarre meals. Maybe it was both. A feeling of invigoration came over him.

He took the fresh painting down and set it against the wall to cure. He sat back down on his studio stool, wondering why he wasn't tired. Now what was he going to do? Start the last panel and finish the project? He was way ahead of schedule.

He heard a light tapping noise and turned to see Candace standing in the doorway. He frowned, but invited her in.

She sat on the cot, looking unhappy and pensive. "Thanks for letting me into your private studio," she said. "I snuck a look at your artwork the other day and couldn't believe how good you are. I'm sorry."

"I just said that to keep you out because I felt violated. Anybody can come into my studio." He looked at her slumped posture. "Are you feeling all right?"

"I'm just thinking about everything. I'm tired of thinking, but I feel great. I'm bored, and I want to do something happy or exciting and dump these black residues out of my soul. I know we can't go out. I'm a prisoner."

It was funny that he felt the same way. He needed a break. Fishing was his only escape, but that was once a week. He hadn't sailed his boat in awhile. He was energized but also bored out of his damned mind.

"I'm stuck in a rut, too," he admitted. "I feel good, and it's going to waste."

She stood up and stared at him. "You wanna know something? I have an idea that will be fun and exciting."

"I'm all ears."

"I've never been painted before. I would love it. You could stash the painting somewhere, so nobody could find it. Maybe when you look at it you'll think about me when I'm gone."

"Hell, why not? I can always say you were a portrait for a romance novel. I've done a lot of those." He looked at her meager clothes. "You don't even have a nice dress to wear."

"That won't matter. I'll be your model." She lifted her T-shirt over her head and unsnapped her brazier in one move. Both fell to the floor.

He glared, rising out of his chair. "Wait a minute. That's not in the deal!" He noticed she had high, perky breasts with nipples that stood out like thimbles. She had an overall tan. Incredibly, she had rows of muscles over her stomach. She was a lesson in solid anatomy.

She faced him full profile. "What's the matter with you? You're a professional artist. You must have painted models in a class at art school or in college."

"I did. But those were mandatory assignments." He closed his eyes, feeling a groan coming on.

"You never paint anything for fun, huh? I saw a painting in Billy's boat.

It was a beautiful painting of the Shamrock. I'll bet you did that for him for free."

She had him. There wasn't really anything he hadn't painted. Only this was something different in many ways.

Candace put her hands on her hips. "Well? Are you squeamish? Afraid? I can't figure out what's bothering you so much. It's just another painting."

Why did she have to remind him of that? "Since you're calling the shots, what now?"

"Just stay calm." She pulled her shorts down and kicked them off. The purple thong that he'd seen her wearing went next. She slid it down and stepped out of it. She straightened up and smiled at him.

"Oh, for crying out...loud. Put your clothes back on!"

She put her hands on her hips. "Then you're an amateur."

"An amateur? Did you just call me an amateur?" *Amateur* was not in his vocabulary.

"If the shoe fits."

Ryan sat down in a huff, training his eyes on his target model, detaching himself from the subject as he had dozens of times before. It wasn't working like it should have.

He had never seen such a beautiful female body in all his life. She was completely tan with strong, rounded hips and a pronounced pelvic mound. Her pubic hairs were shaved down like fresh cut grass into a perfect triangle. Her legs were powerful, but elegantly shaped. When she turned a slow circle for him and asked him how she should pose, he stared at her gorgeous, heart-shaped butt. She had back muscles that rode up to her shoulders. This woman, he decided, looked like something Michelangelo had carved out. The only thing she had on was a diamond ring.

Candace waved her hands. "Well, how do you want me to stand? What's wrong?"

He sucked a breath. "Just let me adjust some things here." He grabbed some brushes and paint tubes. He readied a pallet with different colors. "There's nothing wrong. It's just a job. Give me a three quarter profile— this will be a medium full length shot.

"What's that? Show me."

Show you. Just like that. He slipped off his stool and walked to her. He positioned her body angle and then put a cocked arm on her hip. When he took his seat, he pulled a fresh canvas from the side of the table and mounted it on the easel. He decided on an easy beach scene and quickly painted the background panorama. The white sand would contrast with her tan. It was easily rendered. He painted the sky. It looked good with some cirrus clouds and a few seagulls. He looked at her, noticing she hadn't changed her pose. He began to paint her from the feet up. He used tiny dabs and swirls, swapping his view between her and the painting.

"Am I a good model?" she asked. "You're grunting at me."

"You have good bilateral symmetry." He cleared his throat. "Sorry about the noises. It's my style."

"What is bilateral cemetery?"

"Bilateral symmetry. It means both halves of your body match." He didn't say *perfectly* match.

"Tell me what you're doing. I've never done this before."

Neither have I. At least not with a model like you. If I do this quickly, it will be over quickly!

He glanced at her. "Right now, I just brought out the definition in your calves, and I'm starting on the thighs."

"Yah. This is so neat!"

It took him an hour to finish the torso from the groin up, stopping at the neck. He had to change her position. "Okay, turn your head and look at me. I want to catch the green eyes." *She does have pretty eyes.*

It took him forty minutes to get the face and hair right. She hadn't moved a muscle or asked for a break. He used some heavy shadowing to bring out her contours. When he put his brush down, he said, "Got it. You can relax and get dressed."

She didn't pick up the clothes but stepped up to the canvas to look at it. She stood inches from his right shoulder. He could feel the warmth radiate off her body—smell her fragrance. She had long, curved eyelashes that stuck out like little wings. The caste to her face had flushed a tan-pink. He had never been so aroused in all his life. The great horny god had a firm grip on his whole body.

"Wow," she said. "It hardly took you any time, and you did *that*! I look pretty, don't I? You could paint pole dancers and strippers all day long and make a ton of cash. The girls would go crazy for it."

He couldn't look at her. "You're a good subject. You made it easy."

"Incredible," she said and turned around. When she walked across the floor, he stole a glance at her. She didn't bounce. She rippled. He couldn't draw his eyes away and watched her don her skimpy outfit. She took a long time adjusting her thong. Then she leaned forward to drop her breasts into the bra cups. She arched her back and fastened her bra. She didn't put the T-shirt back on.

It was all he could stand. He felt lightheaded. His member throbbed inside his pants. He was so hard it hurt, forcing him to shove a palm over his crotch. Next, he felt a case of blue balls coming on and had such an urge to masturbate that he began to tremble. Then his mind wandered, and he got off track.

He wondered what her measurements were and how much she weighed. She had a balance, grace and poise he'd never seen in a woman before. The irony was that she hadn't realized what she'd done to him. Not even a clue. She stood next to the cot thumbing through an art magazine, paying no attention to him.

"Go make some damn coffee!" he snapped.

She gave him a double take but nodded and bounced out of the room. He heard her fly down the stairs. He slid off his stool and limped across the room. He ducked into the third floor bathroom and ran the hot water. He pulled himself out. He soaped a hand and gave his shaft savage strokes. It didn't take him long to erupt. It was a violent orgasm. He clamped a hand over his mouth to muffle a howl. Just as he thought it was over, his legs and butt tightened again, and he let loose with a hellish burst. "Oh, Einstein on a wagon wheel!" he swore under his breath. A running dribble from his cockhead brought sweat to his temples, and he thought his heart would blow out of his chest.

It was all her fault, he decided, and toweled the bathroom counter, removing the incriminating evidence. *And that's what happens when you've been kicked out of the bedroom and forced to sleep on the couch for three months— all loaded up.* He washed himself and then stowed the limp monster back in his pants. He drenched his face with cool water and stared at his reflection in the mirror. *What's the matter with you? Where in the hell did that come from?*

Wednesday blurred into Thursday. Ryan and Candace were watching a romantic comedy at nine in the morning when the picture signal snapped off. Ryan tried to reset the TV using the remote, but he kept getting the *Signal Lost* notice.

He got up. "I'll bet one of those blasted seagulls hit the dish again. It's happened more than once. I'll reposition it on the roof. You holler up to me when you get a clear picture. Got it?"

"Okay. I'll stand in the back yard so I can see you and the TV."

Ryan headed up the stairs until he reached the third floor bedroom, opened a window and climbed out onto the steep roof. He walked up to the top spine and followed it to the end of the house where the satellite dish was located. He undid the quick release handle and moved the dish. He called down to Candace who said there was no change. He looked at the pivot joint and could see where the dish had pointed because of the clean spot on the adjustment slide. He turned the dish down and temporarily locked it. He called down, "How's that?"

"It's closer!" she yelled up, then disappeared from the backyard.

Candace stood a dozen feet away from the TV and watched the pattern. The hissing noise rattled her nerves so she turned the volume down, concentrating on the crosshatched patterns of lines that blended with the fuzz. After a few minutes, there was still no change. So far it looked hopeless, which meant it could be something inside the TV causing the disturbance. But she was no electronics expert or TV repair person.

She put a hand on her hip and shook her fist at the wide screen monster. Just then she heard the purr of an engine outside. She trotted to the living room drapes and saw a white Cadillac in the driveway. The driver's door flung open, and a tall redhead exited. The trunk lid popped open. The woman cornered the car and pulled out a large suitcase, then slammed the trunk lid.

The wife!

Candace thought about running out into the back yard and yelling up a warning to Ryan but nixed the idea since it was too risky. Instead, she ran across the living room, hurdled over the couch, then dashed to the laundry room where she slipped through the water heater door and closed it. She had to position her body just right, having burned her butt and boiled her breasts the last time. A minute later, the front door slammed. Candace heard a husky female voice call out. She couldn't make out the words.

Ryan made five adjustments and couldn't get a clear picture. He adjusted the dish in smaller increments, then swiveled it on its lateral axis.

He'd been on the roof for fifteen minutes. He called down again. Candace didn't answer. He figured she had to visit the bathroom, so he sat down and looked at the beach and out into the ocean. He saw some sailboats tacking against the wind and what looked like a coastguard patrol boat. He wished he had the time to sail more often, but he was a slave to his work. In fact, being up on the roof was a minor vacation for him.

He loved the salt breeze against his face. When he looked down at the shingles, he saw a white feather stuck on a splinter. It confirmed his suspicion—a gull strike.

He waited fifteen minutes and then yelled for Candace. There was no answer.

Gloria picked up her suitcase and walked to the garage windowpanes. Ryan's car was inside, which gave her a warm feeling. She'd caught him at home. There couldn't be a better time for a surprise visit and a 'cuddle night' in the same bed. She could get the rest of her things in a day or so. The most important thing was to show him that she'd forgiven him—that she believed in him and was willing to make it work—hopefully for the rest of their lives.

Gloria reminisced. Ryan Barlow had a sultry way about him. His light blue eyes had turned more than a few ladies' heads. He was imposing, but gentle and soft spoken; that's when he was in normal, non-monster mode. But he had an aloofness that caught women's attention.

Ryan sometimes had a funny rasp to his voice. He often grunted for no apparent reason. His enigmatic smile seemed to hide a depth no one could easily penetrate, not even Gloria. He was just a basic cute guy, easy going and courteous to a fault. One young lady who worked at the art supplies store had asked him if he was single and found out he was married to Gloria. Ryan always thanked her for keeping his supplies in stock, especially his favorite colors cobalt, violet and quinacridone magenta.

He seemed resigned to being a homebody, busy with his work and only once in an odd while joining Billy and Ross at the White Horse Saloon and Bar for drinks and billiards. Of course, there was the weekly fishing trip on Billy's trawler. Minus that, Ryan enjoyed hanging out with Gloria and massaging her feet. She was grateful for his loving attention since her feet tended to ache after a day of standing on them at the salon. She had complained that he hadn't planned the European vacation he'd promised her. He wanted to sail but was still getting his large sailboat in shape. Gloria rarely went out sailing with him. She couldn't stand the choppy waves and bouts of seasickness. Now, a major airline flight to Greece? That was something she could handle!

She thought he was actually becoming a bit more reclusive now that he was going through counseling with their therapist Joyce. But things never looked better for a full reconciliation. Gloria would welcome him back to their bed, and that meant she was in for a wild ride. Her tall man had more moves than a jungle snake.

She walked around and keyed herself through the front door. The TV was on, but the picture was messed up. *I never watched you anyway, idiot box. Serves you right for having a fit.*

After leaving her suitcase in the foyer, she called out, "Ready or not, here I come!" She walked into the kitchen, glanced in the laundry room, and then opened the refrigerator door. It was packed with unrecognizable produce. She whispered the items: "fat cheese, whole raw cow's milk, fresh goat cream cheese, blue cheese, defrosting fish, organic blueberries, tofu, avocados, kombucha tea, tart cherry kefir, and raspberry-lemon yogurt." There were enough greens in the lettuce crisper to feed a stable of horses. She looked toward the back. "And what the hell is ginger X-two?" She shut the door and opened several overhead cabinets. After closing them, she headed up the stairs.

She found the second story guestroom door open and walked inside. Several of her old sportswear outfits lay out on the bed and when she looked at the dresser, she found the top right door open. She looked inside and thumbed through the jumbled contents of some laminated cards and loose one hundred dollar bills. She picked up an atomizer bottle and a round plastic case. She set them down. When she entered the guest bathroom, she found a large pearl-shaped diamond ring in the soap dish. She gasped at the size of the diamond. The clothes hamper was half loaded. The shower sink pan was wet.

On the third floor, she walked into Ryan's studio, expecting to find him there. What she saw on his easel took her breath away. "Oh, Mother Mary," she gasped and smudged a finger on the painting; it came away tacky. It smelled fresh, too. A cheap pine frame held the canvas with staples. She pulled it from its perch and walked down the stairs with it until she reached the kitchen.

There was no one in the backyard that she could see from the slider window. He wasn't in the garage. He could have possibly been at their private beach in the back. But then she heard heavy thumps coming down the steps. She braced herself against the kitchen counter.

He'd been on the roof for nearly a half hour now, having lost track of time. He walked bowlegged across the roof spine, watching his footing. He entered the bedroom and walked slowly down the stairs. The living room was empty, and the TV had a slight fuzz to it. He wondered if Candace was sick somewhere and called out to her.

"In here," said a voice.

Ryan walked into the kitchen and froze. Gloria stood by the sink. She had one hand flat on the counter and another hand holding the painting. She gave him a steely-eyed look.

"Gloria, you're early," he said.

"It's a good thing I was early. I wanted to be with you. I came in and looked for you, then headed upstairs. Low and behold, I found this painting in your studio. It was sitting on your easel. It looked damn fresh."

"It's a cover for an erotic publication. I'm getting two thousand dollars for it. I painted it a day ago."

"What's with my old clothes strewn about in the guestroom? There's my compact and one of my old perfume bottles on the dresser."

"I was just going through some stuff."

"Did you go through the I.D. and money I found in the top drawer? Did you see the driver's license that has a brunette's picture on it?"

"I didn't know there was any such thing in there."

"Care to explain all that weird food in the refrigerator and cupboards? Did you turn into a health guru or something? That's not you, Ryan. Not by a long shot."

Things were going south fast. Somehow Gloria had arrived early, let herself in and looked through the house while he was on the roof.

"Have you been listening to the news or watching TV?" Ryan asked.

"You know I don't watch the TV." Her eyes turned to slits. "What's the difference anyway?"

Candace must have seen her or heard Gloria arrive and ducked away somewhere. She was most likely in the water heater closet where he had hid her before.

Gloria hadn't lost her steam. "An extra toothbrush...a diamond ring as big as a grape in the soap dish in the second story bathroom...my perfume lingering all the over place and my sandals on the living room floor. There's nothing you can say. I see it on your face. Is it your old crush from high school?"

"How long have you been here?

"Long enough, dear husband. It took me only minutes to see how this house had changed. Lots of changes. Too many."

"I thought I would—"

"Come here and look me in the eye."

Ryan crossed the floor and stepped up to her. Meeting her gaze was difficult, but he stood his ground. He knew what was coming. Gloria reared her hand back and swept it into his face with a loud crack. The slap rocked his head. Her eyes were moist and filled with hurt. She backhanded him again and then crossed it back for another blow. His ears rang.

"Where is she, Ryan? She doesn't have a car here, and yours is in the garage."

"I dunno what you're talking about." He rubbed the side of his face.

"Who in the hell do you think you are?" she screamed and raised her hand for another strike, but when she swung at him, he grabbed her wrist in a death grip.

"Don't do that again, Gloria," he warned, dropping her arm.

"You no good lying son-of-a-bitch! A woman knows when there's another female in the house. It reeks of it!"

Ryan heard a door squeak, looked toward the laundry room, and saw Candace padding lightly over the floor. Gloria followed his eyes and saw the young girl approach and stop ten feet away.

Gloria crimped her eyes shut, a vein showing on her forehead. "I just knew it." She opened her eyes and glared at Candace. Then she brought the painting up, looked at it and said, "Oh my gawd. This is you!" She waggled the painting. "You little whore. Did you think you were going to get away with this?"

"It's all my fault," said Candace. "He didn't do anything wrong. Just don't hit him again."

Gloria cocked her head. "Oh, hell no. You're *jailbait*." She turned on Ryan. "What the hell were you thinking, you spastic asshole?"

"I ran away, and he found me on the street," Candace offered. "I told him I was alone and hungry, and he helped me."

Gloria pulled a carving blade out of a knife block, which made the other two flinch and back off.

Ryan's wife stabbed the painting several times, leaving slit-like holes. She tossed the knife in the sink. "So! Did you fuck this little girl, Ryan? She's a looker. It wouldn't have been hard for you."

"If I tell you the truth, will you believe me?

"No!" Gloria grabbed the painting and bulled her way past Ryan. She crossed the living room, opened the front door, picked up her suitcase in the foyer, then marched out of the house. "I'll be taking this painting as evidence, you adulteress pig!"

She left the door open. A moment later, the Cadillac started and pulled away. Ryan walked to the door and gently closed it. He crossed the room, sat in his recliner, and stared at a television picture that had snow and lines running across the screen. He had no words for what had just happened. This was the icing on the crap cake.

Gloria would divorce him for sure. Everything they'd worked for was now a shattered dream. How could he ever make it up to her and clear the air? This was the second time in a row he'd been accused of adultery. He felt Candace's eyes on him. He didn't want to talk right now. He picked up a glass of tea from the end table and threw it across the room. It broke on the fireplace mantel. He looked for something else to throw, decided on a shoe and pitched it in the fireplace. His other shoe joined the first.

Candace eased up from the couch and walked up the stairs. Ryan hadn't even seen her sit down. She came down five minutes later in her shorts and a dirty T-shirt. She carried a small plastic sack. It looked like a little hobo bag.

She placed her ring on the sofa end table, slipped the sandals on and said, "That's the least I can do for what you've done for me. I'm so sorry I got you into this." She walked toward the front door.

Ryan looked at the ring and then swiveled his head. He watched Candace open the door. He leapt to his feet.

"Don't go out there, Candace! It's not safe!"

"It doesn't matter anymore." She walked out and shut the door.

Ryan ran after her, swinging the door open. He caught up with her on the lawn, yanked her up in his arms and carried her back in the house. He sat her on the sofa and handed the ring to her. "This is yours. You keep it. Stay here for now. The worst of it's over. Gloria won't tell anybody about this."

Candace sniffled and patted her moist eyes. All he offered her was a head pat. He wanted to stroke her hair and pat her cheek. But doing that would make him out to be the worst hypocrite in the world. Now he really didn't know what to do. He found a box of tissues and handed it to her. Then he got her a glass of fruit juice.

She clamped her hands on her temples. "I didn't mean for any of this to happen."

"I was more to blame. I got you down out of the tree. I interfered and started all of it."

She looked at him with pink eyes. "You don't hate me?"

"Look, I've never hated you. You irritate the shit out of me. You're different. I've never met anybody like you. I mean the whole package you."

"I didn't think you cared about me."

"That bastard Madera is full-on dangerous. You wouldn't stand a chance with him."

The TV suddenly cleared, showing a focused picture. He turned the volume up. "Well, what do you know about that? The electronic gods are at it again."

"Yeah, funny how that works." She gave him a tepid smile and blew her nose. "I'm so glad you don't hate me."

"Candace..." He moved to the edge of his seat and clasped his hands. "I've never hated you. Truth be told..." He gulped. "I think you might be a good friend for me. I mean, I noticed you from the start and all that stuff...and I think I've done something bad because of you."

"You haven't done *anything* to me. Why do you feel bad?"

Confession is good for the soul. I've told so many lies to women it's gotten out of hand. I'll never be believed if I can't man-up and tell the truth. She thinks she's guilty. She has no idea what I did to myself. I'm no saint. She needs to know that. She's so naïve and unassuming she can't see the whole picture. Ryan looked into the kitchen, thinking about what Gloria did to the painting.

"Candace...when I painted you with your clothes off the other day," he began, "I got to the point where I couldn't think straight. I mean I really messed up. To my way of thinking, that is."

"That was the most beautiful painting ever. There was nothing wrong with it. I *loved* what you did."

"No. You don't understand. I got distracted when I saw you. I couldn't believe it. You're just..." He couldn't say it. "I've never seen such a..." He was beyond flabbergasted. He couldn't, shouldn't get those feelings out. *It's no surprise that half the world wants to find you. The slobs at the gentlemen's clubs would claw to get at you.*

Candace looked at him sincerely. "Oh. I thought you were all straight laced or something. I guess I went overboard. I didn't think I had that effect on you." She took a deep breath and exhaled slowly. "Other men are easy to read. They've always swarmed me. You didn't do that. You talked to me. You never groped me or harassed me. You're new to me, too." She wrung her hands. "I hope I don't make you uncomfortable. How bad was it, if you don't mind me asking?"

He noticed a gentle side of her coming out. "It was an out-of-control moment. I told you to get coffee because I had to be alone. It's never happened to me before. It was a crazy moment."

"You thought this because of me? Not some fantasy?"

"Yeah. 'Fraid so."

"Oh, gawd. I can't keep my secret any longer," she said. "I have a confession to make. I've been loading you up with aphrodisiacs. It's in the food and the herbs I've been serving you. They make you get hot around the opposite sex. I learned about it in the clubs."

"You did that to me?"

"I didn't poison you, Ryan. It's all good for you—soy sauce, lemon juice and oysters spiked with wood herbs. I eat those meals too, and I got a little...out of my head, frisky."

"But why? You set a trap for me. I didn't stand a chance in hell of fighting off that feeling. You *knew* about my marriage counseling."

"I knew about your counseling, but you didn't look happy about it. I planned the painting session. I wanted to get a reaction out of you. Women can only handle being ignored for so long until they go out of their minds. I couldn't...bear that you didn't find me...desirable." She sniffled again, while a fat tear rolled off her cheek.

"What did you want to do to me? Or me to you?"

"I can't." She closed her eyes. "It wouldn't sound good. You're married, and I knew I had to respect that. I didn't want to take you to a place you didn't want to go. I just wanted to know if there was an opening somewhere. I craved your attention."

He couldn't believe what he was hearing. He hadn't a clue that she had any real feelings for him. It didn't make sense. She'd led him down a path. He was ignorant of her thoughts. Under her sassy exterior, she had a kind spot. She had some morals and, considering her occupation, that seemed so out of place.

"I didn't know that dancers had brains," he said. "I thought they were evil bitches who took money from men and squashed their hearts. I didn't believe they had personalities or feelings. My mother taught me that women like you were filth and not to be trusted. I think I've had a little awakening. But it doesn't mean shit. Okay?"

"You are one plateful, mister. You are the opposite of what I've seen all my life. Were you an Eagle Scout?"

"How did you know that?"

"Believe me it shows—does it ever!"

"So what's so interesting about me?"

"You don't take any crap from me. Underneath it all, you have strength...and conviction, I guess that's the word. You're loyal to your woman. You're not an alpha—one of those loud-mouthed control freaks. There's an easygoing, gentle side to you."

Ryan knew that an alpha male in a wolf pack was the leader. He was the strongest one and fought for the pack. But he didn't like center stage; it was too much limelight. She was right about one thing, though—he didn't take crap off of any person.

Candace was like a little showoff. She had a wild side. It wasn't easy to understand that she might have needed to be under a man's direction and care. He could ramp things up a notch to get closer as friends. There wouldn't be any physical contact as that would be plain wrong. He was still married. He would have to set up rules. He was honor bound to keep her safe. But if she ever experimented with him again, he would lace her up one side and down the other. He would have to give her the boot.

"No more of those special ingredients," said Ryan. "That's over!"

"I promise—no more." She crossed her heart. "By the way, I know what you see in your wife. She's very attractive and has a rack to die for."

"Don't remind me."

CHAPTER ELEVEN

Ryan had just finished panel number seven. The series assignment was over. It was one o'clock in the afternoon. The collection could be hand-delivered to the publisher's office. Billy or Ross might transport them to New York City if they were headed in that way for anything. It was a relief to know the work would bring in a nice paycheck. It wasn't like he needed the money, but he did want to do some restoration work on the Shenandoah.

He pulled a new bottle of champagne out of the fridge and headed downstairs. He knew Candace didn't ordinarily drink, but he thought she might make an exception for a special occasion. He felt like celebrating just enough to appease his ego.

When he got to the second floor, he tapped on the guest bedroom door. Getting no answer, he entered. The last time he'd talked to her, she'd told him she was planning on a nap. The window blinds were open. He set strict rules not allowing any type of view into the house. He went to shut them and then looked out.

Candace was in the backyard standing over the fire pit. She must have lit it because the flames were three-feet high. Her wedding dress ensemble was piled next to her feet. She picked it up and tossed it into the pit. The hot fire ravaged it, sending up an orange glow and gray smoke. She backed off from the heat and stood there with her head down. He could only see her back. He wondered what she was feeling. Her shoulders quaked, which meant she might have been crying. She could have been angry or even laughing.

A somber feeling touched him deep inside. She was a pretty little gal who had just burned her wedding dress. He tried to imagine how that felt. It had to be devastating. Women planned all their lives for a beautiful wedding and having all their family and friends in attendance. It was the one time in their lives when they felt like someone special—when their dreams came true, and they were princesses for a day.

Candace watched the flames die down. The dress had turned to black cinders and ash. There was nothing left. She lingered for a full five minutes and then turned to walk back into the house. He could feel the slight vibration of the sliding door closing.

After walking back upstairs and opening his small fridge, he grabbed another bottle of bubbly and headed down the stairs. He looked for her on the living room sofa. Not seeing her there, he found her sitting at the dining room table with her head down. She had a towel in her hand. She raised it and wiped her eyes. He walked in and sat down at the table opposite her. He placed the bottles on the table top and waited for her to look at him.

She raised her eyes, gave him a crooked smile. She'd been crying. Her voice cracked. "I just had to do something, and it didn't make me feel good. I'll be all right in a minute." She let her eyes fall to her lap again.

"I saw what you did," said Ryan. "You don't have to hide your face or be ashamed." He waited for a response, but none came.

He tried a different approach. "I just finished my assignment. It was fast, but grueling work. I thought you might tip a few back with me. I don't mean to make an alcoholic out of you, but it might change your perspective on...things. I think I know what you're feeling, and it's not good to keep it inside. Like you said about those bad residue things?" He pushed a bottle across the table. "That's yours for what ails you."

He went to a kitchen drawer and pulled out a cork screw. After a moment, he had both bottles opened. He clicked his bottle against hers. "Cheers. We can let our hair down. We sure as hell deserve it." *To hell with the glasses.*

Her smile widened. They took long pulls on their bottles. Candace burped. "Oh, the bubbles! It's been awhile since I had this stuff."

"Drink up. There's plenty more where that came from."

They did drink up. They polished off half their bottles in five minutes. Ryan got up from his seat and walked to where Candace's painting had been knifed. He picked up some slivers of canvas and let them run through his fingers. It made him think of a wounded animal. The damage to the painting was meant as an insult to the younger, more attractive woman. He didn't think Gloria hated him as much as she hated Candace.

He felt violated and accused. "That rotten witch! We'll do another painting even better."

She sneezed. "Are you sure you want to make another one?"

He joined her at the table. "I'm fine with it, and it will burn Gloria's ass."

After they finished their bottles, Ryan went to the liquor cabinet and made hard liquor drinks. He used glass jars to hold an extra fill. They each took a hefty pull and clinked glasses.

Candace looked at him cross-eyed. "I am so hot and bent."

"I'm not exactly sober, but I have no regrets." He traipsed into the living room, turned the TV on and found a rock 'n roll song for her which he let boom through the house. He next opened the slider and said, "Let's take this outside. Screw the inside."

They walked tipsily out the door to the backyard and flopped on the sand. Candace kicked off her sandals and ran her toes into the warm grains. Then she held her face up to the sun, sporting an ear to ear smile. It gave him a chance to look at her again. He could paint her just like that and it would be a masterpiece.

"Do you think your wife will divorce you?" she asked.

"She'll take me to the cleaners for this. I expect to get served any day."

"I can't believe I was the cause of all this. I'm so sorry."

He told her about the reunion incident with the old flame and how he had been set up. He described Gloria's reaction to it and how she had jumped to conclusions. He didn't leave out any of the details. She gazed at him with rapt attention. When he finished the story, Candace shook her head with an aching slowness.

"So it was no different this time than when she accused me earlier," he stated matter of factly.

"You haven't done a damn thing, Ryan," she said, scrunching up her lips. "How could she be so wrong about it? She's evil, Ryan. She doesn't trust you."

"I've finally come to that conclusion. She could have given me a break the first time. No such luck. You know, I'm glad it happened."

She weaved. "So am I. Ghargh! I mean...I'm running my mouth!"

Drunk and bedazzled, he wondered what it would be like to kiss such a mouth. He hadn't been kissed in a long time. Instead, he had an idea. He wanted to do something for her. She looked like a little vagabond. He could remedy that.

He let out a raucous burp. "Yah. You need some clothes. I mean you really need some nicer things than what you're running around in. I can make the trip."

"You're kidding." Her jaw dropped.

"No, I'm not. I'll record your sizes and all that. You can tell me what kind of outfits you like. The treat's on me."

"Oh, wow. I have money to help with it. If you mean it, you'll have to write it all down. Have you shopped for women's clothes before?"

"I did it for Gloria a couple of times. Let's get in the house."

They rose and walked back into the dining room. Ryan got a pen and pad out of a kitchen drawer and sat with her at the table. She'd brought in the drinks.

Ryan poised the pen over the pad. "What's your height and weight?"

"I'm five-four and I think I've gained some weight...so make it one hundred and twenty pounds."

She gave him her shoe size, asking for a pair of high heels and Adidas tennis shoes. She added her dress and pants size and a few clothing styles that she liked. Then she hesitated.

"Something wrong?" he asked.

"I'm not sure about my measurements. It's been a while since I checked them."

Ryan went to the laundry room and returned with a cloth measuring tape. He had her stand up.

Candace stepped away from the table and spread her arms out. "Wait. Do you want me to do this?"

"No. I've got it." He suddenly changed his mind and threw the tape measure to her. "Maybe you'd better do it."

She took the three vital measurements with as much care and precision as she could, considering she was nearly falling down drunk. She wiggled and laughed and kept dropping the tape. When she finished, he wrote the numbers on the pad: Thirty-six, twenty-five—thirty-five and a half—C cup. He waggled his head. *I'll never get those digits out of my head.*

He stowed the tape measure and looked at his notes. He laughed. "Now I know everything about you."

She sat down at the table and leaned forward, palms under her chin. "What color hair do you like?"

"Puss hair!" He slapped his hand on the table. "Gak! I'm just kidding." But he had her laughing like a hyena. "Okay, for real. Honest to God, I have a fetish for platinum."

"*No shit?* Platinum it is then. Get Revlon." She jabbed a playful finger at him. "But you're not going anywhere now, Mr. Ryan Barlow. You've been drinking too much to drive." She hiccupped.

"Gotcha! I'm going to take a nap. I'll be all right in about five or six hours." He wobbled to his feet and staggered across the kitchen tiles. He held onto the handrail on his climb up to the second floor. When he got to his room, he collapsed on the bed. A moment later he heard a knock. When he turned to see what it was, he saw Candace giving him an impish look. She dropped to her knees and stretched out on the floor.

He fell back and stared at the ceiling.

It was close to nine that evening when he got back from the mall. He hefted three packages and got them into the house. Candace waited for him on the couch. When she saw the shopping bags, she perked up and launched off her seat.

"I got everything and then some," he said. "And I've got one hell of a hangover."

"I made you a hangover remedy and put it on your end table there."
She pointed.

"No funny stuff in it, right?"

"I drank mine an hour ago. I'm fit as a racehorse. It's got fresh
blended tomatoes, fresh lemon juice, Worchester sauce, one raw egg yolk,
black pepper, green Tabasco sauce, a couple teaspoons of olive oil, a dash
of horseradish...and I added a clove of garlic, too."

"No wonder you had me buy all those things." He dropped the
packages on the sofa and helped her empty them.

Her eyes lit up. "Oh, my...this is just...more than awesome! Look at
the *colors*." She began separating the items, undergarments in one place,
dresses in another, sports clothes in yet another. She held up a box of hair
color and then a straight-hair platinum wig. She found two pairs of large
framed sunglasses and a make-up compact. "You thought of disguises."
She held up a lavender bikini swimsuit. *"Just perfect."*

"It doesn't mean we can go out on the town. You still have to stay off
the streets."

She stepped up to him and gave him a bear hug. His chin rested on
the top of her head. He smelled her essence again and gently pushed her
back. She resumed organizing the clothing.

She took a handful of items and dashed into a first floor bedroom.
When she exited the bedroom, she showed off a teal sundress and white
high heels. She went back into the bedroom and came out with another
outfit, this time black leather pants and a matching vest.

Ryan drank his hangover concoction and watched the floor show from
his recliner. He spilled his drink on himself when one of the outfits struck
him dumb—the lavender bikini. Everything fit like magic, and he couldn't
help thinking that Gloria looked like a sow next to Candace. He vowed he
would give his little roommate some art lessons, eat the food she made for
him and show her some respect. Maybe they could become lifetime
friends.

Candace came out with a strut, modeling a white, V-cut cocktail gown
with the white high heels. She wore a pair of sunglasses and the platinum
wig. She did a slow turn around for him. "How in the heck did you get
these sizes so dead on?"

That's the look. That's the major hit. You could start a war with that outfit. Any woman could!

"I had three female employees figure everything out." He laughed. "They even fought over the selections."

He watched her model every one of the outfits, except the undergarments. Until at last, she came out in a pink, form-fitting jogging suit and white socks. She sat on the couch and looked at him lovingly. She blinked back a tear, a happy tear. After she wiped her face, she said, "Antonio never bought me anything like this. He only bought me the wedding dress. I have all my other clothes and furniture in my apartment. Velvet is my roommate. She'll take care of it." She blew him a kiss.

He wanted to catch the kiss, but he didn't. "Hey, no skin off my nose. That's what credit cards are for. And your cash made a big dent."

"These things must have cost a fortune. I don't know how to repay you for everything you've done for me."

"I had the money in the bank," he said, with casual indifference. "Besides, you've already paid me back."

"How did I do that?"

"You made me feel young again."

She cocked her head and studied his face. She then scrunched her brows, seemingly trying to put it all together. It looked like his statement had gone completely over her head.

"I know you're not that much younger than I am," he said. "But you're young at heart. I'm an old reprobate WASP compared to you. You once told me I was sheltered and a prude. You were right. I had a strict upbringing."

"How old are you, Ryan?"

"I'm thirty-five. My wife is forty-two."

"She's your cougar. You know, you are a very beautiful man. The goatee, the sandy blonde hair, and those blue-gray eyes, just like a beautiful Malamute. It all knocks the socks off me. Are you German?"

"Scandinavian. I have Norwegian ancestry."

"Yuumm. *No wonder.*" She almost swooned. "I want to kiss you so badly right now. I can't hold it in any longer. Just on the cheek."

He allowed the kiss. She lingered next to his face, and he felt her hot breath on his cheek. She retreated to the couch.

No man in his right mind would have brought this woman into his home had they known what she did for a living. She was so misunderstood—accustomed to being used and abused which had turned her body into a weapon. Candace Dee Sabella had not often been shown true kindness in her life, it seemed. She didn't live life as much as she attacked it.

He had the feeling that he was asleep in a heavy fog, but the images that flashed through his mind were in color and had smells. He willingly acted out in the beautiful dreams, imagining he was a hero of an emergency or some Don Juan lover on an island of women. Then things changed. The scenes and images that flashed before him were now dark and ominous. He saw them from further away but did not pull out because of morbid curiosity. He saw an image of Margaret Hamilton acting out the part of the wicked witch in *The Wizard of Oz*. She had a pointed black hat and sinister grin. Her face then changed to the sour face of his wife, Gloria.

Gloria kicked him and rolled him off the bed. He asked her why, and she told him he stank like a pig. He tried to apologize in the dream, and he pleaded with her. He next found himself on the cold leather cushions of the couch, drawing his knees up into his chest.

Next he was in a famous publisher's office, talking to the CEO, Raymond Curtis Swartz, about a trilogy order of covers that were unacceptable and downright inferior to anything Ryan had ever done. He was told his art was nothing more than paint smatterings and dirty smudges. Raymond, a squat man with sad eyes and two tufts of hair over each ear, spat across the desk and pointed to the paintings against his office wall, which he had shredded.

"Oh, God, no!" Ryan said. "You've got to give me another chance. I'm not losing it. I just missed my stride. Give me another chance to prove myself."

"You're washed up in this business, young man," Raymond said and chortled. "I'm washing my hands of you. And I'll make sure that your other clients get the news of your substandard work."

"You can't do that to me!"

In the dream, Ryan felt the couch under him again and opened his eyes to see Gloria standing over him. She glared down at him and unsnapped her brassiere. Two enormous breasts flopped free. "Do you want some of this, buddy boy?" She didn't give him a chance to answer and brought a hand around that held a spatula, which she used to beat him over the shoulder. He tried to grab her, but she stepped back just out of his reach.

"Why are you doing this to me, Gloria? Why this?" He kicked and rolled over, exposing his back. He moaned with each painful swat. Images flew in and out of focus until they blacked out. The weight of his body returned, and there was no more feeling of flying. Cold sweat clung to his chest hair.

Something cool alighted on his forehead, and it felt like fingers stroking his hair. From the dim light bleeding through the blinds, he saw a small body and face in silhouette. The small figure sat on the bed. An outstretched hand stroked his cheek. It shocked him at first; he wondered if it was an angel, but the image did not blink away. Maybe it was a ghost? "They were beating on me," he told the fantasy figure.

"I know, honey," said a female voice. "It's going to be all right now. Shush. Close your eyes."

Ryan did as he was told, blowing out a great sigh. Then he heard a sweet humming sound; it was so soft and comforting that he let go of his feelings and surrendered to it. It was a tune that he vaguely remembered, and it seemed like it took forever to recall it. It was a lullaby. Then the melody clicked in his mind, and he found himself humming along with it. Now he knew it for what it was.

Beautiful Dreamer.

CHAPTER TWELVE

Candace had breakfast waiting for him when he came down the stairs. A lion-like yawn escaped him as his feet slapped across the kitchen tiles. He stood at the edge of the table and admired the spread: lean, rare min-steaks, rye toast, cottage cheese in a tossed salad with croutons. A pitcher of fresh squeezed orange juice sat in the middle of the table.

He stretched his arms. "Yo. I could really feast on this."

"Ah...I could really feast on *that*," said Candace under her breath, having just placed cloth napkins on the table. She turned away. "Ryan, your bathrobe's wide open."

"Guh!" He flipped his robe together and tied it off. They sat down together after he apologized. She waved it off.

It was when he sampled a bite that he noticed she had dyed her hair. She was platinum blonde! Her lips shone with a glittery pink. She had green shadow on her eyelids, and her lashes looked like they could swat flies out of the air. She wore the teal sundress. She did not look like the same woman—even her brows were lighter.

"Ryan, you're staring at me again."

"Just checking out the new look. I wasn't paying attention to anything."

"You can say that again."

Next checkbox marked—a sense of humor. Of all things, he'd flashed her.

He never tasted anything so good. The food woke up his tongue as though it had been sleeping all his life. Candace could rock the world as a gourmet chef.

Gloria was in direct contrast. She had served up regular staple meals that never changed in taste or ingredients. He knew them by heart and the days they were served: salmon patties, fried chicken, turkey chunks and macaroni, spaghetti, beef enchiladas, ham and vegetable stew. The side dishes consisted of mashed potatoes (all the time), green cut beans, peas, and corn. He had to beg for macaroni and potato salad to break up the monotony. Milk and water washed everything down, with tea on special occasions. They splurged on Neapolitan ice cream once a week. The regimen never changed, and it was doubtful that Gloria had ever wavered from those dishes because they were main course selections at her mother's house.

"Something's wrong," he said mid-bite. "You don't look happy."

She pushed a crouton around on her plate. "I can't stay hidden forever. I'll lose my mind. If I go out in disguise, he could still find me. That could happen if I stay here long enough. We're not really that far from the church."

He understood what she was saying. His neighbors were not accustomed to seeing another single woman enter and leave his house no matter how many times it happened. Gloria had always parked her Cadillac in the driveway and only moved it into the garage on special occasions. It had sat out on the driveway like a neon sign for the past two years. Now it was gone. Maybe that was reason enough for his neighbors to suspect something was wrong. He'd never been able to gauge how observant his neighbors were. He'd gotten the occasional wave when he watered the grass or drove off in his car. He only knew two of his closest neighbors, but they rarely visited him. The only safe time to move Candace would be at night, in full disguise. Even that would pose some risk. It was the only option they had.

A loud thump and crack came from outside. Ryan left the table and walked to the living room drapes. He peeked out. A car had rear-ended another just yards down the street. Something clicked in his memory.

He'd seen one of those cars before because it was a maroon sedan with blacked out windows. While he was cutting the grass yesterday, he'd seen that car cruising down the street very slowly and stopping on occasion. It looked like a small compact car had plowed into the rear of the sedan.

Candace approached the window, but she did not ask to peer out. He gave her that look which meant something was out of place—not normal. He tried to change the mood and gave her a small, reassuring smile. She had her fists clenched and a stern look on her face.

He looked outside again and saw two dark-suited men at the driver's window of the other car. One of them rapped hard on the window, prompting the driver to back down the street in panic, flip a U-turn and gun it in the other direction.

Ryan let the drapes close. He turned around. "Could you recognize any of the cars that were driven by Antonio's men or even *his* vehicle?"

"What's wrong? You saw something."

He explained about his sighting of the dark sedan the other day and its reappearance just now.

"Antonio has one of those big jungle green Hummers," she said. "Tony the Twister has a blue Mercedes. Two other guys usually drive together in a gray Nexus. Alphonse and Jeppo double up in a dark purple sedan. They change cars a lot. They have a whole fleet. I can't remember all of the rest of them."

"Jesus, I saw a green Hummer on this street two days ago."

"That could have been Antonio."

"Would that sedan be maroon with blacked-out windows? And would the drivers wear dark suits and ties? Why would they be dressed like that?"

"Oh, yes. That sounds like Alphonse and Jeppo. They would pose as detectives with fake IDs so they could shake down the homeowners or search the house." She looked at the drapes. "Did they wreck?"

He told her about the collision.

"They were 'snailing' it then—making a sweep," she said. "I heard them talk about doing drive-bys on drug houses so they could steal the stash."

It was not good if Antonio's men cruised the neighborhood. He couldn't imagine how they'd zeroed in on him. It had been seven days since Candace made her escape. Ryan wondered if a church cam recorded his car, possibly revealing his license plate number. It seemed unlikely that such focus could be picked up at the distance from his car to the church building. He didn't remember seeing any camera poles along the church road.

Candace slapped her thigh. "Oh, boy. I hope they didn't find the veil on the way in here. It would explain a lot. Especially if they picked it up from the gutter."

Ryan remembered the veil tossing incident. He'd been unhappy about it, but he'd reacted too late. It was a spur of the moment thing on her part. He could hardly blame her. Now he had to think of some type of get-away spot that was safe and secluded—a hideout away from his house in case they were closing in on him.

Candace knew they didn't need thugs breaking the door down and finding them. Antonio had muscle and would stop at nothing, even if it meant turning every house in the neighborhood inside out. He was ruthless. He wouldn't care who got in the way. But he could cover his tracks and keep mouths shut through death threats. He often sent out his meanest boys to revisit people who had been previously warned. His threats were not idle. The visitations were frequent, like he'd stamped people and neighborhoods with his name all over them. Only the old time Mafia had so much cunning and organization. People knew him but looked the other way when his henchmen surrounded him. Most of the local police jurisdictions turned a blind eye on his activities—lots of them had dirty dark secrets that Antonio knew about or had outright caused by entrapment. Even small bits of insider information were enough to make the numerous authorities hesitate in launching a full investigation on him.

He'd been in the porn industry for nearly thirty years on the East Coast, owning everything from porn video stores, to topless dance bars, to full nude exotic establishments and a string of live sex theaters. He had gotten away with his empire because there were too many high profile people, including women, who would suffer for their betrayal. Just one open mouth could start a landslide of revenge, causing hundreds of lawsuits, firings, scandals, divorces and even suicides. His girls might have owned thousands of hard-ons, but he had all the balls and ovaries in a vice, ready to squash them if so much as a peep was heard about his activities.

On the plus side, Antonio Madera was a friend of the homeless and provided good income for moms who had to supplement their income or find steady work. He believed in family, higher education and the joy and innocence of children. Both his parents had passed away, but he found a family life amongst all his employees, from strippers to confidantes and bouncers. He was not alone—they looked up to him for comfort and advice. He was a successful business man who was surrounded by respectful and loyal people.

Candace knew about some of his background activities, but not all of them. Antonio had never revealed too much about his upbringing and early history. He claimed to be Puerto Rican, born in the city of Las Mareas on the Caribbean side of the island. Then he'd moved to San Juan with his parents when he was ten years-old. As the story went, Antonio's mother was an English teacher in her young and middle-aged years. She insisted on the Catholic faith for their small family, consisting of only three members, Antonio being an only child. Her favorite services were held in the Cathedral of San Juan Bautista. She taught her young boy English as a secondary language to the native Spanish. She loved the writing of the author Alonso; she'd read some of his greatest works to her boy while he grew and entered his teen years. Antonio always spoke highly of his mother. He enjoyed her cooking, soon becoming fat with her shellfish and pig roast plates smothered in sweet tubers and rice pudding.

His father started out as a child laborer in the sugar cane fields and then enlisted in the United States Army, which took him to many foreign countries and ports. His wife suspected him of having numerous affairs while stationed at the many bases, and it caused some of the most violent arguments in the household.

Antonio's father hated him and started beating the boy in his teenage years for joining gangs and stealing. Antonio had confessed to Candace that he had suffered lifelong scars from a stiff iron rod switched across his back and buttocks. All of the punishment sessions took place during the playing of loud Reggae music so the boy could not be heard crying out for help or yelping from the pain. Candace was not sure of the time when Antonio's father left the family for good, but she guessed it to be around his eighteenth year from what he told her.

Antonio Madera struck out on his own when he turned twenty-one years old. He had power on his mind, needing to find occupations that put him in charge of people. He needed people to think like him and do what he suggested and then later ordered.

He'd visited his first gentleman's club when he was twenty-two. Fascinated by the music, the gorgeous women and the money flowing so freely, he decided to work in the industry. He later began to create his own little empire when he turned twenty-five. His brand name shops, clubs and theater shows began popping up in Boston, gradually sprouting out to the other surrounding cities. It didn't take long for him to dominate and eventually buy out his competition.

Candace recalled Antonio seeing her for the first time in a small dive of a club, remembered his conversation with her when he ordered his first private lap dance from her. She had just finished her routine and stood nude over him, panting, and glistening with a light sheen of sweat.

"Now you're something out of the box," he'd said. "You've got me dribbling all over the place."

He'd given her a sizable tip, which was kind of a surprise since the guy had a face that would make a child cry. Yet he looked prosperous, wearing an expensive three-piece suit, several diamond encrusted rings, accompanied by Italian shoes and a solid gold watch.

"Then that's a good thing," she had told him, but she didn't really take kindly to either of his statements, especially the crude remark.

"You know," he'd said, "you've got something dynamic going on. I think you need a leg up, pardon the pun." He gave her the once over from her toes to her head. "How much are they paying you?"

She told him, and he laughed, his pot belly jiggling. "You have to excuse me," he had said. "This club doesn't fit you. You're too damned hot for this mud hole."

"I don't have any choice," she had explained.

"I'll pay you three times what they're offering you. Plus, you'll have carte blanche of my flagship club, the finest meals, escort service and choice of your working hours."

She remembered looking at him with suspicion at first. Then her curiosity came to the surface. "What do I have to do for all this?"

"How long have you been here?"

"I just got here a week ago."

"Then you can give them notice next week. They'll hardly miss you."

"Are you telling me the truth about all this?"

"I want to headline you at the Kitten's Revenge. You'll get the rank of sugar shack queen."

He'd laid out another thousand dollars on the table for her.

Her eyes had brightened. Her heart skipped a beat. "It looks like you have a deal."

"Fine, fine. Excellent. You're my girl. Before long you'll be running the place."

She remembered the crater-faced man offering to shake her hand, but when she bent over, he fisted one of her breasts and plied it with his stubby fingers. She rose up, feeling a little resistance in his grip, wondering what she had gotten herself into.

"I'm Candace Sabella. You are...?

"You'll be 'Candy' for your stay at my club. I'm Antonio Madera. Pleased to meet you."

She recoiled a smidge. That name had crossed a lot of lips from girls and bouncers she knew on the East Coast. He was a major porn king. That much she knew and wondered if she'd just stepped through a door into hell.

CHAPTER THIRTEEN

The more Ryan thought about it, the more he worried about the presence of Antonio's men on his street. Too bad he hadn't gone back for that veil. Ryan and Candace had just finished loading up her new clothes in three trash bags and burying them in the backyard. All of her personal belongs: make-up, I.D. hair coloring and other items had been included. Her favorite brand name foods that Antonio or his men might recognize were buried in a separate pit.

Ryan set out all of Gloria's clothes and items throughout the house, including her make-up, notes, photos, and portraits of the two of them together at favorite vacation spots. He made sure Candace kept her engagement ring on her finger and emptied her clothes hamper.

Ryan brought down a large Sierra pack from a hallway closet and loaded it with every survival item he could think of, including a small one-burner stove, first aid kit, map, water, packaged dehydrated food, canned goods and other essentials. He gave Candace a large satchel so she could carry her old over-sized clothing items and sandals. He tied two sleeping bags to the pack frame and threw it over his shoulders.

"Ready?" he asked. She gave him a nod, and they stepped out of the door at two minutes past nine in the evening. The back slider was left open. When they passed through the backyard gate, he shut it and kicked a mound of sand against it to jam it closed.

He marched south-west, headed in the direction of the Gay Head Lighthouse. He wore a pair of board shorts, a T-shirt and his basketball shoes. Candace was similarly dressed and carried her sandals in one hand. He glanced at her under the three-quarter moon and could see her outline and a slight shine to the top of her wig. Remembering to erase all clues of her habitation at the house and fake a vacation took meticulous planning. To miss anything would ruin the plan.

Candace reached out for his hand, and he took it. He rather enjoyed pulling her along in the sand.

After thirty minutes, they came to a dark set of hillocks that sat at the base of some clay bluffs. He knew the way into a maze trail and found a little niche he had visited before. It was a small oval patch of sand surrounded by irregular dirt and rock walls. The secluded spot kept a body hidden in near daylight. It was a bit hard to see down into the covey from the overhead bluff, but it was possible.

They laid their gear to the side and spread the sleeping bags out, nearly filling up the open space. It smelled good here. Green shrubs and mesquite gave off subtle odors. There was just enough light to see by, and the temperature was cool. He'd brought a tiny keychain light along and tested the beam inside the small clearing. Gay Head's lighthouse's beacon shone faintly out to sea, under-lighting the low hanging clouds with a slow and faint strobe effect. They couldn't have asked for a more secluded spot, night or day.

Candace rubbed her thighs, but she made no sign of being cold. "Is this the place where you and your wife stayed?"

"Naw, a couple of hills over. She never did like to lay out in public. This place we're in now was my secret hideaway. I used to come out here and sketch, although I had to keep my shirt on because I burn so easily."

"Yeah, you are a pale-faced Scandinavian. But that's okay. You won't wrinkle fast." She found his face in the dark. "I didn't ask you what you were up to with this trip out here. I knew it was important."

"I'm just making a wager against something. Don't ask me to explain. You don't need to be fretting over it, and I want you to enjoy your stay."

They lay back and gazed upward. The sky looked like black velvet pepper shot with salt. It was quiet. There were no voices or sounds of street traffic. No dogs barked.

Candace pointed to one of the larger pinpoints of light and said, "I wish upon that yellow star."

Ryan grinned. "That's not a star, Candace."

"Why not?"

"Stars are small, white and they twinkle. That one is large, yellow and steady. It's either Mars, Jupiter or Saturn."

"Then I can't wish on it?"

"Wish upon one of the little white ones."

Candace waited a beat. "Okay, I did it."

He could imagine what she wished for. There were several choices. She could have been thinking about ditching Antonio for good, having him arrested, moving away, or getting back to her place. She probably wanted to work again.

"Sweet dreams, Ryan."

"Night, little one."

Candace didn't fall asleep right away. Instead, she gazed up at the heavens, watching the stars flicker. The smallest white stars didn't seem to blink in and out as much as the larger ones, which shimmered in and out of focus. There were also green and red-colored stars that were faint and harder to see. Ryan would know the reason for the different colors. He knew a lot about such things and was a good teacher when it came to science and art. Learning was fun with him. He had a good eye, able to pick out details that others might have missed or ignored. His painting of her showed how much attention he gave to the smallest of things, like shadows and skin color. He had told her later that her eyes had 'popped'. The meaning was unclear, but she reasoned it must have been a good thing.

Thinking of the nude painting session made her bite her lower lip and squeeze her eyes shut. The whole idea of it, which was really hers, made her feel embarrassed and sorry for having to resort to such a trick. She'd never had to use such tactics before. She wanted to show him all of her. There was no ogling, crude remarks, or unwanted advances. She remembered the scene in the movie *Titanic*, where Jack sketched Kate, his soon-to-be lover. It was erotic. She enticed him, moved him with a show of naked beauty. Maybe Ryan really thought she was beautiful and irresistible.

You respected me. Instead of acting out of control, you became shy and confused —the little boy came out, not to play, but to hide. Nothing was expected. No favors were asked. But you were not the only one who felt the heat of desire. I had to play it down, sweet man. I wanted you to make a pass and take me. Oh, you'll never know!

Maybe one day I'll tell you just how I felt. I came so close, but you were so far away. I knew why you were so far away, too. Because you have a beautiful heart wrapped in a gentle soul, and it makes me want to melt in your arms, surrendering everything I have to you. I don't know how much longer I can hold out. I'm losing everything that I've kept to myself for so many years. I would die of loneliness without you. I'm changing, Ryan. I can't catch my breath anymore. I tremble when you are near me. I see you everywhere I go and wherever I've been. I'm breaking down right in front of you with no way to stop it. I'm so afraid of losing the most precious thing I've ever felt in my life.

When she turned her head to the side and gazed at his form in the sleeping bag, she wept. She was not certain whether they were happy tears or a flood of sadness. She thought just maybe it was both. One bad bone of contention though—she could not stand his meal selections. Ah, but the remedy was easy.

Ryan let Candace sleep in while he boiled a meager ration of Top Ramen noodles and peas in a tin skillet. It would have to do as breakfast. He had two Boy Scout mess kits that came with all the utensils, with everything weighing mere ounces. The water and canned goods weighed the most which made the Sierra pack heavy to lug. If they stayed long enough, after eating several meals, the trip back with the lighter load would be a cinch.

Candace stirred and opened her sleeping bag. She propped up on her side and crinkled her nose. "I thought I smelled preservatives. That's the noodles with that seasoned chalk."

"It's lightweight and filling. We've got peas."

"Ryan, how could you? My system will get all bollixed up with that food. It'll drag us down and make us tired."

"Hey, it's the best we've got."

"Do you want me to get dysentery and poop in this sleeping bag in the dead of night?"

He'd lost this one. He felt a pouch on the pack and opened it up. "Okay, I've got the solution. Just let me eat before I go out." He ate the noodle mix with six massive gulps and wiped his mouth on a washrag. He pulled out a small plastic case filled with tiny lures, and then a closed reel compact pocket fisherman. He clamped some split shot on the line and tied on a lure. He climbed out of their hilly circle.

"Where are you going?" she called out.

"To the fish store. Stay there!" It was the least he could do since he and Candace would miss out on the great Sunday fishing trip with Billy and Ross.

He had called Billy before leaving to say that he and Gloria would be away for a while. He hoped that Billy caught on to the subterfuge. When he waded in past the surf line, he telescoped the rod out and gave it a strong overhead cast into the waves. He used gentle tugging motions as he reeled it in. He cast a second time out past the breakers. With no luck, he walked further out into the water and tried again. He snagged something on his second tug, then reeled it in. The fish only weighed a pound or so, but he was happy with the catch. He returned to their hovel, found a flat stone, and filleted the fish.

Candace rose to her knees, having gone back to sleep. "Ooooh...what's *that?*"

"Sand perch. I think you'll like it." He started to place the fish slices in the tin skillet, but she stopped him and bit into a raw slice.

She waved a piece of fish at him. "You have to remember that cooking removes vitamins, nutrients and minerals. You should try it this way. It's a poor man's sushi."

He hardly had reason to argue with her. She had to be doing something good to remain so healthy and fit. She also had more energy than he did. He gave in and tried it. Once he got past three bites, his palate adjusted somewhat.

"Slimy, but it's okay," he said.

They had the same food for lunch. He caught a small flounder for dinner. He cooked his. She ate her share raw.

They fell asleep under the stars again that night, relishing the quiet and solitude of the Bluffs. He could hear the lullaby *Beautiful Dreamer* somewhere off in the distance. It soothed and caressed him. Ryan did not wake up babbling and soaked in sweat.

They arranged for 'his and her' latrine locations and took care of business when the need arose. Only a few couples and one family passed by on the beach. Someone stretched out in the nude fifty yards away. Several powerboats and sailing vessels crisscrossed the waters, some of them moving very fast and recklessly.

Candace insisted on sunning herself and began to remove her shorts and shirt.

"Please don't do that," Ryan said sternly.

"Don't panic. I came prepared just in case." She showed him the top band of the lavender bikini he'd bought her.

"You're a little sneak."

"A girl's gotta do what a girl's gotta do."

He started pulling items out of the pack. He knew the basic contents, but he hadn't checked the three side pouches. He found extra toilet paper in one and two paperback books in the other. He remembered that Gloria had brought the reading material to a pond during a previous vacation. Neither of them had read the novels. He found a small transistor radio in the third pouch. The radio would work fine for some much needed entertainment. His believed his phone could be traced and had shut it off. A small radio couldn't be traced. He turned the radio station on to his favorite music channel and turned it to low volume.

Candace had just finished applying some suntan lotion and stretched out on her back. "What kind of music do you listen to anyway?"

"Mostly blues, and rhythm and blues. Right now, you're listening to Charlie Musselwhite. Can you roll with that?"

"Honestly no," she said flatly. "It's depressing. Even jazz is wonky and for older people. Haven't you ever gotten down with rock 'n roll, metal or even hip-hop? You know, like *Angel and Rag Doll* by Aerosmith, *Moving* by Kate Bush, *Still Loving You* by the Scorpions or *All Mixed Up* by the Cars? Heck, I showed you the moves."

"Aerosmith."

"Oh, *you*. Get out your Eagle badge and polish it." She asked for the radio, and he gave it to her. She expertly dialed in a station and raised the volume a notch. "Now here you go...this is *Too Deep* by Genesis." She sat up and showed him some body gyrations. "Listen to the backbeat of the drums." She bobbed her head to the little staccato thumps. "You gotta let it get inside you."

Candace dialed in the music for the next three hours. He began to understand what she meant. It wasn't as though he hadn't listened to such music before. He just hadn't made a steady diet of it. He would have run the risk of making spastic brush strokes while listening to a heavy metal band. On the other hand, R & B let him execute brush strokes smoothly and gracefully.

When Candace turned to get some sun on her back, she placed one of the paperback books in front of her and began to read. "What kind of a title is *Ghost Lover?*" she asked.

"Dunno. I haven't read either book. Mine's called *The Witches of Warwick House*. What do you think about that?"

"Good luck."

Some distant voices carried on the wind from the ocean, mixed with the thrum of a powerful engine. Ryan rose to his knees and peered out into the water. A police patrol boat sat anchored off shore. Two officers hurled grappling hooks overboard from the port and starboard gunwales. They were dragging for a body, and he had a good idea of whose body they were searching for.

"What is it, Ryan?"

"Dunno. I'm not even paying attention."

They had run out of clean drinking water and their food stores were hitting rock bottom. They had been in their little divot in the sand castle for six days: it was now Friday evening. Ryan thought that a quick swim wouldn't hurt to ease their boredom so waited for the sun to drop below the horizon.

Ryan kept his boxer shorts on, and Candace removed the long wig. They went out far enough to dunk under and swim around. She splashed water in his face several times. He swam after her to do the same. But she used a freestyle stroke to easily out distance him until he tired of the chase and retreated to sit on the berm line. She joined him on the sandy bank a moment later, shaking her hair out.

She planted her palms in the sand behind her and looked up. "What's that box thing?" She raised a pointing finger at a group of clear stars.

"That's the constellation called 'Orion the Hunter'. See the shoulders up on top and the legs down below?"

"Yeah. Is that his huge manly member hanging down?"

Ryan rolled his eyes. "No, it's a sword hanging from a belt. He's a hunter and warrior." He showed her some more clusters and star groups. By the time he was finished, she'd learned about the Big and Little Dipper, the Seven Sisters, the Orion Nebulae and where to find the North Star. She showed a genuine interest in things astronomical. He was glad he could impart a little knowledge to her, knowing that she was no dimwit.

They left the shore and snuggled into the small clearing. Ryan explained that he would be back after checking on something. She begged not to be left alone but relented after he told her he'd be back quickly.

He only carried a pocketknife with him when he headed east up the beach.

CHAPTER FOURTEEN

When Ryan left their hiding place in the Bluffs, he only got a dozen yards before he turned around to look back the other way. He could see Candace on her knees, watching him depart. She looked so small, helpless, and alone. The sight of her pulled at his heart strings, and he quickly walked back to the clearing. He didn't want to risk her being left alone. He made a snap decision. They couldn't stay on the beach forever.

"Let's gather everything up," he said. "You're coming with me."

It didn't take them long to put everything in the Sierra pack and load her big purse. They buried all the evidence of their camp site, including used toilet paper, food wrappers, cans, and the fish bones from their meals. They dressed in the clothes they'd started out with and made good progress through the thick sand, although the moon was nearly full and casting some unwanted light on them. The three-story Victorian house came into sight. Ryan had left all the lights off and was glad to see nothing had been turned on.

When they arrived at the back of the property, Ryan saw that the mound of sand holding the gate closed had not been pushed aside. After clearing the mound, he opened the gate slowly, took a long steady look and motioned for Candace to come through. Since the back slider was still open, they crept into the kitchen with as much stealth as possible. Ryan pushed Candace underneath the dining room table and whispered, "You stay here until I come back." She gave him a reluctant nod.

Candace couldn't figure out why Ryan insisted on making her hide under the dining room table. A lot of good she could do if the house was loaded with bad guys waiting in the dark. Her favorite man wouldn't stand a chance if he got ambushed; he could get himself knocked out and/or killed by a surprise attack. He wasn't using a light to find his way, so how could he find anybody in the near total darkness? What if the bad guys had night vision or laser beam guns? They wouldn't have to turn the lights on to see him. One shot and he would be down. The thoughts made her feel hopeless and angry at the same time. She wanted to storm out, chasing after him to back him up.

She was not one of those cringing, whining damsels in distress. Fighting had come with her job description. Hundreds of customers had rushed her stage, and she'd had to handle them before the police or security arrived. She could throw a punch, kick a groin, trip, flip and go down in a wrestling hold with the best of them. Self-protection was one of the first things all the girls learned.

The bouncers taught all the girls disabling moves, how to break holds, gouge eyes and get out of the toughest arm locks. There'd been many times when drunks or druggies had gone for the cash in the girls' garters. The girls learned how to bring a swift knee up under the chin of the assailants.

Any girl caught in a hold was to wiggle out and use pressure points. After breaking free, they were to run away as fast as they could. The fleeing dancers were seldom caught. If the opportunity was there, many girls had climbed their poles to the top and stayed there. Few of the drunken louts had the skill or strength to climb up after them. The ones who made it close to them got heel kicks in the face.

Candace felt perturbed that she had to remain tucked away. Then again, she knew that Ryan lived by a code of chivalry, respecting the fairer sex, because he was most likely brought up with such manners. The thoughts of his behavior brought back a final scene from the Titanic movie where Jack gives up his place on the floating wreckage to Kate because it couldn't keep both of them out of the water without sinking. Jack sacrificed for her, giving up his life to make sure she lived. Candace had no doubt that Ryan would make such a gesture to protect a woman, the elderly, or children.

After thinking about it for awhile, she could hardly blame him. A good part of her anger began to fade. It wasn't really his fault. He'd been taught to be self-sacrificing, even courageous, at the risk of his life. His old school ways had a touching sentimentality to them and, surprisingly, they were unexpected traits that should have belonged to an older generation. When she thought about his actions again, her heart softened because he was now keeping a very close eye on her and she considered that heroic. He did care—he wanted to safeguard and protect her. That gave her a warm feeling throughout her whole body. It eased her. It calmed her mind.

It's not my fault. You're making me love you more and more.

Ryan searched the laundry room first, including the water heater closet. Next on his list was the foyer and living room. He checked the rooms on the first floor and then climbed the stairs, trying not to make the steps creak. He slid into each room and searched behind and below the beds and closets.

It was difficult to see in the darkness, but he managed to pick out solid objects before stumbling over them. He saw no sleeping bodies, but he saw other evidence that he suspected would be there. He tripped over several strewn items lying on the floor and ran his knee into an open bathroom sink cabinet.

After he cleared the three second story bedrooms, he headed up to the loft and peeked inside. There wasn't as much as a mouse breathing in his studio. But things were out of order and arranged differently, making him skirt around them or push them aside. When he looked out the loft window, he saw no suspicious cars parked on the street in either direction. He descended the stairs and walked into the kitchen where he snapped a light on. He turned on the dining room and living room lights, illuminating the interior.

"It's clear. Looks like they ransacked it all right," he said, hands on hips. "Most of the drawers have been opened, the sofa is upturned, opened cupboards, mattresses yanked aside. They even went through my art supplies."

Candace crawled out from underneath the dining room table and straightened up. She looked around with wide eyes. "I knew that you were baiting them. I didn't want to say anything to mess up your juju. Did they break anything?"

"No, they didn't bust things up. It would make too much racket. They probably wore gloves—no fingerprints that way.

"What do we do now?"

"We can relax a little. They've combed through everything and found nothing. They won't need to search this house again. We're clean. At least for now." If only he believed what he'd just said. Why would they make a return trip? He wondered if Billy and Ross had stopped by last Sunday for the fishing trip. Had they come calling before the break-in? Risking a call, he dialed Billy's number and waited for the answer. It came on the fifth ring.

"Hello, there my friend. Enjoy your vacation?"

Billy Powell wasn't letting out any personal information, which was not a needless precaution.

"Just took Gloria to the mainland for a change of pace," said Ryan, substituting Gloria's name for Candace, hoping that Billy got the drift. "Got a little hot here when the air conditioning broke down. We did all right, but the food was rotten."

"So how is Gloria anyway? Did she adjust to everything?

"Just like a trooper."

Billy got the name puzzle.

He went on, "We went fishing Sunday. Caught some prize bonitos and the biggest grouper you ever saw. It snapped the top of Ross's pole, and he had to hand-line it in. We missed you."

"We caught some fish off the pier. I had a little pocket fisherman. We got us some nice sand perch and a diamond turbot."

"Just ring me," said Billy, "if you need anything. If that car breaks down again, I'll bring my truck and help you transport your art."

Ryan understood the coded conversation. He knew Billy and Ross would help get them out of any tight spot. Billy and Ross probably knew why Ryan and Candace had left the house.

"I'll see you if I need you," said Ryan, ending the call. He called Ross next and swapped dialogue with him. The results were the same—the big guy knew the score and gave his assurance that he would help out any way possible. Ryan snapped his phone shut. That was that!

Candace looked out the slider. "If I could dig up everything, maybe some things haven't yet spoiled or been ruined."

He had to stop and think about that for a minute. If they needed extra food supplies, he'd have to make a trip to the health store to buy replacements. That would mean leaving Candace alone and vulnerable. Antonio and his men had paid the house a break-in visit, which meant that they wouldn't likely make a repeat trip. He thought he could propose a safe plan.

"Make up a new grocery list for me. Include everything perishable. I'll make a fast dash in the morning and pick it up. Then you can dig up the goods and clothes. But if somebody shows up besides Billy or Ross, beat feet out the back fence and run to the secret place. If you get caught in the house, get up to the studio and lock yourself in. It's the oldest part of the house with the strongest door and lock."

She picked up a pad and a pen out of the kitchen utility drawer and sat at the dining room table. It took her awhile to list the items. He stuffed the list in his pocket. Their eyes met, lingered. It was unimaginable that any harm should come to her. He would never forgive himself.

"We ought to get some sleep for now. We have plans to make."

Ryan arrived home with the groceries, greeting Candace in the living room. He imagined she'd spied out the drapes and saw his car. They stacked everything in the fridge and cupboards except for some camp-out grub and water which he loaded in the Sierra pack. He set the pack by the rear slider for easy access. Most of her new clothes were laid out on the sofa from her digging venture, and the washing machine thrummed away in the laundry room. She had dressed in a lavender sun dress and black slippers. He told her to package some clothes up in plastic and place them inside the pack just in case they had to make a fast getaway.

Candace turned on the radio and danced to some rock tunes. Ryan watched her out of the corner of his eye while he watered the house plants, which he had neglected to do before leaving. He called Billy and asked him if he could take his painting series to the mainland, and he would spring for his lunch and the ferry cost. Billy agreed and told him he'd be over in the afternoon. Meanwhile, Candace invited Ryan to dance with her. She told him she would show him some moves.

He watched her carefully and tried to mimic her body motions. He jerked his head and flailed his arms. She said the song was called 'Come Undone' by Duran Duran. He remembered the group name because he was certain he had painted an album cover for them about ten years ago, one of his first high-paying assignments. Then he remembered that the band name came from the movie 'Barbarella' starring Jane Fonda.

"Ryan, you're dancing the frug! Stop that and get close to me."

He moved in for the kill and turned his side to her. She gave him a queer look like he was nuts.

"Now you're doing the bump."

"I can double bump," he offered.

"I don't care if you can quadruple bump. Face me and do what I do."

He started to get the hang of it. He watched her hips, arms, legs, and head and tried to sync with her. He felt like an oaf, but he gave it everything he had.

"That's it," she said. "Now you're getting it."

She wasn't satisfied with just the fast moving stuff. She spent the next hour teaching him the two-step and the waltz. She explained that ballroom dancing was very elegant and that she had entered many contests. Right when he thought he had mastered the slower dances, she shocked him back into the faster rhythms.

Going into the third hour of nonstop gyrations and movements, he begged off and collapsed in the recliner. She showed him her signature moves with a ceaseless, boundless energy: the fist pump, body wave, boob pump and the worm.

"Now this one is called the 'swing'—my favorite.'" She hiked up her skirt, knotting it at her waist. She then turned a slow circle and rolled the lower half of her body around in an orbital motion.

"Now watch the hips rotate," she breathed.

And that's my favorite, too. Dear God, help me to not break into a sweat. He couldn't believe she danced this way for men up close. Of course he'd seen films with club dancers before. Very few dance bars had garnered his patronage during his college years. But a TV and movie screen was no comparison to a live performance. He felt entertained, but at the same time teased. It was everything he could do to keep himself composed.

"Candace, you'd better lay off a little, or things are going to go wrong here. I mean it's great and everything, but it's sort of wrong for me. I need a breather."

She changed the channel and lowered the volume. After fanning her face, she said, "I wasn't thinking again. I'm used to teaching other girls how to dance. It just comes naturally. Do you understand now?"

"Yeah, you've painted the picture for me with bold colors."

She took a seat on the sofa. She wet her lips with her tongue and grinned at him. There was something coy, almost flirtatious about her performance. It almost seemed that it was meant to arouse him. Of course, wasn't that the whole purpose of an exotic dancer—to stir up the juices? She got high marks for that.

A light tapping came at the front door. Ryan looked out on the street and could see Billy's truck parked at the curb. Ordinarily, Billy and Ross had permission to open the door and step in. Considering what had happened, his friend acted respectful by knocking before entering. Ryan let him in and motioned to the sofa. Billy took a seat and raised an eyebrow at Candace, who gave him a warm smile, then wiped some sweat from her face.

Ryan excused himself and went up to his studio where he picked up the bubble-wrapped pictures and brought them downstairs. He set them next to the front door and then handed Billy a hundred dollar bill before taking a seat.

Billy cocked a thumb at Candace. "She looks great. What gives?"

What do you mean what gives? Ryan sighed. "Just a little a wardrobe change. We can't have a girl running around here looking like a hobo."

Billy exchanged looks between the two and then faced Ryan. "You guys aren't...uh...are you sweating? I mean, is it time for a celebration or something with you two?"

There you go again, you nosey Welshman. You'd just love to jump to a hasty conclusion. "Billy, I love ya, but it's none of your business. We had a close call over six days ago and had to split fast. I'm sure you figured that out."

"I take it you got a visit."

"Yeah, they were here."

Billy stood up and crossed the floor, reaching into his back pocket. He pulled out a harmonica and a two-inch Smith and Wesson revolver. After he placed the gun in Ryan's hand, he tightly clamped his fingers over it.

"Buddy boy, you'll need this if things get complicated. I know you don't like guns, but tough shit. I don't want to read about either of you two in the obits."

Not giving it another thought, Ryan pocketed the gun. It did not take a convincing speech to know that the weapon would afford much needed protection if it came down to serious violence. If bum rushed, Ryan would fight his way out of it.

"I don't know if keeping your car in the garage makes any difference," said Billy. "I would keep your lights down. If you need to haul ass out of here, I'll come and get you and take you aboard the Shamrock. We can put out to sea if we have to."

"You're a good friend, Billy. I don't want to involve you too deeply in all this. Although if we need help, I'll connect with you as fast as I can. I'll even get a message to Ross."

Billy gave him a nod, picked up the paintings and left.

CHAPTER FIFTEEN

Gloria rode her paint horse abreast of Joyce's palomino. She felt good being out in the sunshine, not thinking of Ryan and his adulteress escapades. The man was clearly an unfaithful lout, having tested her patience twice and lied about it. To think that he ever wanted to reconcile with her had been a nasty ploy, an attempt to ward off a divorce settlement. He could not contest his guilt now. She had saved his first act of debauchery on her Facebook page and buried the dirty picture in her website for future reference. She had a second piece of evidence in the form of a nude painting featuring, in all likelihood, an underage school girl. Gloria thought about all the disrespect and abandonment.

So I was your dreamboat cougar, huh, fella? That was until you tasted the forbidden fountain of youth. All those night sweats and moans were nothing more than your dissatisfaction with me. You chased those women in your dreams and caught them and had your way with them. As if I didn't give you enough love. Was I your practice dummy? You threw me and your morals right out the window onto the curb next to the trash.

"I hate to ask you," said Joyce, her face glowing in the sun. "But what are your intentions? I don't see reconciliation in it this time. You're grinding your teeth down to chalk, Gloria. You're letting the hate inside you grow and wedge itself inside your heart. You have to acknowledge the anger and hatred without letting it fill you up and take control. Just know that it's there but choose to feel the love within yourself."

"Joyce, with all the therapy sessions we had together, I just can't believe he would do something like this. It's hard to let the love in or out when I consider what he has done to me. This was not a drunken one-night stand. They shared our house and probably our bed for God only knows how long."

Both women reigned in. Gloria looked off toward the horizon. "All of this has been percolating inside me for months. His infidelity. I really needed to trust him this time."

"You can't hold the bitterness within you," said Joyce. "It will eat you inside out. That's why we've taken these rides. Enjoy the scenery. Go ahead if you have to talk it out."

Gloria kicked her mount, running it up the hill. Joyce followed close behind. When they reached the rise, they could see out over the vast Atlantic Ocean and could pick out the tiny white sailboats. Up here, the breeze was warm and lively. They dismounted and sat on the sandy ground, leaving the horses to graze on some nearby grass.

Gloria closed her eyes and rocked gently. "How could I ever compete with someone like that?"

"What attracted him to you in the beginning? Can you remember that? Where and how were you when those first seeds of love were planted?"

"He told me that he had hit the jackpot with me and that he preferred an older woman because he liked my maturity." Gloria shifted her butt. "He said that I had stature and elegance—a refined poise. Of course he liked my figure. I found him obsessed with it. It makes me wonder if I was just a ride."

"Do you think he's completely flip-flopped in these feelings for you?"

"Consider the other woman. Or should I say, girl?"

"I would not have expected him to go through midlife crises at this early age. Although there is no set age limit for such a transition."

"No age limit. But he did jump the gun as far as I'm concerned."

Joyce reached out and patted Gloria's arm. "Do you believe you might have been mistaken in his intentions with this other female?"

"Joyce. My hand is still bruised from striking him."

"Then your reaction was very heated."

"I have never cursed and become so violent in my life."

"Then you are convinced this was no mistake?"

Gloria met her eyes. "I saw too much there to ever believe that I was reading the wrong signals. It didn't seem to me that he was harboring a homeless girl. If you have any doubts, you should see the nude painting of her. She is beyond beautiful. I have the painting at my house. Well, most of it is intact, anyway."

Joyce cocked her head puppy fashion. "What are you going to do about it?"

"This situation doesn't call for a no-fault divorce. I deserve to get something out of all my efforts and contributions to the household. I'm going to obtain a good lawyer and find out what I'm entitled to."

"Then you are going all the way this time?"

"I have to. I was such a fool, Joyce." Gloria backhanded a tear. "What was I thinking? What do *you* think I should do about this?"

Joyce cleared her throat. "You never heard this from me and it's against my principles, but I think you should have an affair."

They didn't share another word before they heard the thumps of a horse coming up the rise. They turned to look, and Gloria saw that the rider was Stephan Vonderhellen, the son of the owner of the horse farm. He had a wrapped package on the front of his saddle.

"Maybe you're right," said Gloria in a low monotone voice, still gazing at the man. She watched Stephan dismount and carry the package to the women. Then he sat down and opened it up. He pulled out several plastic containers, paper plates and utensils and began making up portions. It was lunch.

"I thought you ladies might like a bite to eat while you were relaxing. The stew is still hot, and the lettuce is crisp. I hope you like lemonade."

Gloria did not mind his intrusion. He seemed so warm and inviting. She also knew he was gracious. She'd only seen him during three trips to the stables, but she'd seen enough and felt enough of an attraction to him. Likewise, he had followed her on the trails and always gave her a happy greeting. Gloria realized that Stephan might have a crush on her, and she might not be able to resist the subtle advances. He was the perfect solution for an ailing heart. He could be something in her life, but she would have to beat her way out of a bad marriage and take what was rightfully hers from an adulterous husband.

"Riding is great therapy," said Stephan. "It is a communion with animal and nature."

Joyce took a bite of her stew and waved a finger at Gloria. "That is exactly what I told this woman. She has suffered through a failed marriage, and she needs to open up and breathe in the start of a new life."

Gloria had not noticed before, but the serene man had a grooved scar on his forehead above the left brow. If anything, it gave him a look of distinction. She could only guess that it might have been the result of a horse's kick.

Stephan wiped his mouth. "I am sorry to hear that. I can't understand any man's indifference to you, Ms. Barlow."

He remembered my name from the stable register. I'm so confused I don't understand my feelings. All of my emotions are in a gang fight. How could this be happening so fast? I'm still legally married and don't know what to do. Joyce says to give in. God help me!

"Stephan, you are a mind reader," said Joyce. "Gloria has had it rough, and she is at a temperamental stage in her life. This is a time for reinforcement and a change, so she can leave these pangs of hurt and betrayal behind her."

Gloria finished her stew and started on the salad. She couldn't help but notice Stephan stealing glances at her. He did not favor Joyce with such looks. Gloria looked at his hands. They were thick, with stout fingers. *There! He did it again. He looked at my bosom. Without a doubt!* Just to make sure, she drew her shoulders back. *Uh huh. I caught you again. But I don't mind. You can take in all the scenery you want. We can dinner date, but nothing is going to happen until I am legally divorced from my husband. You can be first up to the plate. But I warn you about wandering. Don't do that to me, handsome.*

"I don't mean to pry," said Stephan, "but is this marriage annulled or finished with the divorce proceedings?"

Gloria explained as much as she could about the state of the divorce, leaving out the more intimate and private information. Stephan nodded his head slowly, every once in a while, holding his head back and shutting his eyes. When Gloria finished the story, Stephan sighed, and this time shook his head. "And you are going through with a full courtroom divorce then?"

"I am. I have enough evidence for the jurors to reach a verdict in my favor. I intend to go to the limit this time. There will not be a no fault divorce proceeding. I'm sorry, but he will pay for his transgressions through a legal suit. Enough was enough, and then there was too much."

Joyce leaned forward with an eager gesture. "So, Stephan. What is your story about this beautiful horse ranch?"

"My father is seventy-eight and still owns and maintains the ranch. It was Dad's idea to turn the property into a healing retreat since the earliest days. My mother used to help out, but many chores went to my younger sister—today she tries to get in a full shift, taking some of the burden off me."

Joyce nodded. "This sounds like a very nice place for you."

Stephan looked down at this lap. "A stint in Vietnam gave me PTSD. This environment was meant to be. I fit right in with the animals. They saved my sanity."

Without another word, Stephan packed up the lunch gear and strapped it to the saddle horn. He walked back to the ladies just as they stood up. He slipped his palm under Gloria's and kissed the back of her hand. "It's been a delight to see you again. Keep me informed about your status." He looked into her eyes. "Be sure to come back soon, Ms. Barlow. This is the place for healing and forgetting about troublesome times. I'll wait to see you again."

The women watched the handsome troubadour mount his white gelding and then gallop off. When the horse's hooves kicked up the sand, it blew in a dusty cloud that settled with an eerie stillness.

Joyce couldn't keep the awe from her voice. "Did I just see what I think I saw and heard what I think I heard?" Joyce flicked Gloria's shoulder. "Hey! Are you listening to me? That man has designs on you something fierce, and he doesn't care who knows it. I'm a marriage guidance counselor and didn't see that one coming."

Gloria looked up into the clouds. "I didn't see it coming either."

CHAPTER SIXTEEN

Tony the Twister drove his boss to the Mermaid's Salon, a hair care center Antonio had recently started patronizing. Antonio had an aversion to the blonde mermaid seated in an oyster shell that was painted on the front of the building. It looked too girlish. He slipped in the back door, not wanting any of his boys to see him entering such an establishment. He liked the pretty gals who waited on the customers, even though it was only his third visit. There were six barber chairs, and he never had to wait. Leaving a large tip was his trademark signature. A few of the girls knew what Antonio did for a living, but they never questioned him about it or gossiped with the customers about such things. An employee told him that her boss had made it plain that her girls should not spread rumors or become nosey over someone's private affairs. That appealed to him—sealed lips.

Antonio walked down a narrow hall and entered the main salon. All the chairs were occupied except for one at the rear, and there was no stylist stationed at it. The other girls smiled at him in turn and continued on with their work.

"Please have a seat, Mr. Madera," said the stylist from chair five. "I'll have somebody with you in a moment." The older brunette rinsed her hands and scurried down the hall.

Tony the Twister sat down in a chair that was too small for his six-five frame and tried to spread his legs. Upon seeing the finely dressed, black-haired giant, the girl at station number two dithered and knocked over a shampoo bottle. A moment later, two women appeared from the hallway, one of them being the previous employee and the other one an elegantly dressed woman whom Antonio had never seen before. He liked her style. She wore her red hair up, and she had a presence about her—almost a regal air. She was not outfitted as a hairdresser. She looked like she was ready for dinner and cocktails after an Academy Awards show. He found her breathtakingly voluptuous.

The elegant woman introduced herself. "I'm Gloria Barlow," she said. "Welcome to the Mermaid's Salon." She pulled an apron around him and tied it off. "How can I help you today?"

He could smell an intoxicating perfume wafting from her but couldn't make out the scent. He knew nearly every brand of cologne and perfume that his dancers wore.

"A regular boy's haircut and leave some pompadour," said Antonio.

She patted his thinning hair. "I'm sorry, but—"

"I'm kidding! Just a trim around the edges." He tried to look backward, but his short neck hampered it. "I'm Antonio Madera. Why haven't I seen you here before?"

"Would you like a shampoo and conditioner treatment?"

"No, I'm fine."

"I've been in the back room doing the bookwork. I get behind if I don't stay on top of things." She ran a comb through his thinning hair and made a snip.

"Ah, a bookkeeper who doubles as a barber."

"Actually, I'm the owner."

Antonio looked across the floor. "Tony, did you know this? This woman is the owner here."

"No, boss, can't say that I did. First time I've laid my peepers on her."

Gloria swung her head around and peered at his face. "Wait. I've heard that name somewhere. Ah, you are the big tipper that my little hens have clucked about?"

"I wouldn't say big." He sucked in his paunch, aware of his big stomach roll. "But the service is primo here, and that's why I come."

"Then it is *more* of a pleasure to meet you. We aim to serve."

He wouldn't mind having this woman serve him. She was more of the age he had in mind for a wife, as opposed to one of the young dancers he babysat at his clubs. She was a business owner and not a potential drain on his income, unless she was incredibly high maintenance. It was not like he couldn't afford her. However, he didn't need her spending extravagant amounts of his earnings. And there was the problem of Candace Sabella, a marriage out of convenience that had some heavy overtones. The young half-breed stripper was a thorn in his side that he would have to find and deal with very soon.

"So what is your story, Mr. Madera?" asked Gloria. "Are you a fulltime resident here?"

"I am. It's beautiful here, and I wouldn't live anywhere else."

"And how is everything going?"

He liked her chitchat nature that made him feel at ease. "The usual, I guess. Business is fine on the plus side. On the not so good, I've had a spousal disagreement that has forced a separation. Or should I say an engagement that hasn't gone well." He hoped he wasn't revealing too much. The information kind of slipped. *Am I looking for sympathy from this woman?*

"You don't say. I've had that misfortune myself." She lowered her voice. "I had a complete marital breakdown just recently."

"Small world, Ms. Barlow. What happened, if you don't mind me asking?"

Gloria Barlow kept her voice down, but once she started talking about her up-and-coming divorce, the sluice gates opened and out poured a tale of woe and misery. He found it hard to believe that a woman as pretty as she was could have been duped twice. She finished her story just as she made the last few clips.

Antonio let her remove the apron, and then he stood up so she could brush him down. He looked in her eyes even though it was a slightly upward angle. "It sounds to me like this shyster, er, gentlemen needs to be wrought a heavy hand."

"He certainly does. I'll need a lawyer that will not only go to bat for me but knock it out of the park. This man will not get away with what he's done to me."

113

Antonio dug into his wallet and checked his pants and shirt vest pockets. He snapped his fingers. "Tony! Do you have one of Ardi Kastrati's cards?"

Tony rummaged through his clothes. "Can't say that I have, boss."

"What good are you?" Antonio turned on Gloria. "You'll have to forgive me, but I'm a little caught short. I could drop the name of one of my best attorneys, but I think that your case is special, and I would like to see him in person and set up a conference for you."

"You would do that for me?"

"Certainly. Why not? I aim to serve, ha! I'll get the information and appointment details to you on my next visit. That is, if you are not in a rush."

Gloria gave him a small shot of men's cologne and handed him some business cards. "Mr. Madera, you—"

"Call me Antonio."

"Dear Antonio, you cannot rush excellence."

He pulled two hundred dollars out of his wallet and placed it on the counter. Her eyes lit up. Tony stood up and escorted his boss down the hallway.

CHAPTER SEVENTEEN

C andace had just brought coffee up to the studio loft when Ryan put down his charcoal pencil and gave her a welcoming smile. Yet he noticed something terribly out of place with her. Her face looked like it had been finger-painted by a bunch of kindergarteners. Her make-up was smudged and cockeyed, giving her a ghastly appearance. Her hair was wild, stringy, and frayed. The clothes she wore looked like cutout potato sacks which gave her a bloated appearance. In fact, he recognized the outfit. She had squirmed into one of his old cotton jogging suits that was ten sizes too big for her.

He accepted the coffee. Taking a sip, he felt the cup warming his fingertips. He couldn't help but comment.

"What have you done to yourself? You're a wreck."

"I'm just trying to help things along." She pulled up a stool next to him.

"Yeah, but you're not helping yourself. What's up?"

"I just don't want to encourage you. You really get undone sometimes looking at me...and you know...that leads to other things."

He thought he knew what she meant. If she was ugly enough to make a freight train take a dirt road, it might stop his thoughts of lust. In this case, she had succeeded and wiped them out.

Ryan set his coffee cup down. "Okay. Mission accomplished. For what it's worth, it works pretty well."

She patted his shoulder. "I'm glad then. You don't need to be uncomfortable."

"Candace, what's that smell?"

"I just rubbed some onion on me. And I stopped brushing my teeth."

He laughed. "So now you stink. Will wonders never—"

"Believe me, I didn't want to do it. But our friendship is important."

He looked at the ghastly little clown face and shook his head. She tried to use a deterrent. It meant that she was thinking of him—tying to guard his feelings. He still liked her in spite of the disguise. She'd made a horror show out of herself to keep his eyes off her. She knew the powerful effect she had on him. He would never have expected such a thing from any other woman. It was endearing, but funny at the same time.

Candace shifted on her stool. "See? It's working. You're not looking at me with that other face."

"I'll go along with that. Thanks for thinking of me."

"Yoooooou are welcome!" She gave him a jaw-splitting smile.

Candace Dee Sabella was beautiful and bizarre. She was as smart as could be and knew nutrition inside out. She had to be the healthiest woman he had ever known. But one thing kept popping up in his thoughts while she'd been with him. It was time to let the cat out of the bag.

Ryan took several sips of his coffee and picked up his charcoal pencil. He made some strokes on the paper. She watched him with intense interest. Now was the time.

"You once said that you had something on Madera," said Ryan. "You said it was dangerous information, and it had something to do with his need to kill you. You never told me what it was."

"I didn't want to tell you because you would be involved if you knew what happened. I think he would have to kill you, too."

"Fine. I'm not afraid of the SOB. So tell me the truth. I don't care if it marks me for death."

She took a deep breath and said, "I can visualize the scene all over again in my mind." She closed her eyes. "It's coming into focus now, and I can see it in color. It all started when..."

And so Candace began her story:

As she drove into the front entrance parking lot of the Kitten's Revenge Gentleman's Club, she noticed the front lot was nearly full, which meant a good tip shift. Actually, a huge tip shift. A crowded club meant money. With Antonio paying her three times the regular shift amount plus her tips, she was getting that much closer to her dream of auditioning for Cirque du Soleil in Las Vegas. Hell, Vegas, Broadway—it didn't really matter!

She drove to the extreme corner of the lot and parked in the employee section. She grabbed her purse and keys and headed for the rear door, walking down the side alley, and arriving at the back entrance. After identifying herself, she was buzzed through. She walked down the main hallway, passing four anti-rooms and arrived on the main dance floor.

The club was swimming with customers, especially the seats next to the three stages. The elevated stage platforms had two poles apiece, but the front areas were occupied by free-style dancers, two per stage. In total, twelve bodies gyrated to music from the lively Dolby speaker system. *Sara* by Hall and Oats was playing. Candace had some favorite girlfriends who worked with her. Whammy Tammy was upside down on her pole, legs spread horizontal. Velvet, Cha Cha Suzy, Smitten Kitten, Dendy, and Lori were dancing up front, free-styling the hell out of themselves. Velvet's bikini bottom wasn't visible due to the bills stuck in her band. She looked like a budding green flower.

Some of the girls waved and blew kisses to her. Candace waved back, turned around and headed down the hallway. She made a left and climbed a narrow row of stairs to the second story. She went into the dressing room and glanced at the dozens of racks holding dance outfits. Some were custom-made. Many of them were tailored for holidays. The Christmas theme was sweet and fluffy, while Halloween was dark with a wild blast of blacks and oranges.

Antonio Madera's office sat to the right. The dressing room on the left butted up next to it. He could keep his eyes on the girls that way. And Candace had heard a rumor that there was a peephole somewhere.

She walked to her rack in the right corner of the room and pulled out her red sequined bikini top and bottom, changed into it and walked down to the main floor. She went to the VIP backroom and asked the guys if they wanted a table dance. Two did, and she gave them identical slow strips, shoving her pelvis in their faces. She finished up her act with deep knee bends and bent-over butt wiggles. She pulled fifty dollars from each.

She went to an open pole on the main floor and gripped it, running her hands up and down it like it was a cock shaft. Then she climbed it hand over hand to the top. She loved how she felt when she spread her legs wide open and slowly slid inverted down the pole. Her crotch muscles tightened, then she relaxed, and with one hand, pulled her top off first, followed quickly by her bottom, letting them fall to the floor. She had taut abs and showed them off. She rolled her head back and saw that all eyes were on her, waiting for her to give them a glimpse of her satin mound. She felt beautiful, powerful, and excited to be alive performing her craft. Her skin gleamed from the overhead lights. Her C cup breasts wobbled provocatively, moistened with sweat. One of the older customers was so mesmerized that he stood up and held his crotch with both hands.

She cocked her knees and did a rollover back flip onto the floor, legs spread wide. Her pelvis made a thump as she landed. The whistles and catcalls shrilled loud in her ears, and she moved to the edge of the stage and walked sideways down its length, giving the juiced up guys clear frontals. All the stage row men stuffed bills in her leg garter. There wasn't a slacker or cheapskate in the bunch. One younger guy yelled out, "You're a Goddess! Take me home!"

"Get upside down, and I'll go up on you!" a voice yelled from the back.

"Eat a beaver, save a tree!" she yelled back.

Candace switched to freestyle dancing on the front of the stage and kept it up for hours, teasing, appeasing and driving the men crazy when she did close-up squats and lay-over splits. At one point, she saw her boss, Antonio, staring at her from across the floor. He looked puffed up and happy.

She moved to the edge of the stage, turned her back and spread her legs. She bent over head to ankles and looked through her legs at the crowd. Antonio was smiling at her from a front row seat now. She returned the smile and spun around to give him several hip grinders. He reached out, stroked her thigh and then slipped several hundred dollar bills in her garter. He moved close to her. "You're my baby, Candy. Keep it up, and you'll have anything you want." His words energized her for the last hour of her shift. She felt light and free, proud of herself and totally sexed-up for reaching the height of her talent and appeal. Her dream was that much closer.

When closing time came, she sat down in a VIP chair, kicked back and relaxed. She woke up some time later and realized it was almost 3:00 in the morning. The club floor was deserted. She walked sleepily up the stairs, holding onto the rail.

Upon reaching the top floor, she could hear a loud discussion coming from Antonio's office and wondered if the boss was firing one of the bouncers. She recognized a few voices, like Antonio and Tony the Twister, but the other voices were unclear.

When Candace changed into her street clothes, she could still hear an argument in Antonio's office, but the volume had risen, and it sounded like furniture was being thrown against the walls. She heard a muffled scream and then something heavy hitting the floor. It sounded like a brawl. She swallowed dryly as the fight continued. She was scared to death to move or make a sound. Two or three voices shouted orders, and the other was pleading.

The next thing she heard was the office door swinging open and hitting the wall. Then some shuffling and scraping followed by moaning. She could hear the voices more clearly now since they were on the top landing. Heavy footsteps were followed by a dragging sound.

Morbid curiosity drove Candace to walk to the cracked open door and see what was going on. She only saw the back of a large man, probably Tony, descending the stairs. It sounded like there were men in front of him. She was nervous and shaking and trying to calm herself. When big Tony was involved, it meant trouble. Big trouble. The tall, good-looking man functioned as Antonio's right hand thug.

Unable to resist, Candace slipped out of the door and peered down the stairway. She saw four men dragging an older man. They reached the bottom and disappeared around the hall corner, headed for the back door. She ran back into the dressing room and tried to get her nerves to heel. Moments later, a loud clang came from outside the window. It sounded like the old fire escape frame. She chanced a look and saw Tony standing under the metal ladder rubbing his head. Three other men standing in the middle of the narrow alley hoisted an older man to his feet. The dim back lot bulb shed enough light to see the identity of those involved. Antonio stepped up face to face with the man and hollered at him. Tony cornered the man and held him by the back of his collar. Two others, Jeppo and Alphonse stood on either side acting as back-up.

The beaten man was somebody Candace recognized. He was Randy Hoffman, the seventy year-old owner of the Crazy Daisy gentlemen's club in Boston. She had worked there for six months two years ago and knew all of the employees. Right now, Randy was being strong-armed, and she thought she knew the reason why.

Candace had heard a rumor that Antonio had created a monopoly by buying out other strip joints, dance bars and live sex theaters. He had several porn book shops in Massachusetts and New Jersey. He forced the owners to hand over titles for undisclosed sums of money. He might have had as many as twenty-five clubs. If the owners didn't negotiate with him, they were forced to by physical means—generally a smacking around or an intense beating. Every one of them went along with the deal and sold out, except for a few holdouts. And what Candace saw below was a hold-out situation. Randy Hoffman was not going along with the program. He was a bloody mess.

Antonio backed away from the man and backhanded him several times. Randy's head rocked, but he lurched forward and spit in Antonio's face. Tony brought a knee up into his back, and Randy screamed, but Tony muffled it by covering his mouth.

Candace peeked from the window's edge, not wanting to be seen from below. She felt sick at what was happening, watching a friend who was getting roughed up—a previous employer she liked and who was defenseless against the four roughnecks.

It happened so fast that she would have missed it if she had turned away. Randy grabbed his chest. His head lolled forward, and he slumped. Tony let him drop to the ground and stared at him. Antonio backed off and looked around frantically, then he waved his arms at his men. Alphonse took off on the run and disappeared around the building. Minutes later, a dark sedan with blacked-out windows backed into the alley. The trunk door was popped open. Tony and Jeppo took the limp body and threw it into the trunk. Jeppo slammed the lid. The car rolled out. The three men followed the car as it disappeared around the end of the building.

At first, Candace didn't know what to do. She'd seen a man possibly die right before her eyes. At least it looked that way. The three men had walked around the building. They could have all piled into the car and driven away. They could be standing somewhere in the side alley. There was no other sound. A minute passed...and then another. The silence was maddening.

Candace grabbed her purse and keys, walked out of the dressing room door, and took swift cat-like steps down the stairs. She scurried down the hallway and onto the main floor. She unlocked the front door with her private key. When she swung the door open and lurched out, she ran straight into Tony's back, causing him to swing around and drop a cigarette.

Antonio was off to the side and stepped forward and grabbed her arm. He pitched a lit clove cigarette against the wall. Her keys and purse hit the walkway. One other male was urinating on the pavement a dozen feet away. He looked like Jeppo.

"What the hell's going on here?" Antonio demanded. "Why are you flying out of here, Candy girl? What are you doing here so late anyway?"

"I fell asleep in the VIP room. I forgot a bag of costumes in my trunk, and then I hung them on my rack." She instantly regretted those words.

Antonio furrowed his brows. He got in her face. "You were in the dressing room. Did you see something from the window? Something you weren't supposed to see?"

"Gah, nah," she stammered. "I wasn't near the window. I was racking my...I mean I was busy changing and—"

"Then you sure as hell heard something." Antonio squeezed her arm, digging his fingers into her flesh. She bit her bottom lip and tried to keep from crying out, but the guilt must have been written across her face, and Antonio knew it.

"You know damn well you're my sugar shack queen," Antonio hissed. "You make more poke than anybody here. I thought you would appreciate that. But now you're running out of here with a dirty little secret. I'm not going to let you do that."

"I promise I won't tell," Candace confessed, her voice cracking.

"You won't tell all right," said Antonio. "A little hometown girl like you wouldn't be missed if you went *poof*. You're not going to have anything on me." He cocked his head. "In fact, you're going to join my Gold Club. You'll never testify against me."

Candace gave a shudder and tried to calm herself, but her hands were shaking like sticks. "I don't understand. I told you I won't tell." Her last words were a plea.

"A wife can't testify against her husband."

"Oh, God." Candace blinked. "You...you wouldn't do that to me!"

"I can, and I will. You'll be my wife, and you'll do whatever I want you to do. I'm taking you as a bride. Case closed, baby."

Tony took a step toward her. "You do what the boss says."

Jeppo, the youngest of Antonio's boys said, "Tow the line, or pay the price, bitch."

Antonio snickered. "I'm sealing the deal on this. Inside!"

The next thing Candace felt was a firm hand guiding her through the door. When they arrived on the main floor, the men escorted her to end of the first stage. She knew what was coming.

"Get the duds off," said Antonio

Candace gave a shiver. "You don't need to do this."

"Get 'em off, and lay back on the stage," said Tony.

She unbuttoned her blouse, dropped it, and then pulled her pink cotton joggers off. The bra and panties hit the floor next. All she had left on were her low-top tennis shoes. She jumped backward onto the stage and lay down on her back.

"You can't do—"

"Shut your mouth," said Antonio. "Get your butt over the lip of the stage, arms out and spread your legs."

Tony and Jeppo stood on either side of her, ready to hold her down if necessary.

The cold stage floor bit into her back and buttocks, giving her the shivers. All she dared to do was strain her head up once to see Antonio move in on her. Candace cocked her head back and could see her favorite pole behind her, the pole she had used tonight to show how graceful and nimble she was—the place where so many men admired her and wanted her—the place where she delighted in the sensation of being naked and free. Now everything had changed, and it had become a dirty place—a place of terror. Eight months of kindness and gifts were now gone.

She scrunched up her face and clenched her fists until they were white knuckled. Jeppo and Tony stared down at her with dirty grins. She heard Antonio's zipper slide downward.

"Don't do this to me," Candace pleaded. "I just can't!"

"You will," said Antonio. "Or I'll hack your tits off and use them for tote sacks. How 'bout I break those dancing legs or dig up your parents and snuff them out?"

His drooling member grazed the inside of her thigh, and she felt him close in on her.

"I'll marry you!" she screamed. "I'll be yours!"

"You're my *property*," huffed Antonio. His face was beet red, and the veins in his neck stood out like fat strings. "Nobody else can have you. I own you!"

"Yes, sir!"

She clenched her teeth, waiting for the assault, but it never came. She craned her head up and looked over the edge of the stage. Antonio had backed away and stood statue-still, glaring at her.

She couldn't believe the rape hadn't come. Then she realized her boss hadn't laid a hand on her because he didn't have to. The threat was enough. He could never be prosecuted for something he did not commit.

Jeppo said, "Shit, man, I'm blistering hard! I gotta—"

"THAT'S ENOUGH!" said Antonio. "She gets the idea. Get her out of here."

Hands grabbed her and pushed her hard across the main floor. She never knew how many steps she had taken before her world went black, and she fainted

CHAPTER EIGHTEEN

Ryan couldn't swallow everything he'd just heard in one gulp. To think that Madera had caused a man to have a heart attack was bad enough. That was equivalent to murder. He vaguely remembered the disappearance of such a person because it had made the news some time back. With Candace witnessing it, the situation became more complicated. It was really more than just a marriage of convenience—it was blackmail. Ryan didn't know if they'd lived together or not. He couldn't stomach what might have happened to her when she had to surrender herself and obey that monster every day and night.

Ryan cleared his throat. "Thanks for telling me the story. It had to be gut-wrenching. I'm really sorry you went through that. I don't regret catching you when you fell out of the tree. I would do it again."

Candace shifted on her stool and kept her head down. "I'm glad I fell into your arms. You were like a beautiful prince. I'm sorry I acted the way I did. Sometimes when I'm under stress, I can't help but explode."

He lifted her chin. "Did he hurt you anymore after that?"

She looked away again. "That was it. He bullied and threatened me from then on. Then there was a certain thing he made me do...the one I told you about. He forced me to get a blood test and fill out some paperwork at his lawyer's office."

Ryan had never known how far out of control and hurtful her life had been until this moment. Rage boiled inside him. He had a hard time keeping his jaw relaxed. To think that she had been threatened with mutilation and murder. The promise to kill her parents was deeply disturbing. He couldn't imagine going through something like that and coming out of it sane.

Ryan extended his arms, reaching for her. She slipped off her stool. He lifted her onto his lap and curled his arms around her. She was so little—such a beautiful, lonely princess. He held her tight and massaged her back. He buried his head in her hair and could feel her shiver. She was not the sassy, loud-mouthed woman she pretended to be. She had a wall up. And for a good reason. Yes, she had a feisty personality, a part of her nature that would never change, despite the trauma she had suffered.

Powerful feelings were leaping around inside of him. He wanted to kiss her so badly it hurt. Whenever she was around he felt a craving to be with her. It was getting to the point where every second of every day his mind filled with thoughts of her, and he was powerless to stop them. He didn't care how ugly she wanted to make herself. Something was happening. He was falling hard for her.

Ryan could always talk to Candace about anything. She'd taught him so much about many things. He tolerated life. She chased after it. Why couldn't he break down and do what he wanted and needed to do with her? His resistance was failing. But he had been raised with Christian principles! He could not have Candace for his own. He was still married. Even though his wife hated him from within the very core of her being, he could not break the bond of his sworn commitment. If he did, it would set him up on the fast track to hell.

She turned around and looked into his face. He didn't see the smudged makeup. He looked right into her eyes, into the depth of her soul, where he lost himself.

"Something's happened to me, Ryan," she said. "I'm breaking down. I can't stop thinking about you, and it's tearing me to pieces. I'm so confused I don't know what to do. I've cut men out of my life hundreds of times, but this is different. I know how you feel about keeping your marriage vows and that we can't be together because you have to obey your feelings. You are so sweet and so handsome. I feel like I'm in heaven when I'm around you. I want you so badly...I'm sorry." She dropped her eyes.

Should he even dare tell her what he thought of her? Would that encourage a situation that could get out of control? Somebody had to put the brakes on this, and it looked like it had to be him.

Ryan let her slip from his lap and pointed to the stool. She sat on it dutifully, letting out a sigh.

He shook his head. "Look, until my marriage is over, I'm bound to honor my vows. I have feelings for you, but I have to keep everything under control. We can go on as close friends and keep a certain distance. I know it's not easy, but I have to obey my heart and my faith. I don't want to be a hypocrite or a sinner."

"But..." She took a deep breath. "Do I really stand a chance with you? I don't need any more heartache."

He knew he had to give that question a straight answer. "I want you to stay with me. I admit to falling in *like* with you. I'm not in love with you. But I feel something coming on, and I'm afraid I might have no way to stop it." *You lying fool. You know damn well it's more than that. So now you're putting up a smoke screen. But if you tell her the truth, you're toast. You'll hurt her if you admit your true feelings and refuse to touch her. She would feel miserable and rejected. We have to keep on this path and resist all temptation.*

"Would you really lose control with me?" she asked.

"If I allowed it to go any further, it would be out of control and wrong."

She frowned. "I don't understand why you torment yourself. Do you love any part of me at all?"

"Yes. Several parts of you. We have to wait. Can you understand that?

"I can wait, Ryan. I'll wait for as long as it takes. I want us to be together deep inside."

He told her to scoot her stool closer so she could watch him sketch a scene. The project was a depiction of a robot standing in front of a field of boulders. It was a quick job meant for a science fiction website that explored the mysteries and realms of the future. He had her stand up, and encouraged her to sketch a few lines, then add some shading here and there. She was careful and used detailed precision. She listened to him and followed his instructions. She could easily have been one of his students. She suddenly stopped and sat down on her stool, handing him the charcoal pencil.

He studied her face, but it was blank. She looked solemn and lost. "Are you okay?" he asked. "You look crestfallen—that means sad."

"I know what it means. Your wife stabbed me in the painting. She put a knife through me. You made that gift for me, and she ruined it. She killed me in front of you."

He gave her a half grin. He was going to take a *huge* chance, hoping against hope he wouldn't be sorry for it.

"Candace, go clean yourself up, and put on some fresh make-up. Brush your hair down and come back here looking spectacular."

"Okay, but why am I supposed to do that?"

He pulled a pallet close and grabbed some paint tubes. "Because I want you to stand on that same floor mark where you were before. Then I want you to take your clothes off."

"Oh! Will you make me beautiful again?"

"It'll be better than the one before."

CHAPTER NINETEEN

Tony the Twister Razzuto pulled into the rear parking area of the Mermaid's Salon and shut off the engine. He and Antonio entered the back door and walked down the hallway. Antonio looked from room to room until he came to a closed door and knocked.

"Enter."

Antonio cracked the door open. The pretty redhead was sitting behind a computer. "It's just me, Antonio Madera, for a routine cut and trim. I thought I might spend a few minutes with you talking about your divorce settlement."

Gloria slid from her chair, primped her hair and cornered her desk. "I'm glad to see you again, Mr. Madera. I'm caught up on the books and can take you on. I frequently stay a couple of hours after closing time to work on my flower shop franchise proposals."

"Fine, fine! I'm very lucky I caught you." Antonio opened the door for her, and they walked down the hallway into the main salon floor. He could see one chair occupied, and the rest were empty. Two stylists leaned up against their wash sinks. They came alive when they saw the two men. Gloria sat Antonio in the last chair and prepped him. While doing so, she ran a breast over his cheek without being aware of it. He didn't need to get aroused right at the moment.

Big Tony shoehorned himself into a small guest chair, splayed his legs and began thumbing through a stack of magazines.

"What will it be this time, Mr. Ma—?"

"Antonio, please. First name basis here, Gloria. The same as last time. A light trim around the edges."

"We aim to serve." Gloria brought the shears in close and made small, slow snips.

"My lawyer, Ardi Kastrati, has agreed to represent you at no cost and charge only a small amount of the settlement items. He can prepare an excellent case for you and take this yahoo to the cleaners. Ardi is Albanian born and can be as fierce as a cornered polecat. I hope you haven't made other arrangements. I'm sorry. But business calls sometimes, and I have to be at ten places at once. Otherwise, I would have been here earlier."

Gloria moved to his side. "That would be wonderful. I just had a feeling that you...would be back with good news. I can't thank you enough!"

Antonio smiled, but when he looked at his bodyguard, his smile sank into a frown. "What's the matter with you, you big lummox? Take a seat and patronize this wonderful establishment."

Tony the Twister stood up and looked at the two stylists and then the chairs. Antonio noticed that both girls seemed dumbstruck by the Romanian giant. They were tongue tied, nearly swooning. Antonio wasn't alone in his observations.

"Barbie, Trixie!" Gloria snapped. "Offer this man a chair before the next ice age sets in!"

"I'm Barbie," said the little curly headed blonde as she curtsied "This station is open, Sir. Please be—"

"I'm Trixie," said the taller brunette. "My station is available, Mr...?"

Gloria put her hands on her hips. "Both of you stop right now! Barbie, take the gentlemen!"

Tony took Barbie's chair and said, "How yadoin', kiddo?"

Barbie said, "Oh...uh...welcome to the Mermaid's Salon. How can I handle, ah, you...I mean help you?" She nearly tripped over his outstretched feet.

"Eh, just trim the stash, I guess. Watch it. I've got one of them little moles on the upper lip."

"They say a mole is a sign of distinction," said Barbie as she threw an apron around him.

Trixie looked daggers at Barbie.

Antonio craned his neck around. "I swear the help today can test the nerves and make life more complicated."

"I totally agree, Antonio. My hens can peck me to death on the worst of days."

"Where were we? Oh, yes! Ardi will need any and all evidence you can bring to his office. He will need the names of any character witness who can provide evidence that might support your case. You don't have to make an appointment. You have priority clearance, so just step right into his office any time you want." He pulled out his wallet and handed her a card. "Remember to say that Antonio Madera sent you."

Trixie went over to the wall and turned a knob, changing the channel and bringing up the love ballad 'I Surrender' by Celine Dion. She went back to her station, leaned on the counter, and stared at the big man in the chair. This got an eye roll from Antonio, who'd had about enough of Tony attracting a female fan club everywhere he went. He had that bad boy persona and a hulking body to match. For the life of him, Antonio couldn't see how Tony could make love to any woman without crushing her to death.

"So how is your relationship progressing, Antonio?" asked Gloria.

"There are still some complications that have to be ironed out. I believe I'll reach a resolution in due time. As for the present, it is rather lonely."

"Oh, I know that feeling. Especially one of abandonment and betrayal."

He didn't feel like delving into her private life just yet. That was not respectful. She seemed so refined and dignified. He wondered about her background and marital history. Did she have children? Where did she live, and what was her ancestral background? Surely someone had to be whacko to cause this woman grief. If Antonio ever found out who that shit pot was, he would have his ass capped, then run through a wood chipper. The idea of fucking over a woman like Gloria Barlow was unthinkable. She was worth ten of his dancers.

When Gloria finished with Antonio's trim, she pulled the apron off and brushed him down as she had before. He felt more than generous and placed five hundred dollars on the counter, then gave her a curt bow.

When she looked at the bills, she said, "Well, that will surely pay for the ferry when I have to pick up beauty supplies in Boston. I don't know what to say."

"Say nothing. Pardon me, but are you of Italian descent?"

"Sicilian, actually. And you?"

"Full blooded Puerto Rican." Antonio broke out one of his clove cigarettes but didn't light it. He wished he had worn his platform shoes. This woman towered over him like a skyscraper.

Gloria turned on her heel and clapped her hands. "Barbie, do you think you've spent enough time on that mustache?"

The little blonde was leaning over Tony's stomach when she straightened up quickly. "I was just—"

"You were just fawning over that man. Please finish up and let him go." She looked at the counter. "And, Trixie, you find something to do, or I'm sending you home."

"Yes, um."

Antonio waited for Tony, then they walked out together. Tony opened the door for his boss, then took the driver's seat.

"Where to, Mr. Madera?"

"I'm thinking about a flower shop." He fired up the clove cigarette.

"Hmm...here you go again. You look like you've got it bad."

"I think maybe I do."

Gloria called Joyce just after lunch and confirmed that the counselor had free time to accompany her to Boston for a meeting with the lawyer. They had planned the trip, but Gloria knew that any type of emergency or rescheduling could postpone the meeting. Joyce told her she had taken care of her scheduled sessions that morning and found a gap in her work schedule from 1:00 PM to 4:00 PM. The trip was on.

Joyce met up with Gloria at Joyce's parents' house, and the two took the ferry to the mainland. Gloria had brought a large rolling suitcase for the needed beauty supplies she would pick up after the interview. They drove to South Boston, looking for the address of the lawyer, Ardi Kastrati.

"Okay," said Joyce. "There's the number. It's that three-story brick building on the right. Gloria pulled over, cringed when she saw the parking meters and squeezed her car into a narrow alley. She followed the small driveway to the rear of the establishment and parked in a little lot filled with paper trash and weeds. They got out, walked around to the front of the building, and entered a pair of double glass doors. They found Ardi's name on a small ledger and walked up to the second floor. The building was ancient and smelled of old wood and cigar smoke.

They found the lawyer's office and entered. A receptionist sat behind an oak desk that appeared to be a hundred years old. She looked up from a binder and said, "Welcome. May I help you?"

Gloria handed the receptionist the business card and introduced herself, being sure to mention the referral from Antonio Madera. The woman behind the desk stood up, scurried to a backroom, and opened a door. A loud voice rang out, and a moment later, a very fat man walked down the hall, swearing under his breath, and left the office, slamming the door behind him. The receptionist appeared and said, "Mr. Kastrati will see you now."

Gloria and Joyce walked down the hall and passed through an open door to find a very ugly man sitting behind another antique desk. Ardi Kastrati had jowls that hung down from his cheeks, a turkey neck, and sad brown eyes. He looked ancient, a bloated man who might not have been able to stand for any length of time, let alone walk for any distance. Gloria noticed mold along the baseboards next to a filing cabinet.

"Have a seat, ladies." Ardi pointed to a couple of black button-tuck chairs in front of his desk. Gloria looked at the seat cushion for any stains or dirt. When they sat down, Ardi gave them a crooked smile that lifted half of his face up an inch. "Now..." He looked at the tall redhead. "You must be Gloria Barlow. Antonio told me about you."

"You are correct, sir. I've come to get your help with legal proceedings...to file suit against my husband for a divorce."

Ardi lit a thick cigar and blew a nauseous cloud into the air. "Hmm...I see. Do you have any papers—title copies of the property, valuables such as cars, bank accounts, tax information, computers, boats, planes, and other such personal items? It looks like you might have brought something."

Gloria said, "Yes. I do." She brought out a thick manila folder from a carryall purse and handed it to him. She watched him put on a pair of glasses, empty the folder and thumb through the numerous pages.

She had come prepared, having saved the paperwork from the first incident. She didn't think she needed all the documents at that time. She surely needed them now. She pulled out the rolled up painting that she had repaired with cellophane tape and set it on his desk. She handed him an enlarged still shot of the reunion incident. He put those items in a lower desk drawer while he continued to pour over the print on the papers. Gloria could tell right away that he was exacting and prone to detail. He ran his fingers over the print, sometimes sighing and sometimes grunting.

Ardi looked at Joyce over the top of his glasses and said, "And you are, Miss?"

Joyce stood up, even though it was not expected of her. "I am Joyce Powell, and I have been Gloria Barlow's marriage counselor for the past six months. I am familiar with the intimate details of her marriage and separation. I am familiar with the personality of her husband, Ryan. I am prepared to testify in a court of law about the particulars of this case and all incidents connected with it." She sat down.

Ardi gave her a tired smile and said, "I wish my students were as well-mannered as you. Thank you for that presentation."

"You're very welcome, Mr. Kastrati."

"You can call me Ardi—I'll keep my formal name out of this. And you can relax. We're not in church here." He turned his eyes on Gloria. "Can you fill me in on a little background? In particular, I would like to hear about your observations of your husband's misbehavior leading up to his infidelity."

Gloria began at the start, over six months ago, describing Ryan's penchant for entering the bed with foul smells and his bouts of night sweats, kicking and moaning. She admitted that she'd resigned him to the couch because of his lack of hygiene and state of emotional turmoil. Then she went on to explain about the reunion incident and how embarrassing it was. She told him about the live-in situation with another woman she had just witnessed. Every so often, Joyce would pitch in, to contribute her knowledge of the entire relationship, citing Ryan's admissions or lack thereof.

Ardi listened attentively. He stopped Gloria several times to ask questions, and she answered as best she could. She explained that Ryan was a freelance book cover artist and that he had many lucrative contracts. She described the home, the property, and the location of their past residences before they were married. Gloria admitted that they had no children because she was sterile.

"Ms. Powell," began Ardi, "can you state for me in your professional opinion if Ryan Barlow appears to be sane and in good health, whether in the past or at this present time?" He glanced at Gloria. "You may also answer this, Ms. Barlow."

Joyce pondered the question for a moment and then opened up. "I cannot think of any mental impairment. In my discussions with him, I have found him fluent, but sometimes unclear and evasive about his actions. He had adequate short and long term memory in my dealings with him."

Gloria sucked her bottom lip in and squinted. "Well, I think, or have always believed, that Ryan's sleepless nights, the moaning, the restlessness and sometimes spastic movements in bed might have been the result of toxins in the body he picked up during his painting. He has formaldehyde, isopropyl alcohol, oil paints, paint thinner and linseed oil that he works with on a regular basis. I cannot say for certain if he has ever taken the precautions of proper ventilation because I seldom ventured up to his studio loft."

"Hmm..." Ardi tapped his fingers on the desk. "We would like to downplay any type of mental disorder or instability that could give him a medical reason for unclear thought processes. He does not need any excuses, especially medical ones, to dodge prosecution."

Ardi took some notes for a full five minutes. Gloria noticed he hadn't looked at the painting or the blowup reunion photo. He'd stored them away. She wasn't about to interrupt him or tell him his business. In fact,

Joyce hadn't even seen the painting, only the enlarged photo. They'd had to pack up and leave at a moment's notice. She never thought about taking a phone shot of the oil painting, and now she could kick herself for forgetting it. But how was she supposed to remember everything? Her life had been turned upside down. This was a time of stress and confusion. Wonder Woman couldn't have gotten it all right!

Gloria inhaled sharply. "He knew exactly what he was doing, Ardi. He had all of his faculties. I should have suspected the worst from the first incident, but I gave him the benefit of the doubt. He violated my trust that kept me completely in the dark."

"This has been hard on her emotional state," said Joyce, patting Gloria's hand. "She was plainly manipulated, lied to and betrayed. As their counselor and advisor, I failed to see any warning signs. I do feel a certain responsibility for this outcome."

Ardi spread his hands over the table and lowered his glasses. "This man was bound to follow his whims and desires. You should not shoulder any guilt from this. Some of the sweetest men and women are capable of the most horrific deeds. Marriage partners have been duped since man stood upright and walked the Earth. Reconcile with yourself and look for a new life and happy outcome."

"Then it looks like we have a very strong case," said Gloria.

Ardi leaned back into the cushions of his high back chair. "Gloria, get a sworn statement from your doctor about your deteriorating mental state during this trial. Give me a list of any prescription anti-depressants or anxiety drugs you have taken to ease your pain if you haven't already."

"Will this divorce go quickly?" asked Gloria.

"Quite fast. As quickly as the law permits. I believe you can expect a fifty-fifty split outcome, and there's a good chance there could be more with a maximum alimony allotment.

Gloria stood up and straightened her dress. "Mr. Kastrati, that is exactly what I wanted to hear."

"Bravo," said Joyce. "It's a win-win for Gloria."

Antonio had just finished a late night shrimp platter supreme in the

Kitten's Revenge VIP lounge when he kicked back and loosened his belt. If he knew what was good for him, he would stop gorging himself and chugging a half dozen glasses of white wine at every sitting.

He fired up a clove cigarette and listened to the main floor music. It sounded like a rock tune, maybe something by Van Halen, but he wasn't sure.

Tony stood behind Antonio with his back up against the wall. Tony always scanned the crowd, serving as the eagle eyes and looking for anything out of place—including impending trouble. All Tony had to do was show his Goliath self to stop any club fights or drunken disruptions.

Antonio snapped his fingers and waved for his large bodyguard to approach.

"Yah, boss?"

"Go, and get that new girl, Leona Moon. I haven't seen her do any table moves."

"I thought she was topless only."

"It's time to change that, isn't it?"

Tony wandered off, wedging his way through the crowd. He arrived back a few minutes later with Leona Moon, who was more of a cocktail waitress than a dancer. She was a Spanish-Hawaiian mix with long legs, honey-colored skin, and wide black eyes. She was rather small in the bosom due to her lean figure. Antonio knew that she had just suffered a divorce and had three small children. He had given her double shift money when she had first arrived.

Antonio looked up at her, savoring every inch. "Put down that tray. Let's see what you've got."

"Oh...ah...but..."

"This might take the shock out of it." Antonio reached into his wallet, pulled out three one hundred dollar bills and pushed them across the table.

Leona set the tray down and stared at the money. She stepped up onto the table and used her shoe to clear a place. Tony turned up the room volume and shut the entrance drapes.

Leona started a slow grind just when Antonio's phone went off. He cocked his head over his shoulder, signaling for Tony to turn the music down.

Antonio looked at the screen and recognized the caller. "What is it, Ardi? I'm busy right now."

"You're going to be busier. I'm sorry for calling so late. But that client, Gloria Barlow, brought in some interesting imagery. There's a large painting of a woman in the mix who is supposedly responsible for her final breakup. She suspects this woman has a live-in affair with Ryan, her husband."

"And?"

"And...either my eyes are playing tricks on me or this portrait shows Candace Sabella as the model. The painting is torn up a little bit, but some of the face and most of the body comes out clear enough."

"Why do you think it's Candace?"

"Antonio, I've frequented your clubs for a long time. The Kitten's Revenge is my favorite. You know that. Your little queen has danced for me about ten times. So help me, I know that face and body. I could never forget it."

Antonio sat up in his seat and fastened his belt. "Ardi, are you sure about this? Is this find really hot?"

"It's nuclear hot."

Antonio looked at his watch. "Why in the fucking hell didn't you tell me about this sooner? You had a day visit with her. Were you whacking it or something? It's too late for the god-damned ferry for me to see Gloria!"

"I had a huge client follow just after her appointment, who was worth seven figures or more. I got caught up in the settlement details. When the meeting was over, I checked out the painting and still-shot photo."

"Gloria Barlow lives and works out of Martha's Vineyard, and here I am stuck in Boston. That means I'll have to see her tomorrow."

"I'm so damn sorry, Antonio. I know I slipped up. I'll stay up and wait for you if you want to make the trip here and look at it. I don't think I should come to you and risk damaging the painting any further. I have it spread out and weighted down on my desk."

"You stay there. I'll be over with some boys. Leave your door unlockedand keep a pistol at your side."

"That's a big affirmative. I'll be here."

Antonio clicked off. He blew a gargantuan sigh and made a brushing motion at Leona, who had been standing on the table frozen in place. She stepped down, and he insisted she take the tip anyway.

Tony leaned in close. "We got trouble, boss?"

"Yeah, we have to verify something. Get Jeppo and Alphonse." Antonio stood up and tossed his lap napkin on the table. "I can't remember who Candace has as a best girlfriend around here. I'm thinking Tammy or Lori."

"She hangs with Velvet a lot. That's her roommate."

"Okay, bring Velvet."

Antonio waited for his entourage to arrive in the VIP room. He had downed three shots of Irish Whisky to calm his nerves. He gathered them around him and explained the short trip they were about to take, and no one was to breathe a word about anything having to do with their little ride.

They left the VIP room as a group and took the back entrance out to the parking lot. Tony took the wheel of Antonio's Hummer, while Jeppo, Alphonse and Velvet piled into the dark sedan. They took off with the Hummer in the lead.

It was a simple drive to ArdiKastrati's office, taking twenty-five minutes. They entered the old brick building and found the office. The door was open, and when Ardi saw the group, he straightened in his chair and nodded a welcome.

Antonio didn't need ask where to see the painting. It took up a good portion of the lawyer's desk. Alphonse, Jeppo and Velvet all crowded around it and listened for any instructions from their boss.

Antonio leaned down to get a better look. Although the painting had been damaged and some parts of it were unrecognizable, it bore a remarkable resemblance to Candace Sabella. The background imagery looked like a beach scene. Yet he couldn't be sure it was her due to some of the missing detail.

"What do you think, Tony?" Antonio asked. "Do you see Candace here?"

"I dunno, boss. It kind of looks like her, but I can't tell how tall she is." He held a hand to his upper chest. "She comes up to about here on me."

Tony had slipped a gear in the great timing chain of life. The height wasn't really relevant with the model in the painting. The facial and body features were crucial and either identifiable or not, which meant the question needed a yes or no answer.

Antonio looked at the youngest man, with a brown crew cut, Jeppo, and his riding partner Alphonse, who was bald and slim.

"What do you men think?"

They both waggled their heads, expressions of confusion chasing across their faces. To Antonia, it looked a lot like Candace—the all body tan and pixie haircut.

Velvet stepped up to the table's edge. "I'm not trying to be a wisecracker, but I can't believe that none of you guys see it."

"See what, kiddo?" asked Tony.

She pointed. "Look at the left hand on the hip—you can see all the fingers. Check out the ring finger. If that isn't Candace's engagement ring, I'll eat my tampon." Velvet looked around at the faces. "Wait a minute. I hope you're not going to hurt her."

"No, kiddo," said Tony.

Antonio stared at the tiny white bulb on the finger. "Shit almighty, it's her! Nobody wears a diamond that big. I should know. I bought it for her!" He placed his fists on the desk and glared at Ardi. "Where did Gloria Barlow get this painting, and who made it?"

"She said it came from her house. Her husband painted it in a small, private studio. It was a little fresh when she took it. According to her paperwork and notes, her husband's name is Ryan, and he's a book cover artist. She suspected him of having an affair with Candace. I've got the address of her house here, plus the current address of her parents' house, which is where she's living at the moment.

Ardi held up a little sheaf of papers above the desk. Antonio took them and thumbed through the pages. He brightened when he found the couple's home address. He broke the silence.

"I know this street. We were there one time cruising the neighborhood. And it says here that the house is a three-story Vic....I've seen this house! It stuck out." Antonio's mind spun. "We hit that place. It was vacant. Nothing showed up. Isn't that right, Jeppo? You were on the ride."

"I sure was. I was with Smoothie and Carl. It took us a long time to search that house. I remember papers in the yard like nobody was home."

Ardi dug in a drawer and pulled out a stack of photos that were paper-clipped. Antonio took them and looked at each one carefully. He recognized the house immediately. He studied the make of the car and, surprisingly, a large, sleek-looking sailboat—a sailboat that was designed for ocean crossings. There were no photos of planes, which would have posed a big problem. It would have given the couple a chance to fly anywhere they wanted. They could have flown to any of the Canadian Provinces. But the sailboat...if they were not at home and the boat was missing, the hunt would go nowhere.

"Jeppo, I want you to take this picture with you and see if that boat is docked at the Vineyard Haven Marina."

"Gotcha, sir."

Antonio shook his head in disgust and looked over Ardi's shoulder. A large copy machine sat in the middle of the back wall. He had Velvet collect all the documents and photos and make copies of them. She went to work.

Antonio stepped up to the dirt-smudged window and looked down upon the lights in the street. He felt Tony take a stance a few feet behind him and knew his giant bodyguard cared about what his boss had on his mind. There was nothing he could do about finding Candace tonight. He could fly to Martha's Vineyard, but that would leave him without a car. That meant that if he went by air he would have to call one of his employees to pick him up. He needed to take certain things and people with him. This hit had to be planned down to a minute and pulled off flawlessly. He had to think everything out, and that meant time. He had time. He could wait this one out and avoid a serious blunder.

CHAPTER TWENTY

After hearing Candace's story, Ryan realized how high the stakes were. He knew they had to prepare for the worst.

Candace had just handed the last fifteen-pound dumbbell up to Ryan. While balancing on a stepstool, he hung the last weight in place over a flimsy nail. He had arranged the six dumbbells to slide off the nails and fall. Ryan thought that it was a clever foolproof contraption—simple but effective. Anyone forcing the door open or breaking it down would get a rain of heavy lead over them. He really didn't expect Antonio to return. But what was that about 'an ounce of prevention is worth a pound of cure'? They needed to get out as fast as they could if Antonio decided to come back.

He stepped down off the stool, then tied off a trigger string to the door knob. He stepped back and admired his work. Motion detectors equipped with bright halogen lights, were aimed at the front yard. Detectors mounted on both sides of the house would pick up anybody on the porch or small path leading to the backyard. Two detectors mounted on the rear of the house eave covered the backyard, including the private beach gate. The bailing wire that Ryan had strung from the side porches to the fences would serve as an invisible barrier and snag anyone coming around the house at a fast run.

The laundry room door that led outside was rigged similarly to the front door, in that it had sixty pounds of weights ready to crash down. The only way out of the house was the garage door and the back slider. The back slider would be cracked open so the house could ventilate. Anyone getting near or on the property would get lit up and set off screech alarms.

Everything was controlled by the remote that Ryan carried, along with his revolver and cell phone. He carried everything essential for the moment in his pockets.

Candace had helped him run wood screws through the frames of all the first story windows so they could not be opened with force. Earlier, he had used tape and thin strips of wood to fashion small square reservoirs at the base of the front door and laundry room door.

As a final touch, Candace handed him cans of motor oil which he used to fill up the stick dam at the front door. When he finished doing the same with the back laundry room door, he stepped away, making sure he didn't trail any oil across the floor. That was it. Or so he hoped.

They met at the dining room table and took seats. He'd hidden the masterpiece painting of Candace in the garage under stacks of collapsible cardboard boxes. No one would look there unless they had a hint about the painting's location. Gloria surely didn't need two of them, but she would never be back anyway. He almost wished somebody would find it and steal it so he could make another one. Then he thought about losing control again.

There you go again, you horse's ass. Do you think you can stop this for a second and give it a break? Or is it going to take a brain wash?

"How about some lunch?" asked Candace. "I can whip up something."

"You never whip up anything—you craft it. But that's a good thing. Let's just snack."

Candace pulled out some celery sticks from the fridge and lathered them with crunchy peanut butter. She cut out small squares from a block of cheese and stabbed toothpicks in them. She made a pitcher of pineapple juice and then set the table and placed the snacks.

Ryan loved the eats because they were so tasty, and the pineapple juice set everything off with a sweet tang. He knew he would drink the whole pitcher.

He waved a celery stick at her. "I think we've got it covered. That was about all we can do unless we had landmines." He chuckled. "But that would make a mess."

"I would use landmines if I had them. I know how Antonio and his men are. They don't know what the word 'mercy' means."

"I know that, honey." He'd never called her *honey* before. It was another slip of the tongue. He was getting damn tired of fighting off what he now considered a hopeless addiction. He'd made her wear one of her favorite sundresses this morning and pin a ribbon in her hair. He'd told her that a little make-up was fine as well. At least he wasn't totally losing it now. His thoughts were somewhat balancing out, and some normalcy was being restored. He remembered that he had been no stranger to lustful ways with Gloria. He'd fondled her at the most inopportune times in public and other places. He wondered if he needed sex therapy sessions to cool his preoccupations with women. *Maybe that's it. I'm a sex fiend and don't know it.*

Candace snapped a celery stick with her teeth and spoke around a mouthful. "I have my carryall purse loaded up. It's at the door right next to your pack. Let me put your phone and gun in double zip locks, and you can put them in that fanny pack you bought me."

"Good idea." She was aware of the danger of moisture and saltwater on guns and electronic devises. He handed her both items, and she went to the counter, bagged and packed them inside her large purse.

She resumed her seat. "Do you want me to follow behind you if we have to get our knees in the breeze?"

"Yeah, I need to pull out first. You follow me out and slam the slider behind you. We'll go out the back fence and shut the gate. Then we'll go lickety split for the secret spot. It'll be faster if we run down the shoreline on the packed sand."

She waved a celery stick at him. "I can run like hell."

"I'll bet you can. Have we forgotten anything?"

"What do we do for night lights? What if we're upstairs in bed and need to see where we're going?

"The shades and blinds will be closed at all times. We can run some extra bed sheets over the windows. We'll run real dim house socket night lights." He waved a celery stick back at her. "Besides, we'll be sleeping on the sofa for awhile. I can get a quick look out the window if I need to. The screech alarm is loudest in here."

"I don't trust him." She clenched her fists.

"That's why we're doing this. He's crafty like a fox and has a lot of influence and manpower."

"He has a hell of a lot of women power, too. A lot of dancers would recognize me."

"Do you think he's got a lot of his female employees looking for you?"

"No question about it. Half of them are single moms who need the income. He takes good care of those girls. They won't bitch about doing him any favors. He might even offer a reward for a sighting. He could give up a truckload of cash for a *capture*. I just hope he doesn't find or mess with my parents. The rest of my family is out of state."

"Where are your parents? Never mind...I don't need to know that." Antonio might resort to beating Ryan to a pulp just to get any information he wanted out of him. It wasn't below a mobster's dignity to threaten any and all persons with torture or death.

"It's okay," said Candace. "My mother was originally from Plattsburg, and my dad was from Boston. They divorced when I was sixteen and went their separate ways. I suppose Antonio tried to run down their current addresses but came up empty. That threat was really meant to get me under control. I was left with my Indian grandparents who lived in Burlington, Vermont."

"That must have been tough."

"Not really. My grandparents were drum makers. Grandmother skived hides and showed me how to boil the brains of a deer to brain-tan the hides for the drums. I helped her paint the drums for special occasions and custom orders. She gave me my first dream catcher and sang me a song when I had bad dreams. Grandfather made the drum frames out of wooden slats and gut strings. He picked up road kill, boiled the carcasses down and made really strange wind chimes out of the bones. They were great tourist pieces, and they even sold their merchandise to other Native American tribes."

"Interesting stuff. What did you do after that?"

"When I was eighteen, I traveled across the country with truckers. I found one I liked. I dated him for four years—Charley Johansson—my

Swedish hunk. He drove long-haul. I kept him company in his sleeper and got to see a whole lot of the country. We drove across Canada and the upper US states a few times, mostly from New York to British Columbia. We would come down through Seattle and drive east through Washington, Montana and the Dakotas. I hitchhiked to Nova Scotia and Cape Benton one time and took the ferry to Newfoundland."

"Do you still see him?"

"He fell asleep at the wheel on a solo trip in Alberta. He was killed. That left me alone. That's about the time I found the exotic dance clubs and began to spend my time on stage."

Not only was Candace smart and talented, but she was well traveled. She had wanderlust in her blood, but the end of her journeying was tragic. She must have rebounded and learned a new trade quickly. It seemed that the cornerstone of her life revolved around men. She sought stability and livelihood in those who were willing to shelter her. He could hardly blame her. Any red-blooded male would have jumped at the chance to share her company. It was hard to imagine what she might have looked like in her teens and early twenties if she looked this good now.

Ryan popped two cheese squares in his mouth and listened to a humming sound. At first, he thought the TV was on, but he remembered turning it off. He looked across the table and saw Candace with her head down, running a finger around the edge of her glass. He realized she was where the beautiful melody was coming from—in an alluring contralto. She was humming a tune he had heard before, but he couldn't place it. Without moving her head, she lifted her eyes up to meet his, and she brought up her volume, every note sounding better than the one before. He felt like he'd entered a dream state, and he couldn't move—bewitched. As suddenly as she began the melody, she stopped and gave him a coy smile. It seemed as though she was casting some kind of spell on him.

"Where did you learn that song?" he asked. "What's the name of it?"

"I dunno."

"What do you mean you don't know? You had to learn it from somewhere."

"Maybe I did, maybe I didn't. I can't remember."

"Never mind."

She could be elusive at times and hide her feelings. That was a little snag in her personality. She was blunt and honest most of the time. Yet he had to admit that she cut loose with whopping tales that could have made a movie. She'd lived scores of lifetimes in her twenty-seven years. He wouldn't be surprised if she continued her wanderlust and became a world traveler and connoisseur.

He gave his head a wag in the direction of the living room, got up and walked that way. "Let's have a TV day," he said over his shoulder.

"I'm just going to clean this up—be there in a minute."

Checkbox marked. She had some homemaker in her—a willingness to tidy up. She'd probably learned most of it from her grandmother, who had instilled lady-like behavior in her. It made sense. The Indian culture was heaped in tradition and routine. Although Candace was a half blood and would not be recognized as a true blood tribe member, she would still have been afforded the teachings of the elders.

She appeared ten minutes later and sat on the couch with him. She sat upright and leaned her head against his shoulder. He missed a few button stabs on the remote, but eventually found a movie that had just started.

His juju had taken a nosedive again. It was a romantic comedy.

CHAPTER TWENTY-ONE

Jeppo, Alphonse, Tony and Antonio drove off the ferry and headed for the Mermaid's Salon in Edgartown. Tony, at the wheel of the Hummer, led the way until he pulled onto the street of the establishment forty-five minutes later. The dark sedan followed behind at a respectable distance. Tony slowed down, forcing the car behind to do the same after it had caught up. Antonia turned in his seat and watched one of his men leave the car, cross the street, and enter the alley at the back of the salon. He emerged moments later and gave the head scratching signal that all was clear. The sedan pulled into the alleyway. Tony backed up and turned to follow the other car. Both vehicles found spots in the back parking lot. The only other vehicle present was a white Cadillac that Antonio recognized from a photocopied picture of the vehicle. It belonged to Gloria, according to the bill of sale.

Antonio was the first one out. He stepped up to the rear door and tried the knob. It was unlocked. He waved his arm for the others to follow, and then he stepped inside. He walked a dozen feet and waited for the others to catch up. He continued down the hall and opened the door that he knew was Gloria's private office. Upon seeing him, she rose up and cocked her head.

"Antonio, this is unexpected. What are you doing here?"

The other men slid into the room like worms through a crack and stood behind their boss. Tony moved to the side of the desk and fixed his eyes on her.

Antonio felt sad and a bit tired. "I've come here because I have questions that need answers. You won't be harmed if you cooperate." He nodded at one of the bouncers. "Make sure it's locked, and the blinds are closed." The bouncer left the room.

Gloria looked at the congregation of mean faces and staggered. "Dear God, Antonio, what is this about? Are you angry at me about something?"

Tony went around the desk and put his hand on Gloria's shoulder. He turned her and walked her around the desk toward the door. Gloria sniffled and gave out a squeak. Her hands shook. She clasped them prayer-like.

When everyone entered the salon proper, Tony shoved Gloria into a chair, causing her to catch her elbow on the armrest. She made a whining sound.

"Easy does it, Twister!" said Antonio. "Ms. Barlow is a lady, and there will be no physical harm to her. I'll call the shots here." He did not leave out psychological terror, which in most cases was enough to break anyone. He had a couple of ideas that might work on a woman of Gloria's caliber.

Tony leaned over, hovering inches from the frightened woman's face. "You'd better do what the boss says."

Gloria muffled a scream. "Ohhh, why?"

"Tony, back it off right now. She can't breathe!"

Antonio stepped up to Gloria and encircled her wrist with a meaty hand. "I'm sorry for the pain, Gloria...but I need to know where Ryan is right now. I have it on good authority that he is hiding my fiancée, Candace Sabella. The painting of her that you turned over to Ardi Kastrati is proof of that. Haven't you seen the news reports about the runaway bride?"

"I haven't, except for some rumors around the shop." Her voice quavered an octave higher and she wiped her face. "I don't watch a lot of TV or listen to the radio. I have discs of National Geographic and listen to audio books."

"Forget about that. I want you to call Ryan right now and find out if he is home. Tell him that you want to pick up some personal items. If he's home, I want you to tell him to stay there and help you with some loading."

Gloria looked at each one of the men in turn. "You're going to hurt him, aren't you?"

"All he has to do is give up my fiancée."

"Then you're going to hurt *her*. Maybe you'll kill them both. I won't have that on my conscience. You are evil!" She rose from the chair, but Tony shoved her back into it.

"I know your parents live in Oak Bluffs," said Antonio. "You wouldn't want anything to happen to them, right?"

Tears streamed down Gloria's face. "You're not a man. You're a filthy beast, and I wish I had never met you!"

Antonio twisted her wrist, making her cry out. Tony laid a slab-like hand across her mouth and then pulled her out of the chair. Jeppo and Alphonse helped guide her over to the counter and duck her head in a sink. The bouncers rifled through the drawers, pulling out products until they had a dozen or so dye packets. Tony took the pins out of her hair and brushed the long strands into the sink.

Antonio stepped up to the sink. "Go along with this, Barlow, or your hair will end up a rainbow. Or would you prefer to be shaved bald? *Everywhere.*"

"Stop it. I'll do it!" Her voice sounded hollow and pleading.

They pulled her head out of the sink and set her back in the chair. Her hair had flopped over her face, but she made no move to lay it back.

"What about the boat?" Antonio pressed. "Would he try and sail away? Where would he go? Don't lie to me."

"It's a forty-one foot Bavaria Cruiser docked at the Vineyard Haven Marina. He might want to go to it. He likes sailing to Woods Hole and sometimes circles the island. His dream was to sail to the Bahamas. That's all I know."

"Does he have any weapons? Any dogs?"

"He's afraid of guns, and he doesn't have a dog."

"What about friends who might help him?"

"Only two that I know of—Ross McDaniel, a big burly man, and Billy Powell who works on boats."

"Does he know any pilots who might fly him out from a private strip? I've had men watching the main airport, so he'll get picked up if he goes there."

"I don't know of any pilot friends. He wouldn't fly in a small plane. He thinks they're dangerous."

"Last question...do you think he would still have Candace with him instead of putting her in hiding somewhere?"

"It looked like she'd been at my house for awhile. I'm sure he's keeping her there. She's very attractive." She closed her eyes and put her hands across her chest. "Please don't kill me. My parents are innocent. As much as I hate those two adulterers, Ryan and that floozie, I hope you won't hurt them."

Antonio paced the floor and stopped. "Where would you like to go, Gloria? You're not going home right now. Don't even try it. You might get overemotional with your parents, and I can't have that. And you're not going to make any phone calls or go to the police with any of this."

"I promise I won't. There is one place I would like to go."

"Fine. Now make that phone call."

Gloria did as she was told. Antonio listened to every word she said, trying to decipher any type of code word that could tip off Ryan. The phone call ended after only a few minutes. She looked at Antonio and nodded. "He's not going anywhere today," she said, still visibly shaken.

Tony, who had been quiet like the rest, said "Now you take your car and get out of here, little missy."

"Just leave, Gloria," said Antonio. "We'll lock up as best we can."

Gloria didn't waste any time trotting down the hall. She hadn't straightened a hair on her head, and her mascara had made black rivulets down her cheeks. Antonio knew that right now nothing mattered more to her than getting away from him and his men.

He didn't hate or even dislike Gloria Barlow. She had been caught up in the middle of something that she had no control over. Antonio wished the circumstances had been different. He'd really taken a shine to her.

Antonio clapped his hands. "All right then. Let's close it down and get some drive-thru chow. We can't pull this off without food in our guts. Check your gear and get it ready. Move it!"

When Gloria abruptly ended the call, Ryan stashed his phone in his pocket. He was still seated on the couch, and Candace had fallen asleep across his lap. He looked down at her and smoothed her hair. Even with the dye job, her hair was as soft and fine as corn silk. Then his heart skipped a beat. *If you only knew what I want to do to you, little one. But right now, I've got to hit the head, and you're making my bladder ache.* He gently lifted her up into a seated position, holding her from falling forward. Her head rolled once, then she blinked her eyes open.

"Auuuhg," she cried. "Ohhh...I must have passed out. So sorry."

"It's okay. I did the same after watching a stupid movie. We've been asleep for half the day."

"So I didn't miss anything."

"Gloria called and said she needed to come over and pick up some stuff. That was a little earlier. I told her it was okay. I'm expecting her."

Ryan made a quick trip to the bathroom and returned.

Candace rubbed her face and stood up. "I have to get in my place." She walked around the sofa, headed for the dining room.

"Where are you going?"

"The water heater."

"You get back here right now."

She returned and stood next to the coffee table.

He jabbed a finger at the sofa cushions. "Sit!"

She walked up next to him, plopped down and then watched his face. "We're going to get in trouble if she sees me."

He gave her a stern look. "I'm tired of all this shit. I've been accused of making love to you in this house. We're a real hot item, don't cha know? I'm going to play the part and hope it rips her guts out when she sees you. Don't take any guff from her. You're the most innocent one in this whole disaster."

"Thank you for saying that." She put a hand on his thigh and quickly removed it. "I won't take anything from her. She slapped you so hard for no reason. Let her try that again, and I'll be all over her like a spider monkey."

Ryan loved her spirit. Dynamite did come in small packages. Candace showed him two sides of her world. He could see the difference plainly now.

He turned down the TV volume in case she had anything else to say. Besides, he was listening carefully for the sound of Gloria's car that should arrive at any minute. He wondered if she would notice the dimness of the house and bitch about it.

Candace went upstairs and appeared five minutes later in the living room. She wore a gray, skin tight, nylon jumpsuit and low top tennis shoes. She did a quick twirl. "How's this look for sleepwear? It's comfortable and light."

Ryan stood up and stretched, but noticed she was braless. Her nipples looked like rocks. Before he could moan, he heard engine noise outside and walked to the front picture window. He pulled a drape back and saw a large vehicle coming to a rolling stop on the opposite side of the street. Another vehicle pulled up in his driveway.

"We're outta here!" He ran to the kitchen and yanked the slider open. Fast feet followed behind him. He passed through the door, pack in hand and heard the slider slam behind him. When he got the back gate open, he pushed Candace through, followed her and shut the gate. He ran as fast as he could, trying to catch up with Candace, who was already on a dead run with her carryall purse swinging wildly. She held back when she reached the shoreline. When he arrived at her side he put the pack on. They took off down the beach. Candace ran so far ahead of him he wished he could get caught in her draft. There were no sounds until they were some distance away. It sounded like his screech alarm.

Antonio made it to the house just as some security lights popped on, illuminating the front yard. A whistling alarm went off. It wasn't too loud from the outside, but it might have been blaring from the inside. Jeppo quickly ran to the bright lights and shot out the lenses with an air pistol. Then with wire cutters in hand, he took a path around the right side of the house. Two bouncers ran around the other side. Loud screams came from both sides of the house moments later. Alphonse and Tony stormed the front door with crowbars and gouged at the seam, splintering the door frame.

Antonio stood in front of the door a few yards back. When they snapped the door open, Alphonse and Tony rushed through it, straight into a hailstorm of heavy objects. Both of them took blows and slipped, going down. Antonio reeled back, knowing that the falling projectiles were dumbbells. Alphonse yelped after a dumbbell hit him on the head. Tony landed on his side and took a dumbbell on the hip and one on the side of his face.

Antonio stole a glance behind him, worried about all the racket and yelling coming from the house. He trotted forward and entered through the door with his hands covering his head. Just as he stepped over Alphonse, his legs split, and he went down hard on the floor. It felt as though he had torn every muscle in his groin.

Tony tried to get up but lost his balance on the gooey floor and came down on one knee. "What the hell did we get into, boss?"

Alphonse lay perfectly still and spoke from the corner of his mouth. "Who the flying fuck hit me? I think I'm bleeding."

Antonio gave up on standing and instead made swimming motions across the floor. "It's fucking motor oil! Get on your bellies and squirm out."

The three men had to crawl a good distance away from door. They tried to inch themselves up to their feet. Antonio heard a voice behind him. "I'm cut to shit, man—ran into a barbed wire fence or something. Louis is down, too."

Tony reared up and then took a step, but his shoes went out from under him. He went airborne and came down on his back. Antonio could feel the floor shudder. The big man lay, splayed out and moaning.

Alphonse pulled his gun out and said, "Where you at, you mutha fucka?"

"Put that gun away!" said Antonio. "We ran into a trap." Just as he finished the sentence, the screech alarm went silent. Jeppo arrived at the front door and stood back, looking at the carnage. He pocketed his wire cutters. Antonio waved him off and said, "Go around and try to get in through a window or something. This house is rigged. Start searching the second you get in."

The planned entry was a straight-up cluster-fuck—a real Keystone cops moment. As Antonio rose to his feet and took his first baby steps across the floor, he made it to the fringe of the thick living room carpet and dragged his shoes over it. Tony made a weakened crawl to the living room and did the same thing to his shoes. Alphonse lay still where he'd fallen.

The noise of the sliding door preceded the arrival of Jeppo, who turned on the dining room light. He said he'd check the place, pulled his gun, and climbed the stairs. Tony made it to the foot of the stairs, grabbed the handrail and proceeded upward at an agonizing pace.

The two bouncers appeared at the slider door, looking cut up and miserable. Antonio ordered them to search the first floor and laundry room. He reminded them to check the garage, bathrooms, tubs, and shower stalls. Meanwhile, he took a seat at the dining room table and rubbed his temples.

This house had been vacated in advance of their arrival. Gloria's phone call to her husband, and the time it took Antonio and his men to arrive at the house, would not have given the occupants time to rig all of the traps. They must have done it beforehand as a precaution. Candace was clever. She would have helped with the plan. Ryan knew his house well enough to cover all the major entry points. To think that he'd been outsmarted by a cartoon painter and a little slut was just too much for him to bear. He walked over to the oven and stove, feeling for just the slightest heat. He found them cool.

Jeppo came down first and reported that he had found a stash of women's clothes under the guest room bed. That prompted Antonio to open up the fridge and freezer. Many exotic and holistic foods were crammed onto the shelves. It was just the type of foods Candace had eaten in front of him before. Ryan and Candace had been nesting here like two little birds. *Dirty little shits*.

The third and missing bouncer showed up and checked the backyard. Antonio watched him open up the back gate and go out. He came back in and shut it. His face said it all: *No signs of them. They made a clean getaway*.

Antonio took inventory of the injuries: Three bouncers cut up from wire, a bad back, sore hip, a concussion, pulled groin, bruised knee and other assorted aches and pains. He found a bottle of Scotch in a kitchen cupboard and downed a third of the bottle. It gave him a nasty but needed buzz—a liquid band aid for his failure and trauma. He slammed the bottle down on the dining room table and addressed his crew.

"Let's get in the wind before the cops get here. Load up, and we'll head for the nearest motel. We'll leave for Boston in the morning. Hit it!"

Ryan and Candace squeezed into their secret hiding place and threw their loads down. She was mildly winded and sat up against a rock wall. He fell on his back, heaving for air. She asked him if she could help him. He couldn't answer. She scooted close to him and held his hand, running her other hand over his forearm with soothing strokes. It took him several minutes to catch his breath and calm the thumping in his chest. He felt certain they'd given Antonio and his thugs the slip. No one had come down the beach looking for them. Their getaway was clean and quick. But something about Gloria's phone call and the timing of the break-in didn't sit right with him. Candace spoke before he did, echoing his thoughts.

"That wasn't Gloria who came to the house," she said. "She called before that, and suddenly they showed up. That was Antonio! What are we missing here?"

"Somehow Antonio got to her. He knew our exact location. Gloria told me to stay home and that she would be right over. She wanted help to move something. Besides that, there was something wrong with the tone of her voice. We've been ratted out—end of story."

"That *pignoramis*. I swear I'm going to use her boobs as punching bags."

"Hit something else. I love those."

Candace laughed, but not too loudly. "Well, here we are again in our little slice of paradise. It ain't so bad here at all. I like it here. We're camping out on Mother Nature's bosom. Hey, you ought to like that!"

It was Ryan's turn to laugh, but he covered his mouth. He couldn't imagine hiding out with anyone other than Candace. Gloria didn't like bugs, dirt, dust, or leaves—anything to do with camping. She hated flying insects that snagged in her hair, and she screamed when mosquitoes and bees were around. She never swam in fresh water ponds for fear of pollution. She did not suffer the smells of the country well, including animal scat, skunks, tree sap, cow's shit, pigs, plowed ground and mold. Candace was the opposite. She could run like a deer, fish with abandon, tan and cure hides, eat raw fish and camp out under the stars. There was no comparison.

He brought out his small keychain light and removed the bungee cord that held the sleeping bag roll to the pack frame. He checked inside the pack and brought out two bottles of water and a small bag of potato chips. He got to his knees and looked over the rock shelf, trying to spot any movement on the beach. There was enough moonlight to pick out good sized objects. He saw nothing, not even the pinprick light of a house.

He relaxed and drank some of his fruit juice. "How's about a snack?"

It's time to bring out the big guns, you handsome devil. I've reached my limit—you can blame it all on me if you want. I can't jump you. It's not ladylike. And there's such a thing as going sweet, slow and easy does it. I'm going to lead you into this, sweet prince. It won't hurt. That's a promise. I'll give it everything I've got and climb right inside you. If we don't surrender to this, we never will. Now's the time, and I'm going to take you straight to heaven. Just ease yourself back, honey.

Candace ripped a snack bag open. The contents flew everywhere, but most of the broken chips landed where she wanted them to. She paused and watched him carefully before she flicked some crumbs from her suit. Ryan helped her brush the broken chips off her lap, and then, with what looked like an absentminded movement, he swiped some tiny pieces off the top of her breasts.

She locked eyes with him. *It starts with touch, sweetheart—beautiful and loving touch. Don't be afraid of passion. You have to let yourself go because you have the right to do whatever you want to do.*

He cleared his throat. "You've got to excuse me for that. I just dove right in there."

"It's no big deal, Ryan. Okay?" She picked up several whole chips, crunched them in her hand and sprinkled them on top of her bosom. "Oh, look. We missed a spot. Would you help me with this?"

He extended a wavering hand.

"C'mon, you can do it."

He managed a slow swipe over the top of her breasts, sliding the chips off. She felt his hands roam over her mounds with just the slightest pressure. He swallowed loudly enough for her to hear. It would have been great to be a mind reader and know his thoughts. Neither of his hands had ever touched her like that. At least she couldn't remember him ever touching her that way.

"Now that wasn't so bad, was it? Little tiny baby steps. That's all for now." She gave him a long sideways stare before she turned her head.

He let out a groan as he rubbed his face.

She hoped the hook she'd baited was strong enough to hold him. She would love to reel him in real slow until he felt relaxed and free. Then she would set the hook, but only with a gentle tug that would not shock him.

From the corner of her eye she watched him dig into the pack, fumbling through the items. He stole glances at her top. At the speed he was moving, it didn't look like he wanted to unzip her nylon suit and pull her out. He looked distracted as if didn't know what he was looking for. *So you want to play first...*

He pulled out a little set of plastic binoculars and used them to look down the beach. "These will come in handy," he said over his shoulder.

"Oh, look," Candace whispered, pointing overhead. "There's Orion. And over there is the Seven Sisters."

He followed her pointing finger. "That's right, sweetie. That's Orion. The Sisters are called the Pleiades. Can you pick out the North Star?" He wanted to test her.

"Let's see. The Dipper bottom points to it...and there it is...right there!"

"Do you see anything else?"

"Uh...those two yellow ones are planets. I don't know which ones though."

"I don't even know that." He shook his head. "You remembered all that. How come?"

"You taught me."

"Oh."

She noticed he looked much more relaxed when he untied the

sleeping bag roll and flung it open. He looked at it and jerked his head. "Mother of pearl!" he cursed.

"What's the matter?"

"We're shy a sleeping bag. I remember folding both up into the same roll. I know I did it that way!"

"That's a shame. One of us will have to go without. I volunteer."

Candace hadn't brought a sleeping bag in her big carryall purse, only changes of clothes, hygiene items and extra rolls of toilet paper. It looked like the other sleeping bag had been left behind.

"No, you won't. I will," Ryan insisted.

"Let's both use it. We can go head to toe."

"One of us might suffocate."

"We can go back-to-back then." That would be closer together than they'd ever been. Full body contact appealed to her. She could already smell the musk of him—feel the heat radiating off of his body. Maybe her hair would entwine with his? What a wonderful way to get hung up together!

A back-to-back? Why did he think he was being sabotaged? Because maybe he was? That tight nylon jump suit. The breast touch. The missing bag. He wondered if he could make it through the night without losing his flipping mind. He didn't have anything against snuggling with her. But that might lead to something else that he hadn't prepared for. No matter what he thought or fantasized about, he could not act on it. He might have committed adultery on paper. He hadn't done such a thing in his heart. And as long as he knew that his conscience was clean, he knew he was doing the right thing. Besides, Candace had said that she would wait as long as she had to. He would hold her to that.

He took one last look over the shelf of rock and then cleared a spot for the sleeping bag. He unzipped it flat out and set the pack and purse to the side. Candace watched, scrunched up against a rock. He invited her to lie down, and she crawled onto the sleeping bag. She gave him a long intense look, but he didn't return it.

He dropped on his side, his back to her and said, "C'mon in, and pull the bag flap over you." He felt her back up against his. Her body heat radiated through him, and he closed his eyes. Sleep would not come easy, but total relaxation might help matters. His breaths went from shallow to long and smooth. When he concentrated on the coldest part of his body like he had learned to do in meditation class, his mind went blank.

When Ryan woke up, he didn't know where he was. It was the kind of state between nothingness and barely conscious. Could it be a dream? he wondered. Why was he sweating, and where were his blankets? He rolled onto his back and opened his eyes. The moon shone down on him. But was that really the moon, that platinum blob that was an out-of-focus blur? The blob swayed back and forth a little. He couldn't get his eyes trained on it. Then a soothing humming voice came to him, and with it, the soft caress of his forehead and hair. It felt so good that he wanted to fall back into a deep slumber again. Yet something held on to him, and he couldn't close his eyes. The cold stung the sweat on his body.

He listened. The tune was a lullaby. He knew that now. He had heard it time and time again in the not so distant past. The name of the song escaped him. It'd had a haunting effect on him but in a good way. It brought peace and calm. Then suddenly, the humming stopped.

"It's okay, honey," said a voice. "I've got you. Nothing is going to hurt you."

The humming melody began again. He rose up on his elbows and looked at a seated figure that appeared in silhouette, save for the moonlight reflecting off something. The figure had a hand on his cheek. It was a she—a petite she. The memory came back in a flood. Now he knew who the mystery visitor was. *It was Candace.*

"What happened?" he asked.

She stopped humming. "You were having a little trouble sleeping."

"You've been singing to me all along, haven't you? I know it now. That song is *Beautiful Dreamer.* You've been in my room before. It *wasn't* a dream."

"Yes, I have, darling," she whispered. "You needed help so I came to you."

"How many times has this happened?"

"As many times as it's had to happen."

"I don't know what to say. I'm embarrassed."

"Don't say anything. You'll get better. I'm here with you, and I won't let you hurt anymore."

The sweet exchange with her nearly brought tears to his eyes. Like a guardian angel, she had come to his nightmarish times of distress. She had laid hands on him—had tried to heal him. Gloria had never done such a thing. She had kicked him and slapped his shoulders. She had told him to move to the couch and stay there.

There were no words to describe what tenderness Candace had in her heart. He had to put a cap on his feelings before he ultimately surrendered. There was such a thing as coming to the end of one's rope and admitting defeat. His belief in the gospel teachings was the last bastion of his defense, and now those ideals were teetering on the edge ready to fall. He knew that he was hopelessly smitten with Candace Sabella. What was that saying about on that science fiction TV show? 'Resistance is futile.' That was it. Although he was not in love, he loved her.

"Lay down, Candace. Face to face with me."

She stretched out and pulled the flap over her. He brought her in close, butting her body up against his and wrapped his arms tight around her. Her breaths warmed his cheek. They both shivered at the same time, but not because of the cold. Before he fell asleep, he heard the words, "Oh…my love.

Ryan caught two fish the evening of the second day away from the house. He'd looked through binoculars every five minutes up both sides of the beach as he stood near the water's edge. As far as he could see, there were only local residents and tourist families inhabiting the beach. He'd counted four beach umbrellas stationed over picnic spots. Only a few joggers had run down the beach, and he watched them more closely than anyone. Candace was bivouacked in the secret spot, invisible to any passersby.

He had three perches when he started back. When he got to the hiding place, he entered with a quick duck down. Candace had set a flat stone off to the side. She did the honors of cleaning and filleting the fish.

They got equal servings. He didn't mind the taste because she said it was sashimi. It didn't matter what kind of seafood it was, he was getting used to it. Ryan brought out a bottle of fruit juice and poured two cups.

"This is an aphrodisiac," she said, chewing a slice of fish with her pearl white teeth.

"Is that for real?"

"I'm just *kidding*." She laughed and spit up some pieces. "You would need oysters for that."

He didn't want to tell her that there would be no reason for any oysters, herbal stimulants, or Viagra pills. Candace was a rolled-up, packaged aphrodisiac in her own right.

"Yeah, well, the oyster thing wasn't fair." He chewed and drank his juice.

"Who said women are fair? We have our methods. I would never hurt or embarrass you."

He studied her face. "Don't tell me. You took the extra bag out of the roll?

"Uh huh. I stashed it in the garage."

"You busted up those chips over the top of your ti...breasts, knowing that I might clean them off." His were not questions anymore.

"Yes, guilty. You can say 'tits' if you want. I'll bet you did with Gloria."

"Why do you torment me, Candace?"

"You torment yourself, Ryan. You have all these black residues stored up inside you, and you're afraid to face them. Confront your shadow and do what you want to do." She tore a strip of fish in half with her teeth and had to wash it down to keep from choking.

"It sounds like you've had courses or teachings."

"It's a new age. Everybody is getting into deeper thoughts and realities."

"What don't you know?"

"I don't know anything. Everybody is trying figure out the whole picture. You have your Bible. Lots of people don't have any guide at all."

"Maybe you're right." He polished off the rest of his fish and washed it down with juice after they'd tipped their cups together.

She assumed a butt on top of her heels posture, lifting herself up. "Let's change the subject. I know you want me because you really like me.

But I'm in love with you, and I can't help it. Now that I've got that out of the way, what is it you *like* about my personality? Just let it rip and tell the truth. Women have to be told these things sometimes. We need reassurance."

"Okay, fine. You're kind, sweet and very...feminine. But you have a mind of your own. I think you're smart and funny. You have a strong will. You've been around the block a few times and come out of it without a lot of damage."

"Anything else?"

"You challenge me. You can be set in your ways and then push my buttons until I'm steaming mad. But I respect that. Feisty, I guess. You're also kind of a gypsy."

"What about my body and face? When did you first notice them?"

"For real?"

"Please tell me."

"You were coming down the tree, and your dress was flared open. You were wearing a purple thong. That was just plain hot, but I wondered why a girl would wear that under a bridal gown. Right after you fell, and I caught you, I looked at your face. The green eyes, long lashes and the bangs. The face was flawless.

"Oh, go on!"

"I felt you under your dress. There was something very fit about you. I sensed it. The whole package—*all* of you was kind of irresistible. I thought you were a beautiful teenager until you told me your age." He had to take it further. "When I painted you nude the first time, I did something that I couldn't help because—"

"I know what you did, Ryan. I came up the stairs early because I couldn't find the coffee filters. You were in the bathroom. I know what happened in there."

"You do?"

"Yes. I have regrets because it wasn't fair to you. But I still love you beyond belief."

He blinked several times, then crimped his eyes shut so hard his cheeks nearly slammed into his eyebrows. An overwhelming pall of embarrassment came over him. Still, he could see the humor in it. But then he stiffened and felt his confidence build. When he opened his eyes, he glanced around and saw that it was past twilight and darkening fast. He turned to Candace and took her hand. He put his palm to her face and said, "I can't stand it anymore. You have to know. I'm in love with you."

"What?" She tilted her head and put a hand over his. "What did you say?"

He looked at her with a burning intensity. "I'm hopelessly in love with you. I want to marry you and live with you for the rest of my life. We can have babies if you want. I mean, if you'll have me for that long."

"I can't believe it." She shook her head, and she scrunched up her face. "You want to *marry* me?"

"I want to marry you. I want to protect you and keep you safe. I can't live without you. I don't want any other man to have you. It's hit me that badly. And I'll say it again...I'm head over heels in love with you, and I want you now." His eyes moistened.

Tears fell from her eyes, and her shoulders quaked. She hung her head and bawled pitifully. She tried to talk, but her voice cracked; saliva dripped from her lips. He brought her into his chest and held her. Her breath hitched in her throat until she took several deep breaths. He leaned her back gently. Her face looked like a mixture of wonder and shock.

"Antonio will never stop until he finds me," she whined. "He'll take me away. Our dream will never come true!"

"Sweet baby, baby, it's okay," he said. "I've got you, and I'll never let you go. It's just you and me and the sea cliffs—you and me under the cliffs. No one will ever find us. Let all your worries go. You're with me now."

She looked at him and burst into a new fit of tears. He had to soothe her for a long time before she stilled her body and let her eyes meet his.

"I love that you love me, Ryan. I'm so happy that my dream came true. I wished upon a little star. *Kiss me*."

CHAPTER TWENTY-TWO

He leaned over and ravished her cheeks with kisses, worshipping, smothering every part of her face, all the while holding and massaging the back of her neck. She felt like a ragdoll under him. He rose up a little and gazed at her, his breath caressing her face.

"Oh, please kiss me! Don't stop!"

"I want to make you feel really good."

He descended again, sucked gently on her lips, then pressed his lips firmly against hers, sliding them back and forth over the wetness. He held her cheeks and parted her mouth with his tongue.

She sank even further under his weight and moaned from the back of her throat. He swabbed the inside of her mouth, side to side, up and down and kept it up until they were nearly suffocating. It was unbelievable how sweet he tasted. He gazed at her with loving, soulful eyes as his body came over her like a cloak, blocking out the moonlight. The sensation of falling into the earth came upon her when he was on top of her, pushing her downward.

I'm falling. Catch me and hold me.

He pulled her up into a sitting position, supporting her back with one hand. With the other hand he ran the front zipper of her suit down to her pelvis and then pulled her top down over her shoulders and freed her arms; her breasts jutted forth. She gasped.

He leaned her forward and cupped each breast, testing their weight with such large, strong hands. He fondled and massaged her until her nipples rose up.

"Oh, they're all yours," she said.

He laid her on her back and swirled his tongue over each breast, soaking them with saliva. His left hand kneaded each mound, and it was wondrous to feel such attention lavished on her body. Every nerve cell in her skin tingled with excitement. She titled her head up, determined to watch everything he did to her.

"Suck on them," she pleaded.

"I need to do this my way, and you need to hold on tight."

His mouth came over one nipple at a time, his lips pursing and pulling up, to cause suction. Her nipples snapped out of his mouth, until finally he brought them both to swollen attention. She could see them in the moonlight. They looked like little upright rockets ready to launch. A cool breeze tickled them.

"Oh, God," she said, "I want you inside me!"

"I don't want to rush it. You get to lay back and languish...and take it all in..."

"Hmmm...mmm..."

She couldn't keep the shiver from her body when he ran his tongue down between her breasts, over her belly and then stopped at the top of her pubic mound between the V slit of her suit. He reversed the direction, and she emitted a deep moan. He kissed her again, and this time she pressed her lips hard against his and reached for his crotch. She reached below and found him, ran her hand over his protruding bulge, unable to get her palm around its fullness.

"Do you want me to take your clothes off?" he said in a deep voice.

"Oh, yes. Strip me!"

He didn't strip her right away but ran the flat of his hand inside the suit and rubbed her pelvis with a gentle pressure. He ran his fingers down as far as could and split her groove, pulling up and fingering her clit. She arched her hips. He pulled the suit down and worked each leg out until she tossed the suit aside.

"Oh, I'm naked for you...take me." She gulped. Now that she was nude, and he was pressing down on her—his hands poised to roam and feel what her body had to offer.

"I'm looking at every inch of you right now," he rasped. "I can't get enough of your beauty. Just let me stare at you for a moment."

There was nothing like being so exposed to the man of her dreams. A thousand eyes in the Kitten's Revenge Club could not match the exhilaration she felt at this moment. His eyes penetrated—his eyes only.

He blew a hot breath between her thighs; his face was only a foot away from her bald puss. He inhaled her deeply, then exhaled upon her again. It was easy to see the gleaming wetness of herself under the soft rays of the moonlight. Only a quick grope allowed her to feel his increased swelling. Just touching him set her off again. She knew she was about to let loose.

He got to his knees and pushed her legs wide apart and then stretched out between them. He shoved his palms under her buttocks, grabbing her cheeks firmly.

"Do you know what I'm going to do to you?" he said. "I'm going to slowly run my tongue over your lovely pearl until you surrender and let it go. Then I'll lap up all your juices—drink you like a fine wine."

"Oh, Jesus," she said. "You are making me crazy. I can't wait. I need you right *now*."

"You have to wait, baby. I'm going to make you flow like a stream."

He raised her pelvis up squarely into his face and then plowed his tongue over her from the bottom up to the top of her G-spot. Next he slathered her labia, first in circles and then crosswise. It felt soaking wet down there, and she hadn't fully let go yet. She propped herself higher up on her elbows to watch him. Her mouth hung open; a pleasurable stupor came over her. His fat tongue worked on her with a relentless intensity, causing her heart to slam inside her chest. There came a feverish heat to her face along with a heightened increase in blood pressure. Her breaths came short and choppy, and her body stiffened, immobilized by his passionate onslaught.

Oh, my dear God, where are you taking me, Ryan? I've never been here before or had such a feeling in all my life. How could you do any of this without me knowing it? Was this a secret buried deep down inside you? How many others have you done like this? I'm jealous of them all! I hope I'm your last, and I pray that you keep me, love me and excite me.

"Oh, Ryan, I'm going numb, and I feel dizzy."

He shot her a quick grin and continued.

She felt a rush to her head, gave out a high-pitched whine and fell on her back with a thud. When she arched her back, her hips shuddered. She lay there with her arms splayed out and fists clenched. He pulled her hips up higher, arching her back even more and ran his tongue more firmly over her. Her pelvis and legs shook uncontrollably. It was then that she stiffened and poured her insides out, knowing that she would drench his face. She tried to scream, but it came out as a hissing blast of air. There was no end to the flood.

She could tell he loved the taste of her because he wouldn't stop.

I didn't expect any of this. You're eating me alive. She pounded her fists in the sand.

"Ghuuh, arrhhhggg. You're a sex machine. Please just *do* me."

"You have to wait. I'm going to take you to heaven. Sound good?"

"Yes, just hurry."

He let her hips settle and tongued her pelvis clean. She rose up and grabbed his shirt, yanking it upward. It came off with a stark tug. Next she unbuckled him and pulled his pants down to his knees. The boxers dropped next, exposing his shaft.

Candace hissed. "I just knew it! Oh, baby..."

Ryan rose up and stepped out of his clothes and turned to her just as she reached out, grabbed his member, and fisted his testicles.

"So you want to own me," he said and watched her hands.

She stroked his shaft from the base to the crown of the head, then rose to her knees, fondling his sack. She leaned forward and took the head in her mouth, filling her cheeks. She plunged forward and shoved as much as she could in her mouth. When she pulled back, it made a sucking noise. She swirled her tongue around the head and pulled off. "Oh, baby, I could do this all day—yum." She fisted his cock and jacked it in and out of her wet mouth.

Ryan grunted, pulled in a chest full of air and held it. Her mouth rode back and forward over him, taking more in.

"You taste sweet and juicy hot," she managed to get out as her tongue rode his length.

It was his turn to moan helplessly.

She switched to a fast bobbing motion. "Mmmm..." The momentum picked up, but she had a hard time getting the proper angle, so he thrust his body forward and laced his fingers in her hair. He pumped his hips forward, plunging his member with shallow strokes several times between her full lips. Her throat muscles relaxed. He drove his shaft deeper into the back of her throat. When she hummed, she felt his body tremble.

She held his testicles captive in her hands, fondling and massaging. Then she looked up at him imploringly.

"No, that's for another time." He clenched his teeth. "You have to let go of me, Candy. I could go right now."

She gave him a mischievous look.

"Leggo, darling!"

He pushed her down, spread her legs and mounted her. Now that Candace had finally released him from her mouth, he teased her by running the head up and down her labia groove, then shoving just the head in and pulling it out. She felt wet again. He plunged in further and retreated.

"Hoooh...damn you. I can take *all of you*."

"Are you my baby? He poked the head in her again and pulled it out.

"Ohooo. I'm all yours, I'm your baby!"

"You want more? I'm going to drive it home deep. Do you hear me?" He ran his stiff length over her swollen clit, then plunged half his length inside her.

"Oh, guh. Please...ahhhh...Ryan, stop teasing me!"

"You want me to give it to you, huh? Is that what you want?"

"I've got to have it. I want you to give it to me bad."

"Then beg me."

"You're torturing me!" She rose up and tried to pull him into her, yanking under his arms. She tugged with all her might, but she was no match for his size. "Okay, I'm begging you!" she whined. "I'm burning between my legs."

"You need to get scorching hot."

"My pussy is on fire, and I'm leaking everywhere. I am so ready!"

He gave her an evil grin. This time he didn't tease or tempt her but shoved it home until he hit bottom.

Her eyes grew wide in amazement. She grabbed his buttocks and pulled him into her.

He began driving his member into the limits of her depth.

"Ahh...ahh...ahh...oh...my...gawd...help...meee..."

Her words matched the cadence of his strokes. *I've gone to Nirvana,* she thought, *andI'm not coming back.*

She was so tight he couldn't have entered her if not for her soaking wet tunnel. His movements became more fluid. Candace writhed under his deep, smooth plunges. She clamped a hand over her mouth to stifle a scream which he could hear escaping through her fingers.

He bent his head and focused on relaxing his pelvic muscles to draw his intense feelings inward. He took slow measured breaths, while he remembered to keep his eyes open. *Tell me when to go, Candace. Can I do it now? Am I ready for it?*

Suddenly, a deep thrust brought him to orgasm; a shot of warm fluid flooded her insides. She yelled so loudly she nearly gagged. He instantly knew that she had cum against him. Still hard, he stayed inside her and increased his rhythm.

"You deserve this, baby," he told her. "I'm going to drown your insides, you sweet little thing. What do you think of that?"

She took her hand from her mouth and shrieked into the night. "Fill me up—flood me!"

He slapped a film of sweat from his forehead. When he pulled out of her, it was like opening a sluice gate. A river of sweet juices of passion ran out of her and pooled on the sleeping bag. Both had lost their breath, and Ryan felt his heart hammering against his ribs. But an ache stirred inside of him, and he shoved it in again. A second discharge let loose inside her. He yanked himself out of her and spurt a stream of cum across her stomach and over her breasts.

"Oh, damn it!" He clamped himself off.

"Oh, you*nasty* fucker!" Candace slapped his butt. "Empty it all over me, darling."

"Oh, you wild little..." He panted and fell on his side.

She blew out a long jittery sigh and rubbed his spent juice over her breasts. "Oh, my gawd, Ryan. You exploded inside me. I'm going to pass out."

"Yeah, my head's spinning. You practically annihilated me!"

"Then you *obliterated* me."

She grabbed his arm. "Where did you learn all of that?"

"A long time ago in bedroom school."

"I won't even ask—just hold me tight," she begged.

He drew her into him. She was so vital and gorgeous. She was his now —the ultimate surrender. Nobody would harm a hair on her head. Now he knew what it felt like to make love to a goddess.

"Sheese Ryan, you're spoiling me." She inhaled sharply. "I feel so *good* inside. I feel like I can't get enough of you. You're my yummy stud muffin. Give me more as soon as you can, and I won't stop bugging you until you do."

"Seriously? I didn't satisfy you enough?"

"You satisfied me so much I'm eager for more of you. Don't worry. It's not because I'm some nympho. It's just that I've never had someone make me feel this way before, and I don't know what it is about you. You plain drive me wild."

He brought his mouth close to her ear and geared up to tell her what she meant to him. His words rolled off his tongue like a stream flowing over pebbles.

"God doesn't make mistakes, my little angel. He brought you and me together and blessed our union. I see that now. The love was *always* there. Now it fills our hearts. You are everything that is good for me. You'll always be mine. I'll always be yours."

Candace whimpered. "Oh, Ryan, that is so, so beautiful. You love me that *much*?"

"More."

She buried her head in his chest and encircled her arms around him. All he could do was smile and run his fingers through her hair. He had such a babe on his hands and just couldn't believe how blessed he was. He caressed her until she fell asleep. He believed there would never be another nightmare in his life again.

CHAPTER TWENTY-THREE

"Joyce. It's me. I'm on somebody else's phone. I had to call you."

"Honest to God, Gloria, you have everybody in an uproar. You didn't show for work. The back door to the salon was open, and your employees went nuts and called your parents. Where in the hell are you?"

"I've had a very terrible experience and can't explain it over the phone."

"I'll drop what I'm doing and come to you. Where? Damn it!"

"I'm with the horses. And Stephan."

"I'm on my way. Don't go anywhere!"

Gloria snapped the phone shut and handed it to Stephan. He put his hand on her shoulder and said, "You are safe with me. We have an alert and alarm system here."

"I might have killed somebody, Stephan. *God forgive me*."

"You haven't killed anyone. You are upset. You need to sit down and calm yourself. I can get you a latte and talk with you. You can tell me what happened. I'll listen to you."

"Okay, that latte sounds good. I missed dinner, too."

"We can rustle something up for you in the ranch house kitchen." He took her hand. "Breathe deeply, and take in the fresh, cleansing air."

Gloria walked with Stephan around the main stables and reached a small walkway that circled an old, two-story clapboard house. The white-washed paint was peeling on the little abode, but the front yard was large and cordoned off to protect a finely trimmed fescue lawn. She'd never visited the house, therefore had no reason to visit this beautiful spot. The small house sat there by default—a little cracker box. She knew the registry trailer and the horse paddock, exercise areas and stables well enough, but hadn't connected Stephan's living quarters to anything so near. And she was dead certain he lived in the little house. She could appreciate him all that much more.

They entered Stephan's house and walked to the back part of the first floor into a long rectangular kitchen. Four tables sat in the kitchen, with four chairs each. The tables sat opposite a long kitchen counter on the back wall. The counter had large double stainless steel sinks. Two old gas burner stoves and combination ovens took up a third of the counter space. Two refrigerators and two freezers took up the left wall.

Two cooks turned on their heels when Stephan and Gloria entered. Six employees, horse wranglers and stable boys and girls gave Stephan hellos and nods as he pulled out a chair for Gloria and seated her at the end table nearest the door. He took a seat across from her.

"What would you like, ma'am? Stephan asked. "It's still breakfast. But lunch is no problem. We eat when we're hungry here."

"Call me Gloria. It's okay. Anything that won't make me cry." She felt her hair and heard the alarm in her voice. "I must be a terrible sight!"

A thin teenage girl got up from her table with purse in hand and walked up next to Gloria. She pulled out a small hair brush and pocket mirror and placed them on the table. She added a compact and alcohol swabs. She retreated to her seat.

Gloria looked at Stephan with a few blinks.

Stephan said, "That's Renee. She is a recovering addict and has found peace and love with us. This is her home. She spreads good tidings to all and is one of the hardest workers at our ranch. Are you surprised?"

"No, actually I have employees of the same nature. I guess I didn't expect to see it here. I'm sorry if I looked shocked."

One of the cooks brought two menus to the couple and went back to work. Gloria could smell a delicious aroma coming from a deep fry basket. She put her menu down. "I'll have whatever that chef is cooking right there." She pointed.

Stephan chuckled. "Those are just onion rings. How about a salami, ham, beef, turkey, or chicken sub? It'll heat right up in the microwave."

"Oh, thank you so much. My stomach is so upset, and my nerves are shattered. Chicken would be just fine."

"Then we'll get you some natural whole milk." He raised his voice. Two cluckers with rings, weeds on side and a glass of moo!"

"Coming right up, Stephan," said a cook.

If Gloria wasn't so stressed she would have burst out laughing at the food orders. Instead, she picked up the mirror and looked at herself. Her face was ghastly, and her hair looked like a tornado blow-dried it. Red eyes stared back at her, and mascara smudged her cheeks. She asked directions to the nearest ladies' room where she wiped her cheeks with the alcohol swab and cleaned the rest of her face with warm sink water and soap. She brushed her hair out, grieving that she had no pins to bun it up. A touch of eyeliner and a smear of lipstick made her look presentable. It still looked like she'd aged ten years. *Just the old fat, wicked cougar, yah?*

When she re-entered the kitchen, she flashed Stephan a gracious smile, passed him and returned the makeup items to Renee with a heartfelt thank you. She took her seat across from Stephan and brushed a few lose hairs from her arms and vest. She noticed his eyes pegging her. She was not in the mood for any type of mutual admiration at the moment. She thought that he sensed that. After all, he was quite the gentleman type, but she did not need any advances or pandering comments.

Stephan laced his fingers together. "You are quite the vision. Now, would you like to tell me your distress? I don't mean to be so bold, but if I can help you, we might find a solution to your problem. I do not mean to pry, of course."

Gloria didn't quite know where to begin. There were more twists and turns in her story than a cloverleaf interchange. It was full of intrigue, danger, and betrayal. Would someone like Stephan understand things?

A cook brought them two large platters, place settings and a pitcher of milk. Gloria couldn't speak before she had something in her stomach. She started in on the big chicken sub and noticed that the 'weed' word

Stephan had called out was actually a small bowl of mixed green salad. She tried to eat like a lady, but it was difficult. Thank goodness they ate in silence. Stephan glanced at her frequently and asked her if she needed anything else. It was a kind and thoughtful gesture. As much as she wanted to leave something on her plate, she devoured every crumb of the sandwich and speck of salad, washing it all down with two glasses of milk.

"Ready to share your story now?" Stephan asked.

Gloria nodded, so he led the way out of the kitchen.

He took her hand and guided her out of the house, across the stone walkway, over a road and to the base of some windbreak trees. They sat down in some tall grass. Gloria was relieved that she had a direct line of sight to the open front gate that Joyce would drive through. She would only have to wave to attract her girlfriend's attention. She knew that Stephan was interested in knowing what happened to her. She saw the concern in his eyes. Empathy practically radiated off of him. "Would it upset you if I waited until Joyce gets here? That way I only have to tell the story once.

Though a moment's disappointment flashed across his face, he nodded. "I understand." With that, he settled near her.

Gloria resigned herself to taking in the scenery and gathering her sanity, if possible, while waiting. Some insects crawling on the ground made her nervous, but that was the least of her problems right now. Still, silence didn't suit her.

"Did you have a happy childhood, Stephan?" She wouldn't mind knowing a little bit more about him. It was an innocent way to pass some time.

"My childhood was rather typical. I really had nothing traumatic happen that stayed with me. My parents have always loved me. My upbringing was very normal with some good memories. But my childhood ended in my teenage years."

"How so? Can you tell me?"

Stephan rolled a blade of grass between his fingers. "This place was great therapy for me after my service in Vietnam. After my discharge, I couldn't be around people that much. I kept seeing Asian faces and the color red. The screams were like white noise, and I couldn't turn them off.

I knew I needed help, and I did seek it. But it was like putting a band aid on a nightmare. That's what action in war does to a person."

"Dear Stephan, was it that terrible for you? I'm sorry."

"There are details to it."

"I can understand that. It's okay. What happened, Stephan? I'll listen." And she would, too. She found herself warming to him more and more. He was so thoughtful and tender.

"Okay. Well, we were told Charlie routinely strapped explosives to themselves, walked up to G.I.s and tripped the devices. Women were especially good explosive carriers because the packages were easily strapped to their thighs, hidden under their dresses. Females were the least likely suspects to carry out such a deed. Young girls, especially, were seldom suspected of having the devices."

"Oh, dear. I've heard about such things."

He went on like he had to confess. "We got intel on a small village near the Cambodian border that was harboring a munitions cache. They sent in a patrol—my patrol. We came down hard on 'em with a surprise engagement. When we busted through the brush, men, women, and children scattered, but they were taken down with automatic weapons' fire.

"I saw an indistinct blur and emptied five shots into it. When the firing stopped, I went to stand over my victim and saw that she was a young, barefoot girl who wore a filthy, gray muslin dress. She had no panties on. I found out later that our body count was twenty-two, and the girl I took out was thirteen years-old. There were no explosive munitions found in that village. Those people were only producing some kind of a speed drug. That was my first and last heroic deed in that war."

Gloria bit her lip and closed her eyes. She couldn't imagine such a horror, and the man who had just relived it was sitting across from her speaking in a calm and soft voice.

Fifteen minutes later, Gloria stood and waved to Joyce who was coming through the front gate. Joyce drove to where the two sat and left her car on the side of the small road.

Joyce scurried up to Gloria, wrapping her arms around her. Her eyes were moist and pleading. "Gloria, what's happened to you? Did Ryan do something bad?"

Gloria pulled her girlfriend down to the grass. "No, Joyce. But I might have done something bad to Ryan and maybe that woman who is staying with him."

Joyce's mouth gaped open. "Oh, no. When you look like that, I know something terrible has happened." Joyce acknowledged Stephan with an absentminded "hello" as though she hadn't seen him at all upon arriving.

"I can tell you the story since you are both here." Gloria began to relive the incident, swapping looks between the two. Both of them listened with serious attention. Joyce showed more emotion as the story unfolded and allowed numerous expressions to cross her face. Gloria tried to get all of the names correct and describe the persons involved in detail. She told them about the threats to her parents and the threats to mutilate her hair. When she finished, she hung her head, fighting back tears.

Joyce rose to her knees with an awestruck look on her face. "I'm going to call Billy. Then I'm going to have Billy call Ross!"

"You can't do that!" Gloria begged. "These guys know where my parents live because that lawyer is connected to Antonio. That's where I took the painting and filled out my paperwork. They could kill my parents. This man is an underworld crime figure. I only knew of his name because he was involved in charities and the homeless. But that was years ago."

"Then we go to the police," Joyce insisted.

"No," said Stephan. "That is an even worse risk. Police officers storm on impulse and lack stealth. The media often follows them because they have scanners tuned into law enforcement frequencies."

"What do you suggest, Stephan?" asked Gloria, wringing her hands, looking from face to face.

"If this Billy and Ross can be completely trusted, we can summon them here and use this location as a staging ground. We are interested in your husband's and his girlfriend's welfare. Is that correct?"

"Yes," said Gloria. "I am deathly afraid of what Madera and his men might do to them. I feel awful that I broke down and pointed the finger at them. I don't hate anyone...if something happened to them...I could never forgive myself, and God would damn my soul."

Stephan cracked his knuckles. "This will take some planning. It's a stealth mission. We'll have to even the odds. I have a few ranch hands who are vets."

Gloria felt Joyce slipping into her clinical demeanor.

Joyce looked at Stephan with a burning gaze. "Why would you help us? Why take the risk?" She caught him off guard. Joyce had baited the poor man. But the truth had to come out either now or never.

Stephan lowered his head but peered sideways at Gloria. "I do not like injustice against anyone."

Joyce nodded. "But especially injustice against Gloria, correct? Do you have feelings for her?"

Stephan drew in a jittery breath. "I am very much attracted to Ms. Gloria."

"Fine," said Joyce, and she grinned at Gloria. "Now that we've got that out of the way, I'm calling Billy and Ross to see if they're available." She pulled her phone out of her vest pocket and speed dialed Billy first, told him the situation in code-like language that all of them had used at one time or another, and then got Ross on the phone and gave him the same spiel. Gloria heard the words *ten-seven*, meaning indisposed, *ten-eight* standing for back in service and available and *ten-twenty* asking for their location. They were cop ten-ten codes, but they were great for hiding civilian info in messages. Joyce had once called her and said she had a *fifty-one-fifty* at her business, in addition to calling the police. That code word meant a crazy lunatic was on the premises, drunk or on drugs, maybe both and exhibiting dangerous behavior. As far as she was concerned, Antonio and his men were all *fifty-one-fifty* cases!

It didn't take Billy and Ross long to arrive at the horse ranch. They flew out of their vehicles and trotted to the threesome.

Big Hoss Ross lifted Joyce up off the ground and held her. "S'matter, honey. Somebody messing with you and Gloria? You said code for bad guys on the phone."

Billy stood a few feet away and said, "I think my sis is okay, but Gloria needs our help. Ain't that right?"

Gloria nodded. "Something's happened to Ryan. I don't know where he is. He could be kidnapped or dead. Gangsters went after him."

Billy stiffened. "Dirty mutha fuckas got my bro? My boy?"

"And that little girl," said Gloria. "Candy or something. The woman that he took in."

"Ohhh...please put me down, Ross. You're breaking my back."

"You got it, baby." He dropped Joyce and then gave her a passionate kiss.

Ross cleared his throat. "Uhmm...okay, that's *Candace*," he told Gloria. "I know her, and so does Billy."

Gloria felt like her brains had just been scrambled in a blender. "So you two know who this woman was and kept that from me?"

Neither man would look her in the eyes.

Gloria puffed, "Oh, dear Lord. I might not be a fishing buddy, but I sure the hell am your guy's friend!"

"That you are," said Billy.

Gloria gave both of them dagger looks. "You kept a lie from me. Those two might get tortured and murdered. Maybe Antonio thinks Ryan stole her from the church."

"What's the bottom line on this?" asked Ross.

"I'll tell you what's going on, and we can decide what to do about it," said Gloria more calmly. "This gang, or whatever, has the addresses of our parents and other family members, so we have to keep that in mind. So listen up to what happened..."

Gloria told the story of the incident just as she had before. She didn't embellish any of it. When she finished, a pall of silence remained as it had during her first recounting. Her delivery had an ample tone of guilt.

"You didn't set this off, Gloria." Billy confessed. "It was a run of bad luck. For your information, Ryan didn't steal that little gal. She got in a heap of trouble from that Antonia Madera dude. That was the runaway bride thing all over the news a month ago. Ross and I knew about it."

"Ryan kept her from getting hurt, and we kept our mouths shut," said Ross. "He couldn't let her go because that guy was hunting her down. Ryan got caught up in it through no fault of his own. And he ain't the type to go pluggin' some strange little pootang."

"Billy," Joyce huffed. "There are ladies present here. "

"Sorry, darlin'."

Gloria stomped her foot. "Oh, great. I'm the last to know everything. We're still going to get them back! Those monsters have to answer to justice!"

CHAPTER TWENTY-FOUR

Ryan rolled onto his back, stretched his arms upward and then threw the sleeping bag flap over to the side. The front of his body and face were hot and sticky. He blinked away the blur in his eyes and looked over his right shoulder.

Candace lay on her side with her arms crooked under her head and her legs straight out. She had her suit on, and he could swear he saw steam rising off it. A slight wheezing sound escaped through her lips. He picked up the binoculars at his side and stole a glance over the rock shelf. No one occupied the beach at the present, and his watch told him it was 8:33 AM.

He reached over and gently drew his hand across her cheek, then he ran his fingers through her hair. "Hey, my little portable heater! You can rise and shine now."

Candace stirred and gave out a whimpering yawn. She opened her eyes and then rubbed her face. "Auuggghh..." Her eyes met his. "It wasn't a dream after all. Good morning, my love. Ohhh...I'm hot."

"You can say that again. It was our body heat. We were overheating. This is a goose down bag."

"What time is it?" she asked sleepily.

"Time to get up."

Ryan watched his little beauty rock her body up into a sitting position. She closed her eyes, leaned toward him and pursed her lips. He fell into her, licking her lips, then closed in on them. Her breath was warm and sweet. He kissed her long and gently, savoring every moment. He massaged her back and ran his hand up to the base of her neck, pulling her tighter into him. She went limp. He laid her down and gave her a good old-fashioned make-out session. He sat up after a few minutes and exhaled a breathy gust of air.

Candace sighed. "You've got my heart beating again. But I'm sweating under my arms something fierce. And I stink. Whew!" she unzipped her suit and pulled her arms out of the sleeves, then rolled the top down. "I'm sorry, but I just have to cool off. My suit is soaking wet."

He grabbed the binoculars. He stole a quick look over the rock shelf and then set them to the side. The coast was clear.

Candace reached inside her large carryall purse and pulled out a cotton washrag. She laid the washrag on his thigh and said, "Will you do me nice, you handsome Norwegian?"

"You don't have to twist my arm." He tried to dry her as best he could but told her to keep her arms down lest somebody see her. He wiped her gently and then stowed the washrag. Then the alarm bells went off in his head. The sun was up, and it was a problem if they decided to get busy with each other.

"It wouldn't be a bad idea to cover up, Candace. No complaints whatsoever." He tried to coax her. "I'm just worried about showing too much body skin at this spot. We're right below the edge of the cliff top. We're pretty tucked in, but somebody might get a little peek at us." He tried to swallow but had no saliva.

"Okay, sweetie." She tucked herself back into her suit top but left the zipper half open. "Gosh, I am so dehydrated."

He laughed. "Well, we did have quite a workout, didn't we?"

"She giggled. "Oh, and it was heavenly. I wish we could have gotten that recorded on video. Can you *imagine*?"

"Don't make me think about it, you little sand dollar." He ran his hand over his face and noticed how moist it was, but his tongue was dry and sticking to the inside of his mouth. He pulled a plastic container out of the pack and took several swallows of fruit juice. He passed it to Candace, but she refused it and asked for bottled water. He retrieved the fanny pack out of the purse and snapped it around his waist. He hadn't thought about calling Billy or Ross because he didn't want them sticking their necks out with Antonio so near. Now he felt it was safe to make contact and fill them in on the recent events. They would go ballistic about the incidents, but after they settled down, they would use logic and tactics to come up with a solution.

He pulled the phone out of his fanny pack while watching Candace rummaging through the big pack. He had no clue what she was looking for. After he removed the phone from the zip-lock bag, he held it up. His finger hesitated over the auto-send button for Billy's number until he finally stabbed it and waited for a reply. His friend answered on the second ring.

"Okay, who is this?" asked Billy

"Who do you think it is?"

"What the hell, dude? I wasn't taking any chances with somebody else using your phone. And you haven't been answering anyway. We got the whole story of what went down, and we know your situation."

"How do you know—?"

"Later on that. Are you safe right now?"

"Yes, for the moment. But it's not going to last. We can't go out in the open."

"What's your twenty? *Careful*."

"You know where you lost your virginity in high school? We're almost on top of that spot."

"Yeah, I remember where that is. Little one must be with you. We thought she might have gotten snapped up."

"Who's *we*?"

"Everybody. Don't worry about it. Tell me what to do." Billy delayed explaining and pushed for any plan Ryan might have.

"Take the Shamrock to your virginity spot. We need a shallow water pickup. Stay off the sandbars but get in-shore as close as you can. Give me three blasts on your air horn. Maybe I'll hear your engines first."

"Okay, I got that. Then what?

"We'll break out of here and hit the surf. Hang your swim step over the rail. We'll board you."

Billy gasped. "You're gonna swim for it? Can little one take to the water?"

"There isn't a thing she can't do."

"Look, dude. I have to drive up-island, then sail back down. I'll take the southeastern route, which means I won't get there until early evening.

"Okay. We'll wait it out. Just step on it."

"Okay. Ten-four on that," said Billy. "We're burning daylight. Ten-eight!"

Ryan heard the phone go dead. He gave out a sigh of relief. He looked at Candace and saw that her mouth was open, and she was staring at him. He knew she had heard every word of the phone conversation.

He gave her a nod. "We're going to make a break for it, sweetie. We've got to get out of here. They might be total morons, but they must know that we escaped out the back gate."

"I get what you're saying. I can swim like hell."

"I'm not surprised. When we're ready to go, we go real hard." Somehow, he remembered saying that to her once before.

Candace stared at his lap. "Yeah, we should go hard. I need some liquid protein right now before I waste away from hunger and dehydration."

"I'm dry, too."

"You're going to be a lot drier."

We'll get something out of—"

"Forget that." She scooted closer and unsnapped his fanny pack buckle, letting the straps fall. After she guided him down on his back, she tugged his legs apart and got between them.

"It might show too much skin, honey," he warned. "I didn't think of anybody looking from the cliff top from just the right vantage point."

"There won't be any skin out here except for a little..." She giggled. "Change that—you'll come out in full, but I'll keep you covered."

Candace began rubbing the bulge over his crotch. She snaked her hand down under his groin and massaged his butt and brought her hand up slowly to feel his tightening groin. "Ohhh...nice and starting to come to life." She ran her hand from his underside to the top of his pelvis again.

She kept it up for a few minutes.

His breaths came short and choppy. "Aah...Candace, you're driving me crazy."

Oh, sweet stud, you are going to get good and crazy. I haven't even started, and I'm going moist. She put more pressure on his bulge, rubbing over it from every angle. "This is all mine now."

"I've got to get it out. It's too tight in there."

"Keep your hands away, baby. I'm going to do this." Didn't he say that to her the previous night?

She pulled his zipper down, slid her hand inside and dug her fingers gently into him. "Oh, you're coming on strong."

"What are you doing to me, Candy girl?"

She could feel his hips pulsate. "Getting ready to give you a deep cream pie. Then I'm gonna lap you up." She curled her fingers around his shaft and pulled him out. His member sprang upward, hitting her chin. She gasped in delight.

"Oh, Ryan, what in the name of...whoa.... Here we go again!" She stroked him with a double-handed grip from the shaft base upward.

"Auuhhg! What's a guh...deep cream pie?"

"You'll find out. Watch for it because you're going to the same place you took me. Heaven."

She glimpsed his eyes fixed on her face and swapped looks back and forth with him. *This isn't a penis—it's a tube steak!* She giggled.

He'd never seen such a beautiful woman hovering over his manhood before. He felt mesmerized and couldn't close his eyes or look away. He watched her slide her hand up and down, pinching the head with gentle fingers.

"Honey, I've got blue ones somethin' awful. I'm aching really bad."

"I'll take care of that," She positioned her face directly over his shaft and took his head inside her mouth, swirling her tongue around it. Then she created suction by mouthing it and pulling up off of it with a squishy pop.

"Guuugh...ya killin' ma." His tongue jammed in his mouth.

She pulled his balls out, filled her cheeks with both of them and then spit each one out with an agonizing slowness. She cupped his sac and buried her face in it.

"Oh, you smell so good." She reared up and drove her thick lips over him down to the base. He felt her chin hit his pelvic bone and knew she had stuffed her throat. He felt devoured, like some beautiful vampire was feasting on him. And this vampire had a skillful hot mouth.

He localized all the feeling deep within his pelvis, down into the prostate and breathed slowly in and out of the crack between his teeth.

She began a steady plunging rhythm. It didn't take long. He clenched his teeth and erupted.

"Oh...holy mother!" he cried out.

She made a moaning sound when the semen ran from the corners of her mouth and washed down his shaft, soaking his thighs. She kept at it.

He growled like a bear, released again. It came fast, furious and as intense as it ever had. When she rose up off of him, his swollen head bubbled up a last few dollops. He settled down, trying to catch his breath. He watched her tongue his groin, licking up all of it.

She looked at him with a nasty grin, her chin glazed.

"That's a deep throat cream pie, you big handsome Viking. It's a high protein meal and good for the hair. You're going to be giving up a lot of that to me. She patted his shoulder. "And you've been drinking pineapple juice. You taste like candy!"

He tried to catch his breath. "Of...all...that is holy and decent. I can't believe you just did that."

"I can't believe you did what you did to me. You're a horse hoser!"

He laughed and scrambled her hair with his fingers. She tucked him inside his pants and buckled him up.

He sat up with a foggy head rush. Some of the most idiotic questions ran through his mind: how many calories had he burned with all this passionate activity? What was the connection between pineapple juice and candy? What in the hell was a cream pie if it wasn't a pastry? Why in the Chuck Dickens hadn't he watched porno so he could have learned more of this stuff? He knew why: Boy Scouts were never allowed to think of such things. And the church was against blatant debauchery and unmarried sex. He'd never felt such pleasure and release in all his life. The excitement factor was off the scale, and he'd never been so much in love—not even with Gloria.

Ryan woke up and turned on his side. After he rubbed the sleep from his eyes, he saw that Candace wore her sheer lavender bikini and was sitting up. She had nearly upended the entire contents of the big pack and had strewn some food items over the sleeping bag. The foodstuffs consisted mainly of pastas: regular and angel hair spaghetti noodles, sauce packets, pita chips with hummus and every energy bar known to man. He also noticed that she had picked out her dietary foods from the rest.

"No fresh fish this morning?" he queried.

"Naw, you don't need to go out just for me. Let's have your favorite dish. Do you have one?"

"The egg noodles and those chicken powder packs. I'd go for that in a heartbeat."

She didn't have to be told how to use the little burner stove that was fueled by a small propane cartridge. She filled a tin pan with bottled water, lit a match and set the pot to boil. After a few minutes, she added the noodles and cream sauce and gave the contents a vigorous stir. She tore open two oatmeal bars and placed them on tin plates.

He watched her every move and couldn't help thinking how skilled and exacting she was even with the most primitive and basic implements. She must have gained loads of experience from the countless cross-country driving adventures that allowed her to camp out and really rough it in all kinds of weather and environments. The journeys she must have taken from one end of the country to the other; the little gypsy hitting the road and taking in the most beautiful scenery imaginable.

He felt insanely jealous of her wanderlust and wished he could have traveled just half the roads she had. Compared to her, he had been cooped up and stagnant, trapped behind an easel and prisoner inside a small, stuffy room. He didn't smell of the country and fresh breezes. He spent his days saturated in oil paints, alcohol and linseed oil. More than half his clothes were ruined from art supplies. On occasion, he'd accidentally smeared his goatee with paints and, as a result, spent the day smelling the fumes wafting upward and then suffered some of his worst headaches ever. Showering and scrubbing seldom removed all of the potent liquid chemicals.

He and Candace were diametrically opposed as far as lifestyle and personal history. Ryan had knocked on the doors of schools, and Candace had come from the school of hard knocks. A yin to his yang—a black to his white.

They finished their meager meal and cleaned up. Ryan had no idea what they were going to do until Billy's arrival—it might be half a day away. He felt sure they could last it out, but Antonia had been so hot on their trail. What was to stop the porn king from setting up camp in his house? He might also check the beach from one end to the other since it was the most logical escape route. In their favor was the fact that a thorough search of the Bluffs area would not likely produce results since their hiding place was tucked into the base of the steep cliffs.

Candace spanked the sand from her hands and looked lovingly at Ryan. "I'm the luckiest girl in the world to have you. I had a dream about us last night."

"And I'm the luckiest man alive to have you when you could have your pick of anyone. So what kind of dream did you have?"

"That's so sweet. I chose you! Well, we were sailing along in this big, wicked fast sailboat, and it was leaning over a lot, and you said for me to get to the top rail to help with the keeling or something. We had the spidicore up and—"

"Spinnaker. The big fluffy sail that catches lots of wind."

"Yeah, that. Anyway, we were headed for Obama, and I thought that was very strange to be sailing to the president."

"Hmmm...I like him as a president. And then what happened?

"We just kept on, and you gave me the wheel and let me try sailing for awhile. When I finished the shift you gave me, you said I had sailed one-hundred and eighty nautical miles, and you said that I was very good for a boats man mate."

"Bosun's mate."

"That's it."

"Then what happened."

"The next thing I knew, everything was white. The sky and the sea and everything on the boat was covered in white. Then the wind picked up and blew everything overboard that wasn't tied down. That was it. I couldn't understand what it meant."

"Sounds like a white squall. It's when the wind and rain comes and the waves get white-capped."

"Ohhh...I see. You are so smart."

He smiled, staring at his lap for a solid minute. When he looked at her, she was leaned back and watching him with her eyebrows raised. He saw anticipation on her face.

"I know what you're thinking," he said. "What do we do now with the hours ahead of us?"

"Yeah, that's pretty much what I was thinking. I know what I'd like to do to burn some time. But that can't happen. I mean most of it." She gave him that coy look again and lifted an eyebrow.

"Disneyland Park is closed except for a few rides," he said.

She gave him a wink, and he returned it. *Now why did I say that? Because I have no willpower!*

She wasn't about to let that one slip by. "What kind of rides?" She rubbed her fingers together and gave him *that* look. The look that said I'm in love, but I'm nasty and mischievous, and you're really going to get it. She had an insane craving for his sexual attention.

Oh yeah, baby. This train is barreling down the tracks, and there's no way to stop it—the brakes are shot. It's totally out of control, and so am I!

They locked in a tight embrace, kissing each other with probing tongues. A few minutes of make-out time and she found that he didn't need any stimulation. Neither did she! He was so into it, he was as hard as a pipe. She hoped it was the sight, the smell and the feel of her that drew him in so deeply. She knew now he couldn't hold his excitement back, and he was mad for her. She would let him lead—feeling powerless to stop him.

After he pulled her bikini bottom off, he placed her on her hands and knees, dropped his pants so he could take her from behind. The first slow thrust made her cry out. She arched her back when he pulled her hips up.

He gave her his length again. Now she was wet and inviting. She heard him sigh heavily when she pushed her chest into the ground and turned her head. He glided deeper into her with smooth lunges until he almost hit her limit.

"Oh, take me good!" Candace growled. "I love you, I love you, I love you."

He pulled out. She could hear his wheezing breath, accompanied by a yawing noise.

"Oh no! Go deep...you brute!"

He plunged again, this time taking it all the way in. Both of them let out loud groans. She saw him throw his head back. Then he let go. Candace made whining sounds, almost like crying. He grabbed her buttocks, causing her body to spasm. A minute later, it was over, and he laid her down on her back. She palmed her pelvic mound with both hands and gazed up at him with amazement.

"You Scandinavian sex fiend," she huffed. "You split me wide open."

"That was the idea." He coughed hoarsely. "You can take it. You're a big girl."

"I'm your girl. I'm your girl *forever*."

It's kind of a shame," he began, "but we'll have to bag the essentials in the zip locks, then stuff 'em in my fanny pack and bury all of this. You might run a shoelace through that diamond ring and knot it around your neck so you don't lose it swinging your arms in the surf."

There wasn't much to do but sit quietly and get some sun during the midday. The most exciting thing that happened involved a pair of seagulls fighting in midair over a large smelt. The gulls lost patches of feathers, dive bombing each other until they managed to tear the fish in half and go their separate ways.

The highlight of their quiet sojourn was taken up by their number of make-out sessions that had them sweating. Afterwards Candace had dug her bikini out of the pack and changed into it while Ryan had stripped down to his boxers. He tried to use a pair of scissors to shear off his goatee and explained that it would cut down on water resistance, but

Candace had vetoed it with some imploring words. One bottle of water was left out for reserve purposes. The fanny pack with the zip-locked bag holding the phone, wallet and gun would go with him. As a last order of business, they dug a deep hole in the sand and buried the large carryall purse and the pack, then covered them over.

"Someone will be mighty lucky when they stumble over this little buried treasure," he had said. "There will be a lot of head scratching going on."

Ryan had started to take regular trips out to the shoreline and aim his binoculars south-south-west at about 5:15 PM. Each time he had gone out on watch, he'd recited a sailor's prayer and hoped that Billy and those on board would be safe.

CHAPTER TWENTY-FIVE

Antonia had been bickering with the Pure Need and Breed Kennel owner for, according to his watch, nine minutes. The ancient kennel owner, who looked like a bag of bones wrapped in cellophane, would not budge on his price, and Antonio was trying to get him to drop another hundred dollars. The kennel had advertised bloodhounds that were available for adoption.

Antonio leaned on the counter, looking at the leashed dog brought by a handler to the front desk area ready for pickup. What a ploy it was, bringing out the animal as though it was a done deal and all they had to do was sign some paperwork and let the animal prance through the exit door.

Antonio could afford the cost of the beast, but that wasn't the issue. It said right in the *Martha's Vineyard Times* newspaper that this place was a rescue and adoption agency for orphaned dogs. Antonio explained that to the owner and then leaned back and rocked on his heels. Tony stood behind him. Antonio glanced at the tall man but shook his head—the sign for *there is no need for muscle.*

"What do I have to do?" said Antonio. "Bring the Better Business Bureau in on this? It's advertised that there are free dogs here. You're charging me for one."

"You said you wanted a bloodhound that was trained and that could 'get on the job'. Well, Banjo here is a sniffer. The rest of them are just huge lap dogs."

"It's highway robbery!"

"It's two hundred dollars."

"All right, all right. One of these days somebody is going to throw the book at you instead of a wallet." Antonio slapped the bills down on the counter. "There! Are you satisfied?"

"Not really."

"What now?"

"The leash and collar costs an extra ten dollars."

Antonia grimaced and paid the extra ten dollars.

"Fine, fine," said the owner. He reached under the counter and slid a pamphlet across the top. "This is a basic guideline for putting your dog on the scent."

"I'm not paying for it."

"It's free."

"I feel a heart attack coming on," Antonio said sarcastically as he stuffed the small book in his back pocket and told Tony to grab the leash.

They left through the front door and walked out to the Hummer. Three other cars were lined up next to his—Alphonse and Jeppo's sedan and two SUV sport models. In total, Antonio had seven of his best men with him, the rowdiest of all his hit men and bouncers. They were known as the Little Madera Mob Squad and were a force to be reckoned with.

They tried to coax the dog up into the back bed of the Hummer, but Banjo just sat on his haunches and slobbered.

"C'mon, girl, up you go," said Antonio, anxious to get on the road.

"I think it's a boy, boss," said big Tony. "You can see right there that's a—"

"I've got eyes. I can see. Throw that son-of-a-bitch in the back."

Tony picked the dog up, shoved it into the bed and closed the door. With Tony at the wheel of the Hummer, they took off for Aquinnah. The dog started howling immediately. It seemed like the clamor reached one hundred and fifty decibels, an uncomfortable sound in the confined space.

"What do you think is the matter?" Antonio raised his voice.

"He might need water or food."

"They feed them there before they cut 'em loose."

"Then he might have to go potty, boss."

"We're...oh, my aching head...not pulling over. Let him do it back there and roll the windows down."

"Yes, sir."

Antonio brought out the pamphlet and thumbed through the pages. Then he began to read the text in earnest, thinking that it was incredible that an instruction manual existed for such a dog. On the other hand, he knew about police using such dogs to track down escaped criminals and sniff out corpses. Cops had probably launched armies of dogs to ferret out the corpses that he and his hit men had left behind.

The howling stopped after twenty minutes of travel, just when they had pulled up into Ryan's driveway. As Tony got out and went around to open the tailgate, he remarked, "I guess Banjo didn't like the car ride. Now he shuts up."

Antonio flipped the last page of the bloodhound pamphlet book and got out of the vehicle. He met Tony around the other side, and they walked up to the front door.

"Just make it look natural," said Antonio. "We could attract too much attention." Which wasn't too far off the truth, what with a Hummer showing up in the driveway of the residence, a giant with a bloodhound on a leash and several cars just beginning to park on the street. In retrospect, they were dressed like detectives, so it wasn't too bad. The few neighbors who were in the area would do nothing more than peek from their windows out of morbid curiosity. What were they going to do? Call the cops?

Antonio looked perfectly natural and relaxed when he knocked on the door. One of his bouncers answered and let them in. The rest of the Mob Squad filed in behind.

Jacques, the French bouncer and door opener, said, "Glad to see you, boss. No visitors and no Candace or that dude showing up. Sorry I raided the fridge, but that stuff tastes like shit." He looked at the dog for the first time. "Whoa, a basset hound. Nice dog."

Antonio turned to his right-hand man. "Tony, keep that dog with you in the living room." He looked at the others. "I want you guys to gather around me and pay attention so I can tell you what we need to do."

His men closed in on him, quiet and respectful. They looked like all ears and no brains, but at least they could carry out the simplest of chores.

"You need to search this house from top to bottom," Antonio stressed. "I want you to find some plastic bags and grab a fork each from the kitchen. Get a small cardboard box to put these things into. Look for any hair in the bathroom trashcans. Bring all the toothbrushes you can find. Look for used dental floss. Fork out any dirty clothes from the bathroom, laundry room or bedroom hampers. Look for gum or half-eaten anything, like candy bars, apples, oranges and stuff like that. Check the kitchen trash for the same stuff. You know, bones, toothpicks. Look for used snot rags."

Antonio waited for a response or questions, but there were none. His men looked shell shocked. Alphonse, the smartest of the bunch, said, "I know what you need—anything that belong to the owners that this dog could sniff. I'll direct the search."

Antonio nodded. "That's what I want to hear. Coordinate the search, my man. Bring the goods to me when you're finished."

The men grabbed forks and a box and broke up into small teams. Most rushed up the stairs. Two began rummaging through the kitchen. They acted as though they were on an Easter egg hunt.

Tony sat on the sofa, holding Banjo's leash. "Do you think this is going to work, boss?"

"It's the only thing that makes sense. We knew they were home. They had to have gone out the back way when we came busting in. We had all the exits covered except for that one. It hasn't rained, so I figure we could pick up their trail. They might be hiding out with a neighbor somewhere on this coastline."

There was no doubt that it was a gamble. No other plan made sense. The couple could not risk being seen on the streets. He had a feeling they were close. He had that premonition in his gut again. He could never let Candace Sabella go. She was the mouth that could turn his world upside down. The fact that she ran from him was enough to know that she disliked or hated him. She was the biggest risk in his life right now, the potential witness to a murder that could put him away in a state penitentiary. He was an older man. He wouldn't last behind bars until he got out, if he got out at all. His empire would collapse without his management. Who could run twenty-eight businesses and keep everything open and drawing substantial income? Who would feed the poor? Who would take care of the young single mothers who needed jobs to feed their children? Who would hire newly released inmates and give them enough wages to rent an apartment?

It took less than an hour for Alphonse to bring back a box filled with what the training pamphlet called 'DNA Samples'. Antonio studied the contents of the box. It seemed to be all there—at least most of what he'd asked for. He told Jeppo to open the slider all the way and do the same with the back gate. When both were opened, Antonia told Tony to bring the dog into the kitchen. After setting the box on the floor, Antonio instructed Tony to rub Banjo's muzzle in the contents.

Antonio stood over the dog. "Just keep it up, Tony. He's got to get those smells all registered in his head. He has to know that's the only thing he needs to look for."

"I'm doing it, boss. He's getting his nose all messed up in it. He's trying to pull away now."

Antonio knelt on the floor and grabbed the dog by its loose neck skin, plunged him back down inside the box and then brought him back up. "Go find 'em, boy. Go find 'em," he said. "That's a good boy. GO GET 'EM!"

The dog wheeled around, sniffed once and lurched toward the slider, its nails gouging for purchase on the floor tiles. Banjo snapped the leash out of Tony's hand and ran out the door and across the backyard, headed for the open gate.

"Christ!" yelled Antonio. "Get after him, you idiots!"

Antonio couldn't get out of the way fast enough and was knocked down in the heated rush.

Gloria weaved from side to side, up and down as she pulled her knees together and spread her arms to grip the sides of the old sofa. At times, Billy's boat, the Shamrock, pitched and slammed into the waves, causing her butt to lift off the cushion. Diesel fumes wafted through the open salon door, causing a nauseous odor and dizziness. Most of the others, Stephan and his twin horse wranglers, John and Regis Remy, were holding on to the transom rail while Ross took a seat on the bow. He held himself down by clutching the cleats. He had a big pair of 8X binoculars. Joyce sat close to Gloria, and every once in awhile they exchanged sympathetic smiles and grasped hands.

Gloria had learned most of the essential parts of the boat while they got ready, just as they left the dock. Billy had said that it would make her feel more at ease about sailing under full steam. The knowledge gave her little comfort. She felt her horse ranch meal fighting its way up her throat and threatening to spew all over the place. At one point, Billy's Rottweiler, Ginger, walked up to her and licked her knee, somehow knowing the stress she was enduring.

"Coming around the Cape of Good Hope!" Billy yelled out. "Eyes should be peeled. But you can stay on your ass if you want."

"What's the Cape of Good Hope?" yelled Gloria. "That can't be *here*."

"Just lingo for we're coming around the south end of the island. Cover your ears. I've got to test something."

Billy gave a couple of blasts on the air horn that made Gloria jump in her seat. Joyce grimaced.

"Sorry," said Billy. "I got the blaster off a train, and it really gets attention."

Gloria wanted to show a little bravery and join the others on the back deck of the boat, but she thought she might fall or get sick. At least in this cabin, she felt somewhat safe and protected from the elements.

Joyce scooted close to her. "Not to bring up a bad subject, but why your change of heart about Ryan? You've shown some unexpected empathy for him and even the girl. I'm not saying it is a strange thing for you to do. It's certainly a humane view of the situation. But I'm curious about your flip-flop attitude."

Gloria looked at her. "Joyce, there is a part of me that still loves Ryan. He was kind and gentle. I feel that I somehow punished him and forced him into the acts he committed or might not have committed—I just don't know anymore! I remember our love sessions, and they will always stay fixed in my mind. Suffice it to say, there was no one else quite like him. He said when he was a kid, he learned all his lovemaking techniques from an older woman named Savannah, and it went on for almost two years." She chuckled. "You know, he worked so hard at times that he used to pass out in his studio. I found him asleep once with his face smudged up against a wet painting."

Stephan made wobbly steps into the salon area. Joyce scooted over, offering him a seat next to Gloria. He took it and held onto the cushions, trying to smile, but having a hard time doing it. He blew out a sigh and spoke up. "I'm used to the movement of horseback riding, but this is quite a different experience. I've never been jolted so much in all my life except in a troop carrier."

Gloria gave his thigh a pat, but quickly withdrew her hand. "Then I'm not the only one who has a hard time out here." She explained her reluctance to sail with her husband on the Shenandoah after her first trips out.

Stephan said, "It looks like we have something in common besides cluckers."

Bless his heart, thought Gloria. He wants so hard to make a connection, and it couldn't be at a worse time. He was kind and polite and seemed to have all the patience in the world. He was aware of her divorce proceedings, which put him in an awkward position. Still, it was nice having a man give her support and a positive outlook on everything.

"Stephan, forgive me, but I hope you know that our relationship can only be as friends. I hope you won't expect too much in the beginning. I haven't officially split from my husband." She knew he was curious about such things.

"I understand. But I would like to be the first in line for an evening out." He grinned.

"I promise you have first dibs on a date." She could see Joyce leaning in to listen carefully to the conversation and wondered why the woman hadn't brought out a note pad and started scribbling away.

"Whoa, Nelly," yelled Billy to anyone who would listen. "I've got some high temp readings. Bringing her down a notch." Then in a louder voice, "I need somebody to man the wheel for a couple of minutes!"

Stephan hesitated at first, but then pushed off the cushions and went to where Billy was standing. Billy pulled Stephan behind the wheel and pointed through the window. Stephan nodded. Billy exited abruptly.

Gloria, with her curiosity and reserve up, followed the route that Billy had taken and ended up at the entrance hatch to the outside of the rear deck. She saw Billy lift up a large deck panel and slide it to the side. He climbed down inside the boat. John and Regis Remy stood over the gaping maw, presumably to help if needed. Gloria had no idea what the problem was, even after hearing Billy complain about something. He might have gone down to check on the engine, if that was where the engines were on this craft. She just hoped they weren't sinking. She couldn't swim all that well and would never last long in these waters without a rescue.

Billy popped his head up, handed a large spray bottle to one of the twins and pantomimed with his hands for him to fill it and bring it back. The man ran across the deck past Gloria and down a flight of steps. Moments later, the man ran back to Billy and handed him the bottle. The task went on for another five times until Billy climbed out of the hatch and reentered the wheelhouse where Gloria assumed he relieved Stephan. Sure enough, she turned when Stephan laid a hand on her shoulder from behind. With the noise louder since the engine hatch was off, Stephan had to speak close to her ear.

"Billy says that the engines are heating up because of going full out for so long. He had to cool down the lines."

"Is that bad?"

"A horse has to be walked when he gets overheated. Water is used to cool him down if he's real hot and sweating. Same with a car engine. And it's the same here."

"We've been going too fast, haven't we?"

"I'm afraid so."

There wasn't anything to do but sit down in the salon and wait it out. Billy had said the timing had to be just right for the pick-up. Gloria knew that Ryan could swim okay, and he could do it for some distance. She didn't know about Candace.

Gloria almost couldn't find it in her heart to condemn someone who had been caught up with the likes of Antonio Madera. Yet she hated Candace living with her husband.

Ross lumbered around the corner and held onto the hatch door frame. He yelled at Billy, "I've got two tiny upright figures near the shoreline about fifteen degrees off the port bow. I think it's Candace and Ryan. I also see some movement further down the beach from them. And I kid you not, it looks like a big dog!"

Billy swung the wheel hard over. "Okay, got it. We're on our way!" He gave his air horn three loud blasts.

CHAPTER TWENTY-SIX

R yan looked south, straining his eyes through the cheap plastic binoculars. He saw two specks in the distance. One of them was taller than the other and further out to sea. He figured that one of them had to be a large sailboat or even a catamaran with tall sails. The other speck had a darker hue and was a safe distance from the shoreline so it wouldn't run aground. As he watched it, he could see a trail of black smoke swirling up from it, which told him it had to be diesel-powered. A dark diesel-powered vessel that could be seen at this distance meant only one thing. It had to be Billy's trawler. It had a noticeable bow wave, indicating it was making good headway through the swells.

He glanced behind him and saw Candace's eyes peeking over the edge of a rock shelf. She'd been waiting there for the past fifteen minutes while he was on his last watch shift. This time he felt that with their saviors in sight, he and Candace would have to make their move. He didn't want to stand on the beach in his boxers any longer than he had to. He looked through the binoculars again, blinking against the sun's golden glare sparkling off the waves.

Now he could see more detail; tall white outriggers swayed on the approaching vessel. As the boat leaned into a shimmering wave, the sun hit it just right—a blue hull with faded yellow trim. It *was* Billy!

Ryan got antsy, swapping looks between Candace and the approaching boat. He would signal her at the precise moment they had to make their frantic dash. Yet as he looked at Billy's trawler, he saw much more black smoke belching out of the exhaust pipes than before, and the vessel was not moving at flank speed. Something had slowed it down. He prayed it wasn't engine trouble. Not after coming this far!

The blue trawler came closer, made a starboard turn, then straightened out.

A faint howling noise coming from the east distracted Ryan. He turned and looked through his binoculars, trying to steady his hands and get a clear focused view. Several images came into view on the beach. There was no mistaking the large hound dog walking up and down the low berm line. It sniffed the sand, raised its head and emitted a whining howl.

At times the dog veered off into the soft sand, then turned back to the high tide line. The most distressing thing Ryan saw was a crowd of people running behind the dog. They looked like detectives dressed in dark suits, but that thought was ridiculous. Then it clicked in his mind. They were Antonio's men, running full out behind the dog.

Ryan glanced at the boat. It was a ways off but still under steam. He suddenly jerked around, waved his arms and yelled, "Whoop, whoop, whoop!"

The dog came on the run and started howling for all its worth. Then it picked up speed and singled out Ryan.

Candace leapt over the rock shelf and launched toward Ryan. Her muscular thighs pumped through the sand kicking up small rooster tails. He waited until she reached him and then ran abreast of her at full speed. She passed him, kicked through the surf and dove into a shallow wave. He waded through the wave and dove over it. He hit the sandy bottom, reared up and dove into the next wave. When he bobbed up for air during his strokes, he could see Candace far out ahead of him, her arms windmilling. Her body glided through the water with the grace of a dolphin. He kicked as hard as he could, determined to catch up.

He couldn't see the boat. He didn't have time to stop and look up, although he did take glances back at the beach where he saw a crowd of men that had just converged on the spot they'd left. They looked in Ryan's direction, threw up their hands and shook their fists. Glancing back again showed them running down the beach, now in the same direction they had. He wondered why they had not fired on him. Then the realization hit him that discharging weapons would summon the police.

"C'mon, baby!" Candace yelled.

She hadn't realized how far she had swum ahead of him. Stupidly, she had neglected to look behind her as she went hell bent out with her fastest freestyle. Why did she assume that Ryan knew how to knife through the water, using the swift Australian crawl? He lived on the water. But what did that mean? Nothing, if he never ventured out into the surf.

She kicked her feet hard propelling her body upward to see him. When she did catch sight of him her heart sank. He looked so tired and defeated, now only wallowing in the water and puffing hard. She could feel a current under her legs, not a swift one, but a steady one with pull. She hoped it wasn't a rip current.

Her mind flashed with a terrible scene—she would see him one minute, and then he'd be gone the next. She couldn't bear the thought of the love of her life going under and drowning. Her world and heart would shatter to pieces. There would be nothing left for her to live for. He was her angel—the champion of her heart—the sweetest and most caring man she had ever known. She was so in love that she could not stand to be out of his sight, and yet she had done just that without thinking.

"I'm coming to get you! Stay with me, Ryan!"

Courage and strength welled up in her breast. She launched herself upward and dove. Her body was a machine now, going full out at breakneck speed.

Ryan swam toward the voice as fast as he could. He could just barely make out Candace's head bobbing in the swells. She signaled him with a raised arm. The boat was further off shore than he thought and still south of him. He felt his lungs starving for air but kept up with driving hard strokes. A mild current set him off course, and he had to swim against it. The muscles in his body began to seize up, and he hoped a cramp wouldn't overcome him.

He stopped to catch his breath and saw a body cutting through the water toward him. Candace swam up next to him and grabbed his hand. She spit water and said, "Just scissor kick, Ryan. Kick hard. I'll pull you."

He didn't expect her to come to his rescue, yet he was glad that she did. She tugged hard on him, and he could feel the underwater wash of her legs thrashing hard beside him. Just the closeness of her gave him a renewed energy, and he gained a second wind. Side kicking through the water allowed him to see the location of the boat. It was still out further than he thought it should be, but maybe Billy was playing it safe and avoiding shallow water.

They both kept driving on harder than ever, the two of them swimming in tandem like one body. He'd lost track of the amount of water he'd swallowed and taken up his nose. Candace's breaths were loud enough for him to hear, and she was starting to chug and slow down.

There was nothing he could do when his body started to numb after twenty minutes. His legs felt like lead weights, and he had a hard time keeping them moving. She tugged on him, kicking the last twenty yards toward their salvation. The massive blue hull of the trawler loomed huge and resplendent. It glided slowly past them. A roped life ring splashed in the water only a few feet from their heads.

Ryan hooked his arm through the life ring and hung onto Candace. He felt manic with elation as those on board the Shamrock towed them up to the aluminum swim steps. Ryan shoved Candace up a rung. Then she started hand over hand up the steps. He followed her up, kicking his legs back to life.

As Ryan looked up, he couldn't resist. "You have a really nice butt for a little gal."

"I heard that!" Candace answered.

Ryan saw heads peering anxiously over the rail and wished he hadn't said a thing. Some faces were familiar. Others were unknown. One of the faces gave him the shock of his life.

Candace pulled herself over the top rail with the assistance of several hands. Ryan slogged up the last steps and stood up on the last rung. Joyce and Gloria gasped.

"Yeah, we're alive!" he yelled cheerfully. "Let's get out of here."

Ross threw him a large beach towel. Ryan stepped down from the railing onto the deck and wiped himself down. That's when he noticed he had lost his boxers and fanny pack and now stood naked in front of all his friends. And a few strangers, too! He quickly covered up.

Candace stood shivering with a towel around her shoulders. "He's a little shy," she said aloud. "But once you crack his nut, he comes out of his shell."

Gloria white-knuckled her fists. "Oh!" she hissed and stormed at Ryan. "Damn you!" She pounded on his chest with both fists. He took a wobbling step back and raised a hand. Joyce ran to Gloria's side.

"Don't you dare hit her, Ryan!" the thin woman demanded.

Gloria stepped around Joyce and pounded across the deck. She hauled to a stop in front of Candace and cocked a fist. Joyce ran to Gloria and got in front of her just as a fist whistled through the air. Joyce took a haymaker in the face—her nose sprayed blood, and she grabbed Gloria's arm and yanked her toward the salon.

"Why did you stop me, Joyce?" Gloria whined. "Oh...I'm so sorry I hit—"

"Violence isn't going to solve anything. And never mind that punch."

Billy emerged from the cabin. "You guys get all your asses planted. We're moving' out, and it's gonna be rough. Somebody, please, take care of these women. Joyce is bleeding!"

Ginger barked her own warning of alarm

The remaining people came up to the couple and expressed their joy in seeming them alive and healthy. They all filed into the salon and took seats. Gloria attended to Joyce's nosebleed with a hanky, begging for forgiveness. "I'm so sorry!" she wailed.

A few sat on the sofa that Gloria and Joyce occupied, and the others sat opposite them on a smaller sofa and three recliners. Stephan checked on Joyce and then introduced himself as the man connected with the horse riding stables. He included his two wrangler employees in the greeting.

Ross made a visit to the forward part of the boat and brought back an armload. He offered some of Billy's work pants, a plaid shirt and some boots and socks to Ryan. Ryan used the head to change and returned to his seat. He pulled Candace back onto his lap.

Gloria would not look up from the deck boards to meet Ryan's eyes. Suddenly, she lurched to her feet and stormed off in the direction of the front V-birth. Holding her palms against the corridor walls for support, she stomped her feet all along the deck.

Joyce shook her head, holding the hanky to her face. But some sympathy radiated from her eyes. She looked both saddened and relieved to see that Ryan was okay.

Candace turned her head, looked at Ryan and said, "I'm sorry. I wasn't thinking. I was just sharing...well, you know...trying to lighten up the mood."

"No fault, babe. I blew it, too. Most of them are still happy for us, and we're safe."

Candace couldn't believe that she'd spouted off like that. She hadn't paid attention to the company that was onboard the Shamrock. She hadn't seen Gloria in the crowed of faces. That was hard to believe because she was a big woman. Maybe she didn't want to see Gloria and had blanked her out of her mind. Maybe she never wanted Gloria to come near Ryan again. Just maybe she might have felt a little jealous of the wife who had lived with her guy for two years. What kind of love had he offered her? Was it the same as she had received? Somehow, Gloria made her feel inferior, not good enough to surrender her husband to a strange woman who had come out of nowhere to tear her life apart. Gloria had called her a whore and believed she was a home wrecker.

In a way, Candace felt sorry for Ryan's wife. Gloria had jumped to conclusions about an affair that had never happened. Candace wondered if she would have handled the situation any differently. What if she had been married to Ryan and found Gloria in her house with a nude painting of her? It wouldn't take any deep investigation to think that something wasn't kosher. The scene would be complicated more with the fact that she and Ryan were in the last stages of a counselor-guided reconciliation.

To think that a couple was struggling and succeeding to patch up their marriage and then have it blow up in their faces had to be wrenchingly heartbreaking.

Ryan was especially desirable—a beautiful person and a great lover. To lose someone like him would have intensified the hurt. She could understand that hurt. He was so special. Gloria had had him for a length of time that would have surely delighted a wife and kept her satisfied. To have the rug pulled out from underneath her so suddenly without warning could have driven Gloria to a state of insanity—an outrage so cruel that she would take out as much revenge on him as possible.

Would Candace have acted any differently? She might have reacted even worse, having her husband snatched away by an older, more refined woman who owned a business, a woman who had influence and social standing in the community.

Would she have given Ryan the chance to explain, or would she have started looking for the nearest gun to shoot one or both of them? Of course, that would be an extreme measure; she would never do such a thing. But her mind would overload with evil, vengeful thoughts. How far would she suffer those hurts if she were in Gloria's place? What if Candace had been pregnant and had to face such a situation? A wife who had to confront her husband's mistress would have brought most women near the brink of suicide.

No. Any woman who knew Ryan for who he was, experiencing his kindly nature and shy attitude, would have had to give him a fair hearing and let him explain. Candace could see the purity in him after knowing him for just a short while. He would deserve a fair hearing. What confounded her was that his wife was so suspicious, dead set in her belief, that it seemed she really did not know her husband.

It wasn't a question of where Ryan had gone wrong. The riddle was how Gloria had gone so wrong. Was it possible that his wife was hasty in her hatred because she wanted to end the marriage? Was there another man in her life? Had there always been a secret lover on the side, or was there another man on her wish list? It did seem that Gloria had kicked her husband out of their bed for reasons that could have been easily solved. Whoever heard of a woman who wouldn't help clean her husband up for good and comfort him during his worst nightmares? That described a true bitch. He wasn't worth the effort? He wasn't worth the time? Was it too much work and humiliation?

The difference between Ryan and his wife was that she had no inner peace. Left to his own, Ryan had a gentle nature and only wanted to paint, make money and be recognized. He wanted to feel accomplished and appreciated for it. He had such artistic talent that Candace was certain that he would be famous one day, only because he was focused. What woman on Earth wouldn't stand by such a mate ready to lavish him with all the encouragement in the world? Why did he deserve mistrust and hatred?

Candace turned and put her hand against Ryan's cheek. She gave him soothing pets and looked up into his eyes. He grinned at her. His expression was one of pride. If anything, she knew it was possible that she was not good enough for him. He was a peacemaker in the middle of a raging war with no way out.

She was glad she had come to Ryan's rescue. It would not be hard to mend the damage to his heart. She was meant for the job. No one else would have a clue how to bring this man back into a happy reality. He was so much worth the effort, but it seemed so impossible that things had been allowed to get so far out of control for so long. She was the right prescription for his illness.

"I'll love you forever under the stars," she told him.

"That's beautiful, baby," he said with a soft smile. "I'll love you in my arms under the moonlight until the end of time."

"We'll travel to the end of time together."

"That's right, darling." He stroked her hair. "And then we'll go on together into infinity."

She wiped a tear from her cheek, then leaned her head into his chest. He smelled like salt and heaven.

CHAPTER TWENTY-SEVEN

Billy swore some unintelligible words that drifted inside the salon. Ryan slipped out of his chair and walked the short distance to the wheelhouse. When he got there, he could see a black plume of smoke swirling in the air through a side window pane. The engine knocked, and the RPMs had dropped.

"She's overheating again," said Billy, nodding behind his shoulder. "Take the wheel, and don't throttle her up."

Ryan did as he was told. Candace appeared at his side a moment later and looked at him with questioning eyes. He shook his head. It did not look good.

Ryan heard a crash, then stole a peek at the transom deck. Billy had pulled the engine covers off and had Stephan's employees filling spray bottles with water, then handing them off to him. It was akin to a bucket brigade—another attempt to cool the engines.

Ryan turned around and straightened the wheel, staying on a steady course. Then there came a sound of hurried thumps across the deck.

Billy popped his head around the hatch door. "We're red-line overheated. I pushed her too hard. I have to keep spraying the lines without hitting the manifolds, or they'll crack. We've got vapor lock something terrible. Just stay on the northern route."

The northern route was the shorter way around to Vineyard Haven, a steam of three to four hours depending on the conditions. Yet at reduced speed, it could be longer. Something told Ryan that their rescue journey would not come out as expected. At least they were together.

Ryan felt a chugging, a surge and then some rattling mixed in with some heavy metallic knocking. He watched both temperature gauges climb over redline and the RPMs plunge. The engines spit once more, then fell silent. The only thing he could hear was a sizzling sound, accompanied by the burning smell of insulation and rubber. They were dead in the water. He knew enough about engines to conclude that both had locked up due to the scalding of the bearings. Billy had just lost his major investment, and it was because of him and Candace.

"Ross! Drop the bow anchor!" Billy yelled. His voice sounded above the near silence except for the waves lapping against the hull. Moments later, a splash and chain rattle signaled the release of the anchor.

Everyone moved out to the back deck. Billy emerged from the engine hatch, steam and smoke roiling up around him.

"She's done for," said Billy, wiping torrents of sweat from his face. He tossed a spray bottle across the deck. "It was my fault for pushing this old bucket beyond limits."

Ross appeared, inching down the catwalk until he reached the others. "Fuck me tender! I just knew those engines were going to seize."

"My ship-to-shore is out again, so we can't call from it," said Billy. His frown deepened.

Ross managed a weak smile. "Maybe we can use a reflective mirror or semaphore."

The comment made everyone smile. Then Ryan saw movement out of the corner of his eye. A fast approaching boat was headed in their direction. It must have been an islander since the size of the craft was enormous, and it was coming on at full opened throttles. The sound of the beefy twin engines reached everyone's ears, and they turned to look. The oncoming vessel was an elegant yacht. On closer inspection, he had seen this ship before and knew her brand and model. It was his neighbor's luxury cruiser—a sixty-seven and one half foot Class D Galaxy Sport Yacht. It belonged to Theo who lived four houses down from him.

The huge yacht cut its engines, made a hard turn and drifted up close to the port hull of the Shamrock. The maneuver was almost ballet choreographed. Theo sat at the helm, and two men appeared from the cabin and cast lines over the sides. Ross and Billy picked up the lines and tied them securely to the fore and aft mooring cleats.

"You're a sight for sore eyes!" Ryan yelled. "The Shamrock has gasped her last breath."

Theo let the engines idle and walked out to the deck rail. "I figured something was up when I saw your smoke signals." He laughed. "Looks like you need a tow."

Ryan felt comforted by the look on Theo's face. Yet something was not quite right. Maybe it was Theo's deckhands. Theo always took his wife Melissa with him on cruises.

Theo shut his engines down and climbed precariously from one boat rail over to the other. His two men stayed behind.

Billy and Ryan greeted Theo and invited him into the Shamrock's salon. Even though they were in a rush, Billy said a drink was in order and then offered his guest a seat.

"Now this is a Welsh drink," said Billy, pulling a bottle from an overhead cabinet. "Condessa makes the finest Black Cherry liqueur in all the United Kingdom." He poured several neat shots in plastic cups and passed them around. They toasted.

"What brings you out here, Theo?" Ryan asked.

Theo knocked his shot back. "Just a fast one to get the barnacles off her hull. No, I'm kidding. She has no barnacles. I needed to run the engines and charge her up." He favored everyone with a polite smile. "And what brings you salty blokes out here?"

Billy walked to the main salon hatch and closed it. "We're just delivering some passengers to their destination. I ran her too hard and fried 'em."

"That's a bit of bad luck," Theo commented. "Both engines?"

Billy nodded. "Both—at damn near the same time."

Billy poured another round. Everyone drank up except Gloria who still remained in the forward section of the boat.

Ryan felt a noticeable list to starboard. The deck yawned with a creaking sound. He figured it might be Theo's deck hands coming aboard.

But two men wouldn't cause that much list, especially as small as those guys were.

He went to the salon hatch door. It flung open and hit him in the chin. Instinctively, he back pedaled and pulled Candace behind him. Stephan, his two men, Ross and Billy formed a barrier between Ryan and the crowd of boarders.

In the blink of an eye, several well-dressed men had climbed over the rails and took positions on the rear deck of the trawler. They drew revolvers and automatics. They pointed the guns at the Shamrock crew through the open hatch door. Theo's two fake deck hands joined the rest of the men on the aft deck.

Theo crushed his hands together. "I'm so sorry, Ryan. They made me do it. They have my wife at gunpoint at the house!"

Now everything makes sense. I should have listened to my gut.

Antonio Madera, recognizable from his short stature and greasy looks, yelled out, "The first one that goes for a phone or runs up to the bow gets shot. Don't fuck with me." He jabbed a finger at Candace who stood behind Ryan. "I want that woman right now. She's my fiancée! I'll say it again. The first one who moves gets it."

No one moved in the salon. Candace hugged Ryan's waist. He backed his arm around to hold her. She was shivering but managed to whisper in Ryan's ear, "The tallest one is Tony the Twister. He's dangerous."

The cap on Ryan's rage popped open suddenly. *This might not go well, but I don't give a flyin'..."*

"You're a real fuckin' brave lot to pull down on women," Ryan hollered. "I know what you did to Candace, Madera. You piece of shit. I really owe you for that. Put those weapons down and take us on like real men. You won't shoot anyway—you'd have a mess on your hands—fodder for the cops and too many witnesses.

"Hand her over," said Madera, "or I'll put a hole in you."

Ross stepped forward. "Come and get me instead. You're a bunch of cowards." He pointed. "I'll tangle with the big boy there!"

Ginger, appearing from the front of the boat, stiffened when she saw the strange men. She barked out several threats.

Tony the Twister grinned. "Boss, I want a piece of that son-of-a-bitch. I'll take him down and all the rest of them."

"What's it going to be?" asked Ryan. "You guys got the stones to take her from me? Man up and go fisticuffs with us. I'm going down before you take her from me."

Stephan flicked his fingers, looking sideways at his wranglers. It was some type of sign.

Billy spit in his hands. "You know the deal, dudes. Come and get your due, you bunch of dung beetles."

Stephan stepped forward. "Yeah, what's it gonna be, hard asses?" he spoke under his breath, "You ladies get to the front compartment."

Candace stepped up to Ryan's side. "Sorry, but I'm not going anywhere. This man is the love of my life. I'll go to heaven or hell with him."

Ryan glanced at the other two women. Joyce puffed up her chest, and Gloria, who had just appeared from the corridor, narrowed her eyebrows.

A knife could have cut the tension in the air. The Madera men shifted their stances and looked to their boss for the answer. They looked primed —ready to go. They also looked seasoned—a very tough lot. Ryan had some doubts about the outcome, but his love for Candace threw caution to the wind.

Madera's jaw muscles clenched, and the veins on his forehead stood out. He finally took a breath, waved his arm and said, "Get 'em, boys!"

Most of Madera's men holstered their weapons and rushed forward. The Shamrock crew met them in a rushing head on crash at the door, knocking a few of the other men's guns to the deck. The women pushed the men forward and then squeezed between them to get in a fist. Ryan saw Gloria with a quick glance when she turned around and ran in the opposite direction.

The fight was taken to the aft deck of the Shamrock.

A young skinhead dove at Ryan and plowed his head into his stomach. The blow nearly knocked the wind out of him, but he managed to bring his fist down on the boy's head and stun him.

Ginger launched herself at the first strange intruder and clamped down on the thug's leg. The man let loose with a high-pitched scream.

Ross and Tony stood face-to-face, trading punches like two heavy weight boxers.

Someone grabbed Ryan around the neck. He flipped the body over his shoulder. A punch came out of nowhere and rattled his teeth. He swung back three times and connected once.

One of the burly men picked Candace up in the crook of his arm and made hurried steps toward the yacht. Ryan grabbed his hair, pulled him backward and gave him two right-cross punches in the face. He felt something snap in his right hand with the second blow.

Joyce tried to tear the T-shirt off one of the fake deck mates. He turned and kicked her in the crotch. Ryan ran after him, caught him, then threw him down. But his opponent gave him a straight-up punch in the face. Ginger bit the man's arm, sinking teeth deep into the flesh.

Ryan finished the man off with three face blows and left him bleeding on the deck from the dog bite. But Antonio slithered through the bodies and groped for Candace. He got her around the legs and pulled her hard. Ryan leapt at him and delivered a front snap kick to Antonio's face, crossing the man's eyes. Ryan watched him crawl away like a beaten dog.

"Candace, you and Joyce get back!" Ryan screamed. "Get out of here!" He didn't know if it would do any good to call the woman out of the fight. So far, they were giving as well as they got. But Candace was so exposed he feared she might be snatched up and taken aboard the yacht. So he fought his way to her and grabbed her hand. He pulled her out of the crowd.

Stephan and his men fought back to back, using combat judo, flipping incoming men on their backs.

And still the brawl continued. Everyone engaged in some tussle or another. Ginger ran around snapping at exposed flesh and dragging bad guys across the deck.

Ross pulled Tony down to the deck and grappled with him. Now they were sumo wrestlers.

Ryan punched any strange face that came within arm's reach. Someone jumped on his back and gouged fingers into his eyes. The person on his back had legs wrapped around his middle like a monkey. Ryan jumped backward in the air and came down flat on the deck, flattening his combatant. When he got up and rubbed his sore eyes, someone hit him on the side of the head, and he went down, seeing stars mixed with lightning flashes. He was punched again, this time in the forehead. He raised his hand up and caught a throat, stabbed it hard with his fingers. The attacker fell to the side choked for air. Ryan rose up and karate-chopped him over the Adam's apple. Candace appeared and stomped on the man's face several times. Ryan pulled her away from the mêlée again.

"I'm fighting, too!" she said.

"You stay back and get the fallen guns—throw them overboard."

"Look out!" she warned.

A large, broad shouldered man with a dark three-piece suit tackled Ryan around the middle. They went down and rolled. Candace jumped into the fray and kicked the man in the nuts, causing him to cry out in pain. But Antonio, still addled, made a desperate lunge for Candace and grabbed her arm. Billy stepped in and kicked Antonio in the groin as well, causing the man to go down into a fetal position.

Ryan saw Ross delivering punches through Tony's crossed arms. Ross's face was bloody, and he looked worn, but he kept on with the relentless slugfest.

After five more minutes, team Shamrock had control of the fight with most of the thugs sprawled on the deck from knockout punches or serious dog bites.

Ginger had torn a combatant's clothes nearly off of him.

Ross got up after knocking Tony unconscious and grabbed a dizzy hoodlum by his belt and the scruff of the neck. He raised the little man over his head, then staggered to the port rail and threw him overboard. "You're outta here, puss!"

Ryan expected to be jumped again, but it didn't happen. He ran to the starboard side of the Shamrock, hearing Candace's steps behind him. He grabbed Antonio by the collar and flung him to the deck. Ryan yelled in his face, "How does it feel, muther fucker?"

Antonio yanked the automatic up from his side. He aimed recklessly, but Ryan swatted the gun out of his hand, causing it to skid across the deck. He grabbed Antonio by the hair and pounded his face on the hardwood planks as hard as he could. "This is for you, you murdering lowlife pig." Ryan let go as soon as Antonio's eyes glazed over, and he fell into unconsciousness.

A gun shot went off. A woman screamed.

Ryan saw Candace standing in the middle of the deck. She wobbled once, then her knees buckled. She fell backward and hit the deck. Billy got to her in a second. "She's been beat to shit."

Ryan yelled for Theo to call the police and Coast Guard. Then he fell on his knees and pulled Candace up into his arms. He grabbed an automatic out of her hand and noticed she gripped it by the barrel.

"Hey, baby darling," said Ryan, "it's going to be all right now." He bellowed for all to hear, "The next thug who tries anything gets wasted!"

Joyce staggered to Ryan and dropped to her knees. Her nose had broken open again, leaking blood. "Oh God, I saw it happen...she's been shot...I saw the bullet come out of her back." She pointed. "She fought with that man over the gun!"

Ryan lifted Candace up gently and saw a pool of blood on the deck. Her eyes rolled to the back of her head.

"Oh, Lord no," said Ryan. "SOMEBODY GET HERE QUICK. MY BABY HAS BEEN SHOT."

Ryan tore off his T-shirt and made two bandages out of it. He tucked one hand under her, compressing the wound tightly and placed the other over the entrance hole in her chest. Her mouth bubbled with a froth of blood. Her nose ran with a yellowish discharge.

"Somebody HELP ME!" Ryan cried piteously and then looked down into the pretty face he knew so well. "You can't leave me, Candace! I can't live without you!"

CHAPTER TWENTY-EIGHT

The Coast Guard and police arrived twenty minutes after the gang fight and stormed both vessels. The cops drew their weapons. Two EMTs went right to work on Candace. The first thing they did was perform a tracheotomy to keep her airway clear. They lifted her onto a stretcher.

Ryan had to stay behind since they would airlift Candace to Martha's Vineyard Hospital. All the protests and cursing in the world would not change the medics' minds.

He could only watch as his little angel was taken away from him. The medics and Candace got onboard the huge Coast Guard cutter via a Zodiac. Rotor blades on a helicopter began to rotate with a gyro hum, then the chopper rose, leaned into a steep bank and flew off toward the island.

The chopper grew to a speck in the distance. Ryan saw his friends stealing glances at him while the police officers interrogated them.

"God help us," Joyce said, sobbing. "How could this be?"

He replied in a strangled voice, "It's all a nightmare. This should never have happened." His hand throbbed and when he looked at it he could see that it was swollen to twice its size. It meant nothing to him. He had to get to the Vineyard as fast as he could to be at Candace's side.

Looking over toward the cabin salon entrance, Ryan saw Gloria standing there, staring at him with lost and sad eyes. She looked like she was shivering. Ross was the next one to hurry to Ryan's side.

"We have to get you off this boat and to the island." He looked down. "Bud, what's happened to your hand?"

"It's broken. I don't give a shit about it."

"That's what we'll use to get you transport." Ross strutted across the deck to an officer who wore sergeant stripes. With a raised voice and pointing a finger at Ryan, Ross explained the situation. "I've got a man with a shattered hand here. He needs medical attention now."

Just as Ross finished his statement, another police patrol boat arrived on the scene and tied off on the first patrol boat. Several officers disembarked with guns drawn and started asking questions. Other cops collected loose guns and interrogated Madera's men.

Ross gave a frantic wave to Ryan, beckoning for him to come to the officer's side.

When the sergeant saw Ryan's hand, he spoke through his mic, reaching the captain of the arriving patrol boat. They helped Ryan cross two boat decks, to arrive on the last one. A policeman gave him a blanket and took him inside the cabin.

"Martha's Vineyard Hospital," pleaded Ryan. "I have to get there fast!"

"We'll get you there, pard," said a young cop as he gently wrapped an ice bag around Ryan's hand. He held onto a support rail with the other hand just as the boat's engines fired up.

Left alone in the silence of the small cabin, Ryan could not think straight. His mind swirled like a tornado of scattered trash. He knew what had happened, but he was unwilling to face it. Nothing seemed real. Only a short while ago, he had held Candace in his arms and spoke of his love for her. They'd had unrivaled and passionate lovemaking. Only yesterday, they had cracked jokes and told stories.

After Ryan arrived at Martha's Vineyard Hospital via an ambulance ride, he went to the in-patient service desk and asked about Candace Sabella and where he could find her. An EMT had followed him, after

Ryan had politely refused transport on a gurney. It was against regs, but the EMTs had heard about the shooting and understood the urgency of Ryan's need to check on his loved one. The EMT behind him spoke up.

"This is Ryan Barlow, and it was called in. He has a broken hand."

Ryan ignored the statement. "Please, first I need to know about my girl, Candace Sabella.

"We have a doctor standing by for Mr. Barlow," said the clerk to the young EMT. "Thank you for the expedite and have a good day."

"And Candace?" Ryan pleaded.

"Yes, Candace Sabella," said the clerk and checked her screen. "She was air-lifted here and taken into trauma surgery. She has a gunshot wound to the upper torso. She is still in surgery."

"Where is that?" asked Ryan. "I've got to get there."

The desk nurse clicked some keys. She looked at Ryan. "I'm sorry, but you are required to have treatment first. Rest assured, she is in the best of hands, sir. And I'm afraid you are not allowed on the surgery floor. I'm very sorry."

An orderly appeared like a wisp of smoke and asked Ryan to follow him down the hall to one of the inner examination rooms. It took Ryan all the reserve he had to obey the young man's wishes. He would do anything he had to do, cooperating with the staff, if it meant he would get his wish. In his heart, he yearned to get to his little gal's side. Nothing more.

After treatment of his hand and wearing a cast, Ryan walked straight to the front desk and inquired about Candace again. There was no news. She was still in surgery. He asked the receptionist where she would go after surgery and was told that she would be assigned to ICU. He also found out some of his friends had been treated and released during the time he had been getting his hand set. Billy had left a note at the desk for him. It read, "WE ALL FIGURED YOU WOULD WANT TO BE ALONE AND NOT NEED ANY GAWKERS OR STALKERS. WE LOVE YOU. CALL WHEN YOU NEED A RIDE. OUR PRAYERS ARE

WITH LITTLE ONE. P.S. I LEFT A PHONE FOR YOU AT THE DESK.

Ryan crossed the lobby and took a seat on a vinyl sofa. He looked at the other waiting room occupants. About fifteen people sat in the room with him. He thumbed through a few magazines and absently read some of the article titles. He'd never felt so depressed in his life. If it took until the next millennium, he would camp out on the sofa.

It wasn't long before exhaustion overtook him. His head lolled forward, and he knew no more.

Some time later, Ryan roused and rubbed his eyes. First, he had no idea where he was. Then it came back to him in bits and pieces. He was in a hospital waiting room. It was dark outside. He counted nine people in the room with him. It looked like all but two or three of them were new guests. The wall clock read 3:35 AM. Grogginess overcame him again, and he passed out.

He heard a voice in the blackness of this mind and flicked an eye open. He saw a crisp, clean lab coat in front of him. His phone went off. He didn't answer it.

"I'm Doctor Daniels," said the white-haired man. "I've been told you are Ryan Barlow, and you have inquired about Candace Sabella."

Ryan massaged his face and stood up. "That's right, sir. How is she? Can I see her? Where is she?" His legs felt like noodles. He felt a head-rush.

"She's in ICU recovery. She is lucid but in and out of consciousness. She has a perforated lung, and we have her on support at the moment. I talked to the head nurse and arranged for you to have fifteen minutes with her...you'll have to be very quiet. She must not be subjected to any excitement." He handed Ryan a slip of paper. "This is her floor and room number."

Ryan thanked the doctor profusely, then he went in the direction of the doctor's pointing finger, which led to a corridor. After getting lost twice, he found her room on the fourth floor and approached the door. He stepped back quickly, noticing that two nurses were inside. Of course, there would be multiple nurses in attendance around the clock, seeing as how Candace was in critical condition. He walked a measured distance down the hallway and waited for the nurses to leave.

Candace found herself in some type of dreamland paradise, floating over a garden of shimmering flowers that gave off the sweetest fragrance she had ever inhaled. A white robed figure joined her, gliding along with her and gesturing at the beautiful flower petals. The figure did not appear to have a gender or any facial or bodily detail. It was only a glowing, comforting mass that seemed to be her host in this strange and beautiful place. Everything around her looked out of focus except for the vivid appearance of the garden. White amaryllis and magnolias were in full blossom, but there were no colored flowers present, and she wondered about that.

The vision around her suddenly cleared, opening up a new vista. The gliding figure pointed off into the distance toward a row of hills that rolled away in a blaze of bright green. She was quickly transported there and found herself over a meadow of wavy grass. Below her, deer, foxes, and rabbits darted about. Their movements looked playful and unafraid. She so much wanted to pet or hold one. But her view changed again.

Her next visitation was over a lofty mountain peak glazed with snow. There was no chill to the air. Her vision of the rocky, red and purple slopes was crystal clear. White cotton-like clouds waltzed in the sky above her.

She was whisked away at a swift and dizzying pace again. Her flight stopped suddenly. The next view below her was that of a deep green lake, pockmarked with ducks and flying loons. The shadows of fish swam just under the water's surface. She could see and hear the squawking symphony of the birds. The scene was magical.

Then she was out over the ocean, flying over white-capped swells, where she could spy small white objects cutting through the water. She imagined that they were sailboats, and she wondered about their destinations. Dolphins and whales breeched the surface, performing graceful dives, making foamy splashes.

Next she flew over the desert, smelling the mesquite and feeling the warmth of the air. After that, she arrived over a thick swamp and catalogued all the creatures she saw there. Waterways and small lagoons formed a tapestry of graceful lines and curves; it was another of nature's wonders.

She was instantly transported back to the white garden. Her heavenly escort, for that is what the being seemed to represent to her, gazed at her and raised a question in her mind. She now knew the answer to the mystery of the fantastical trip.

You have shown me all the beauty of the Earth, she said in her mind. *These are all the places I have been somewhere in the past or the places that I will see in the future. I understand. But where am I now? Have I lost my way? Where is the vision and dream that I love the most? I can't remember where or what it is. Can you take me there, dear spirit?*

Her glowing host lifted its arms. They flew swiftly upward, past the milky white clouds, into the fringe of space and beyond. They arrived at the outskirts of a small, shimmering white star. The glowing figure pointed. She fought hard to understand the meaning of it. She had seen that star before but couldn't connect with its importance to her.

But what does it all mean?

Now they fell at the speed of light to nearly crash into the Earth. They halted suddenly above a grassy lawn filled with thick trees. Her lovely host had vanished from her sight. She knew that somehow, she was back in reality. *But what reality?*

Looking below, she saw one large tree that stood out from the rest. She gracefully glided to it, and then somehow became one with it, climbing inside of it and holding it to her. Something snapped with a flash, and then she felt her body weight return.

The next sensation she had was that of falling backward and being filled with panic. Something caught her out of the air, and she was surprised to have landed in the arms of a person. When she looked at the person, her eyes locked with his for only moment, a feeling of wonder and love shot through her heart and filled her soul. She knew her destiny had arrived. This man would be the champion of her dreams. His name was Ryan Barlow.

I know you, she remembered all of it. *You are what I love the most.*

When the nurses left, Ryan scurried down the hall, his cumbersome shoes making annoying thuds on the waxed floor. He opened the door and stepped in, closing it softly behind him. He had only to part a curtain to see Candace. He tried not to show any dread or fear on his face as he looked upon the scene, but he failed miserably.

It was obscene, looking at all the tubes and lines protruding from her body. She had a tube down her throat and something behind the bed that sounded like a motor pump. He stepped up to the bed and leaned over her face. It tore his heart out to see her this way. He gave her forehead a soothing pat, and then he kissed her cheek. The oxygen tube hissed inside her nostrils.

"Beautiful dreamer, wake unto me..." he began the lullaby, "...starlight and dew drops are waiting for thee..." Ryan finished singing the song to her and then began it again. He was halfway through the third stanza when her eyes opened a crack. She turned her head toward him with a painful slowness difficult to watch. Her eyes found his. His breath left his chest when the corners of her lips rose in just the slightest smile.

He held her hand and broke down into tears. From the expression on her face and the slight shake of her head, he knew she was motioning for him to be of good cheer. She gave out a small wheezing noise around the mouth tube.

"Don't try to talk, darling," he said, his voice cracking, "because you can't right now. Okay?"

She blinked once, and he could feel her hand weakly squeeze his.

"I promise I'm going to be with you through this," he said. "I'm going to stay at your side."

She gave the hint of an eyebrow furrow. And again, the weak headshake.

"The hell with them," he said to her. "They will have to drag me out of here."

Five minutes later two nightshift nurses passed through the door and flung the privacy curtain open. One was tall with a red stacked hair bun, and the other was Candace's size and had short curly blonde hair. The tall one had a mini-laptop.

The tall one spoke first. "What are you doing in here, sir? It's past visiting hours. This lady needs her rest."

221

"Who are you? And why should you be in here?" asked the short one.

"I'm Ryan. Candace is my wife, and Doctor Daniels gave me permission for a short visit." He showed them the little square of paper.

The tall one placed her laptop on the counter and stabbed some keys. She turned her head, a pained look on her face. "Candace Sabella is not married according to my records. The police officers supplied us with that information since she was lacking I.D. for admittance."

"I'm sorry. That's an error on my part. I'm her fiancé."

That's better," said the redhead. "That was a pretty hefty ring we removed that was shoe-laced around her neck."

"Do you own Wal-Mart or something?" said the small one with a giggle. She looked at the monitor. "Still, we'll have to ask you to leave, please. This is against regulations, sir. There is no way around it."

"I can't leave her. It just isn't possible."

The tall redhead cocked her head sideways and tapped some keys, then left. Two minutes later, a security guard stepped into the room and told him to go with him.

Ryan fought hard, holding onto the bed, before it began to slide across the floor. He let go for fear of toppling everything or disconnecting vital equipment. "Don't you worry, sweetie," he said over his shoulder. "I'll be right back!"

Ryan was escorted to the lobby. He sat on the sofa. The phone went off in his pocket again. He ignored it. Again.

CHAPTER TWENTY-NINE

After six days, Ryan Barlow was politely asked to leave Martha's Vineyard Hospital so that he could go home and get some rest. He had seen Candace through the worst of her ordeal and kept her company, often singing to her or reading to her before she went to sleep. He was there for her, helping her anyway he could, changing the TV channels and spoon feeding her. He had smuggled in some of her holistic foods and beverages, without the hospital staff's knowledge. His friends had made regular visits and consoled Ryan, giving him money, and additional phone numbers where they could be reached.

When Candace was discharged after seventeen days, Ryan helped her into the wheelchair and insisted on pushing her out to Billy's awaiting truck. He had taken Ryan to the hospital on her discharge date. He wanted to drive them home so Ryan could comfort her.

Ryan picked up Candace's ring at the checkout desk and thanked the staff for his fiancé's wonderful treatment. He also picked up prescriptions for various meds and a list of some cautions about the healing process. Candace could sign up for a home nurse if she wanted one.

Then he pushed her out of the front doors and into the sunshine. She bridged a hand over her eyes, squinting.

"Ryan, it's so bright and fresh out here. I can breeeathe…"

Billy, who had been waiting at the front curb, opened his passenger door and gave both a fat smile. "Welcome to the land of the living," he said.

Candace refused help out of the chair and rose up to step into the cab. An orderly whisked the wheelchair away, and Ryan slipped in beside her. Although he had already kissed her several times in the hospital, he laid one on her that lasted for a full minute. She came up for air with a wheezing intake of breath. Ryan apologized for the display.

Billy pulled out of the parking lot and headed south. Candace took a deep breath and sighed. She snuggled up next to Ryan. He put his arm around her.

Billy gave them a glance. "Looks like you two are headed for picket fences and babies."

"That's the way we're going to roll," said Ryan. "I've got to wait for the divorce, and that's going to be a mess. I was bequeathed the big house, so there's the matter of how much of it she can take from me."

"Nah," said Billy as he pulled some papers from his door side pocket and handed them to Ryan. "Gloria gave them to me. It a no fault divorce. You don't have to show—she already found out she has no claim to the house. Just sign."

Ryan shook his head. "Why the change of heart? She hates my guts."

Billy cocked his thumb at Candace. "Gloria doesn't hate *her*—she only hates you. Her heart melted when li'l one took a bullet and nearly died. I dunno. It was one of those Christ the Lord forgiveness things. Just sign, and I'll return it to her on my way back to my poor little broken down boat."

Ryan gingerly signed the papers and handed them back. "I appreciate this."

Candace took the ring off her finger and handed it to Billy. "Don't take less than forty thousand. It cost fifty."

"You can't do that," said Billy. "You guys need a wedding and all that!"

"I can go back to my apartment and sell all my things," she said. "You deserve it for rescuing us and putting your life in danger." She squeezed Ryan's arm. "Isn't that so, honey?"

"That's right. You need the Shamrock restored, or you can get a new one. I've got money in the bank and a lot of artwork to catch up on. We'll make the big Vic our home."

Billy kissed the ring. "Wow. Just wow. Thanks, guys!"

Billy dropped the two off at the big, three-story Victorian and sounded the horn as he drove away. Ryan and Candace strolled down the walkway and entered the house. The living room was infested with newspapers, fast food wrappers, beer cans and upended furniture.

"Gee, Ryan," said Candace. "You didn't keep your house up at all."

He kicked a can across the room. "Some of this stuff was messed up by Antonio's thugs. I didn't feel like cleaning up much—I didn't give a shit. There was only you to think about. Now that we're home, I can clean up some."

Candace opened the refrigerator. "Oh, what a mess. My work is cut out for me."

"You're not doing any work."

"Is your car all right?" she asked.

"They didn't slit my tires if that's what you mean. I had a hide-a-key spot and picked up the other set of keys early on. Sorry, didn't do much shopping." His voice saddened. "I've let things go." He fell onto the couch. She walked into the living room and sat down next to him. He kissed her gently, his heart soaring that he had her home. She patted his face, then looked at it more closely.

"Don't you worry," she said. "We'll get everything straightened out and back to normal."

"Hell, I haven't even looked at my mail."

"Baby love," she cooed. "You have so many eyebags your face looks like chopped liver. You're wiped out—exhausted. You have sleep deprivation. Take a long nap, my darling man."

"Maybe I do. But you were worth every sleepless moment. I wanted you home so badly."

A tear dropped from one of her eyes. "I've never had a man in love with me so much who would go through all that." She laughed, but it came out a cough. "Maybe I should get shot on a regular basis."

"Let's not and say you did." His body leaned forward. His eyelids became heavy. He felt small arms around him. A sweet melody drifted to his ear. He knew that song. He'd even sung it.

CHAPTER THIRTY

R yan turned his head around and felt a misty breeze across his cheeks. A thin whitewater trail of bubbles and foam cut away from the stern. Looking up, he could see a slackening in the fore and mainsails, so he turned the wheel, adjusting for it. The Shenandoah heeled over just the way he wanted her to. The large sailboat picked up speed. He told Candace to hold onto the starboard rail lest they tip over. They experienced a brisk northerly breeze and were making good time, considering they'd hit the doldrums twice on the way out. He could see his first glimpse of the Bahamas chain, and he could easily pick out the long profile of Grand Bahamas Island. The couple's best friends would be waiting for them at the docks. Everyone had flown in ahead of them and made all of the preparations.

The boat evened on the keel somewhat, and Candace joined Ryan at the wheel. Recovered completely, she rubbed his back to ease some of the soreness since he preferred to stand most of the time.

"Why do you think Billy gave us twenty thousand dollars back from the ring sale?

"He didn't need all of it," Ryan said. "Twenty grand will fix his engines easily. He didn't want a new trawler. He loves the Shamrock."

"There are some good people in this world."

"Yes, there are." He looked at her. "I found you, didn't I?"

"Don't say anymore, Ryan," she said in a wavering voice. "You'll make me cry again. We have a ship to sail."

"Aye aye, Skipper."

Billy, Ross and Joyce met the Shenandoah at the docks. Ryan tied up his boat and paid the slip fee. He and Candace unloaded a long wardrobe box and two suitcases. They gave the others greetings at the edge of the pier. The three were dressed for the wedding. They all wore white from head to toe.

Billy put his hands on his hips. "You're late for your own G-damned wedding. The preacher's on call. I'll get a hold of him. Your parents are here, Ryan. There are three publishers and your agent in the guest crowd. Why didn't you call ahead?"

"Because we were busy in the bunk." Candace giggled.

"How'd you manage that?" Billy grumbled.

Ryan smirked. "We just put it on autopilot."

"Get in the car!" said Billy.

The friends picked up their luggage and led them to a rental SUV. Ross and Billy tossed the luggage in the back of the vehicle. After embracing Candace and whispering something in her ear, Joyce told the couple to jump in the back and change into their wedding clothes on their way. The engine roared, and they were off.

At one point, Ryan watched Candace pull on her dress and remarked, "Really, honey, a G-string under that?"

"You know that's the way I roll."

They arrived at Lucayan Beach on the south side of the island just before the clouds started to turn pink on the horizon. Everyone rushed from the SUV and walked into the wedding assembly arranged inside several grassy knolls. A white gazebo sat at the end of a long aisle festooned with hundreds of white amaryllis and magnolias. The wedding chairs were white. The preacher, who stood on the gazebo stage, wore white. Ryan's parents were dressed in white, along with the bridesmaids, who were mostly strippers from the Kitten's Revenge. It all looked so pure and innocent. Sadly, Candace's parents were not in attendance because they had boarded the wrong flight. She was not lonely—she had a new family now.

Everyone took their places. Ryan waited for his soon-to-be bride to walk slowly down the aisle, her arm crooked with the best man Ross. A song drifted on the wind. It was *Somewhere*, by Barbara Streisand. Billy played his harmonica in soulful tandem to the song.

Joyce held Candace's bouquet and helped Ross escort her up the steps. The bride and groom stood opposite each other. A tear rolled down Candace's cheek. She closed her eyes as she gave out a long, jittery sigh.

She was overwhelmed with the joyful and reverent spectacle of it all. She found herself in a wedding dress for the second time, only this one she and Ryan had picked out together. This was her princess day, her ultimate dream come true. Before her stood the man who had rescued her. He had wholly invited her into his life. It was unconditional. She would never need to go anywhere alone when she had such company by her side. She would never have to work again undressing in front of men for a living. What's more, all of her friends were here to join in her happiness. They were people who really cared about her.

Today was the first day of the rest of her life.

"What is it, sweetheart?" whispered Ryan.

"It's just...just the first time I've ever been married for *real*."

The preacher cleared his throat and began. "Dearly beloved, we are gathered here to..."

When it got to the pivotal questions, both said, "I do." Then Ryan placed the small gold band on her finger, lifted her veil, and gave her a long, sweet kiss.

The wedding assembly applauded. Handfuls of rice flew over the happy couple as they stepped down from the dais. Candace retrieved her bouquet from Joyce, then tossed it over her shoulder. It fell into the hands of her best friend, Velvet. She looked out into the crowd and saw pairs of proud, gleaming eyes.

The newly married couple hurried up the aisle to greet their friends. Candace met Ryan's parents for the first time. They lingered. The sun was on its way down, painting the sky crimson and persimmon pink. It was all so surreal, like a beautiful fantasyland dream.

EPILOGUE

It was no surprise that Ross married Joyce six months after Ryan and Candace's wedding. They indulged in many horseback riding adventures at the Lofty Pines Horse Stables. Gloria and Stephan exchanged vows three months later. They joined the other two in breathtaking rides, enjoying picturesque vistas of the island. Stephan and Gloria found a specialist that was highly recommended and had plans for her to have in vitro fertilization. They could hardly wait to become parents and start their own family.

Billy got his engines fixed. He jumped at the chance to adopt Banjo, and Ginger graciously accepted him as her new best buddy. Four months after Ryan's wedding, Billy met up again with Nancy at his favorite bait and tackle shop. He had met her at Ryan and Candace's wedding. They hit it off big time, sharing anecdotes about their favorite lures. Yup, Nancy caught a big one when she lured Billy into courting her, and like the gentleman he was, he made sure to treat her right.

With his new bride at his side, Ryan continued venturing out with Ross and Billy on their fishing expeditions. And now Nancy joined in as part of the crew. Once in a blue moon, even Joyce came along, and they all succeeded in robbing the sea of many fine specimens. In fact, they landed a few sharks!

From the eyewitness testimony of Candace, plus the DNA evidence found in Jeppo's and Alphonse's sedan, Antonia was found guilty of second degree murder and sentenced to twenty-five years to life. Tony the Twister Gazzuto, turning State's evidence against his boss, helped seal the lid on Antonio's fate. Tony gained full immunity for his testimony.

Alphonse and Jeppo got fifteen to life for their participation in Randy's death. Several of the Madera Mob Squad received reduced sentences for assault and battery, breaking and entering and other assorted crimes.

Ryan and Candace loved to call each other Mr. and Mrs. Barlow. They enjoyed passionate nights and days making love. Their insatiable desires kept them both feeling more vital and alive than ever before. Their love for one another seemed to come right out of a romance novel.

But the day came that they missed their first Sunday fishing trip with their salty crew of friends on the Shamrock.

The big gingerbread Victorian had the perfect guest room for a special occasion. Ryan painted the most exquisite undersea panorama in the room that anyone had ever seen. The artwork made the front page of the *Martha's Vineyard Times* newspaper.

They knew beforehand that the room would be painted in soft pinks. Their new arrival would be christened Cynthia Joan Barlow.

Mr. and Mrs. Barlow would always have a special song that they shared together. It was old and corny, but they didn't care. And Ryan knew he would never have another nightmare for the rest of his life.

THE END

Don't miss out on your next favorite book!

Join the Satin Romance mailing list
www.satinromance.com/mail.html